Nirvana
Effect

Craig Gehring

FOR EVERY DREAMER.

INTRODUCTION

This in all likelihood is the first broadly published novelization of the events surrounding the rise of the most influential scientist of our times. Although Atlas gave no interview before he died, non-classified excerpts from his journals have recently been released by his foundation. These, combined with unprecedented interviews with both Doctor Knowles and the late Doctor Seacrest, make this fictionalization closer to truth than the many unauthorized biographies that have filled bookstores since Atlas's untimely demise.

The scientific community may find fault with writing an historical fiction on such a figure as Atlas, but one could argue that in order to understand him and gain context to his accomplishment, one must take artistic license to fill in the many gaps. A timeline does no justice to his life's work; a litany of his scientific discoveries does not spell out this man's soul.

On behalf of my research team, co-writers and editors, it is my great pride and pleasure to present to you *Nirvana Effect*.

BOOK ONE: ONE ISLAND

In order for my early decisions to be comprehended, one must look out from the faulty pair of eyes I wore in 2010. I suffered from tunnel vision. If one desires to grasp my thinking at that time, one must feign the same affliction. One must ignore the affairs of nations. One must divert one's eyes from such matters as my International Science Foundation. One must focus only on one island, one near-invisible speck on the globe. From there, one must narrow one's consideration further to a small group of men and women and their conflicting struggles for survival.

This localized viewpoint actually provides the true story of the nirvana effect, all the way up the line to present day — that is, individuals and tiny groups making decisions (with global repercussions, I might add) in their own separate fights for life.

I hope someday that my earliest decisions will be forgiven. Once this journal is declassified, it will be quite plain that my initial actions with the trance substance brought on disaster and unnecessary suffering.

For the gifts I have given Man, I have never desired admiration.

But I hope for forgiveness.

-Atlas
Journal Excerpt, 2023 A.D.

I

A mosquito landed on the anthropology text Edward Styles studied from his lap. The insect was nothing; it scarcely blocked a single character. But since he focused his eyes on it, it was everything. All the world was a blur except that bug.

Much to Edward's surprise, the bug and the text were blotted by the flickering shadow of a man. Edward looked up. He'd heard no footsteps into his tiny bamboo hut, no real warning sign.

Nockwe, the Onge chieftain, towered at the entrance of Edward's dwelling, his dark skin punching out the starry sky behind him. The native's surprise appearance unnerved Edward. It wasn't like Nockwe to enter unannounced. In his six months of work at the Onge village, Edward had never feared for his safety. For no other reason than a poisonous wrenching in his gut, Edward feared then.

Nockwe wore more clothes than Edward had ever seen him in. Besides the staple loincloth, the chieftain wore ceremonial hunting garb: a feathered headdress, a bearskin for a robe, a dagger at the waist and hunting spear in hand. Edward noticed the spear particularly. The native gripped it as though he intended to use it.

Nockwe communicated with signs. He knew little English, and Edward preferred to not let on how well he understood Onge. Nockwe pointed at his spear, its tip glistening with poison. Nockwe then pointed to Edward.

The missionary stiffened. The text in his lap slid to the floor. Neither man glanced as it pounded the dirt; Edward watched the spear, and Nockwe watched Edward.

Nockwe spoke slowly in English: "White man stay hut." He searched Edward's eyes for a sign of betrayal. Edward nodded and tried to make his eyes appear trustworthy. The mosquito flitted past his nose. Edward had no trouble ignoring it.

Edward had a mind for facts. It had served him well in seminary. Facts flitted through his mind like the mosquito through the air. One fact was that Nockwe had become chieftain by dueling three men consecutively in hand-to-hand combat. Another fact was that the village was a forty mile hike from Lisbaad. Another was that Onge custom dictated that only one Westerner be allowed to visit at a time, and that in a village of 1,161 primitives, Edward was the only pale face.

Edward never prayed. He was a priest by profession and creed, and he said the words of the prayers as was custom, but he never put any faith behind his rosary. On mission, alone, where no one could detect him, he didn't even bother rattling off the empty words.

At that moment, though, Edward prayed. He prayed faithfully, as an instantaneous thought. Make him leave.

The chieftain's eyes strayed above Edward's head. The missionary turned to follow Nockwe's gaze. He was looking at the cross hanging from the wall, fashioned of wood and thorns. A young Onge man, Mahanta, had made it for Edward. Edward would have preferred a local craft, but accepted it graciously enough.

Nockwe walked around Edward to touch the cross. He easily reached it and fingered one of its thorns. Edward had used a chair to hang it up near the ceiling, out of his sight line.

Nockwe left abruptly. He swatted a mosquito off his arm on the way out.

Edward slid down to the floor to join his text. He flattened his hands on the hard dirt. The earth felt cooler than the air.

He picked up his book and examined it. One of its corners had dug into the ground. He picked each speck of dirt away and slid the book back onto his cot.

Edward looked outside from where he sat. He could not see far. Onge nights were darker than any he'd experienced. Only the stars and moon lit the village clearing, and even they had a rough go of it through the constant cloud cover. The tropical Isle of Lisbaad rained in seeming perpetuity.

This night was clear enough. He was happy to not have to endure his leaky roof.

Edward noticed that the nearby huts were tinged in the subtle warmth of a far-off campfire.

His mind had started racing for an answer for Nockwe's uncharacteristic threats from the instant the chieftain had swatted the mosquito. The possibilities were few.

Either the tribe had gone to war (unlikely, since the only force to go up against on the island was the Sri Lankan government) or else they were having a ceremony to which Westerners were not privy. The campfire tended to confirm the latter. The lack of war cries, or any voice at all, for that matter, allowed Edward to finalize his conclusion.

He already knew what ceremony. It was Mahanta's coming of age.

Edward lay down. The dirt felt a better pallet than the cot for the time being. The difference in temperatures and the hardness of the floor helped him think. He felt a soft spot where the handle of Nockwe's spear had broken up some of the dirt, and fingered the grains of soil idly.

Edward did not pray, but he did meditate. Meditation was a way of the Jesuit. St. Ignatius would approve. Edward meditated on the ceremony and the dirt, gradually slowing his gyrating heart.

So Mahanta will come of age tonight. His thoughts beat in rhythm to his pulse. He gathered a handful of dirt and poured it out of his palm. *And they don't want me to see.*

Edward guided himself into a light trance as he considered the key events surrounding the ceremony.

Weeks ago, Mahanta had mentioned the ritual. Edward's mind travelled back to the moment.

"In a few moons, the tribe will try to make me a man," Mahanta says in Tamil as he guides Edward through the jungle.

"What do you think of that?" Edward asks, noting the odd way Mahanta phrased it.

11

"Well, I'd like to stay a boy forever, I think," he says.

Mahanta was hardly a boy by any standard. He was a hardened, muscular seventeen year old who could have passed for twenty-five in the West. His dark hands bore the callouses of labor.

"Me, too," says Edward. "How will they make you a man?"

"It is not something for outsiders." Mahanta will not discuss it further.

Edward breathed in deeply and let the oxygen circulate through his veins. Nockwe's threats were fresh in his mind. The more time distanced him from them, however, the more easily he recognized that Nockwe's intimidation act was probably for Edward's own benefit. *Must be some Onge law forbidding outsiders, just like Mahanta said.*

Finally, Edward recalled his mission instructions. He would follow them tonight, not because he really cared what Brother Anthony thought, but rather because they provided a good justification for the decision he'd already made the moment Nockwe had told him not to leave the hut:

"You have too inquisitive a mind, Brother Styles. It is why I'm sending you to the Onge. No white man has ever changed their culture. I know you've heard 'you're not your brother' plenty of times – and you definitely are not Allen. But in this one case, perhaps, it's a good thing. Don't do the preaching that you hate, anyway. Just study, and study well. Teach these people western science - irrigation, basic medicine. Do not fail to learn everything about this tribe - every secret, every way. You must understand these people. Only then can you help them. Maybe after that we'll send in Allen.

"Why did you become a Jesuit, again?" It was Anthony's running joke. He always said it with a serious face and then laughed sharply, in a staccato chortle. "Your heart's in the right place, my scientist priest. I have no doubt of that. God has a purpose for us all."

These Onge had mystified Edward. In six months, he felt no closer to understanding them than when he started. Perhaps Allen would have done a better job after all. The Onge not only resisted change; they rebuked it. Their women lugged water over half a mile from a nearby stream, yet were utterly disinterested in irrigation. They let Edward practice medicine on individual tribesmen, but refused to learn medicine's procedures themselves. If he could just *understand* some fabric of their culture, he could relate enough to help them. As it was, he was planning on packing up, soon.

He would not miss this opportunity to observe them. Nockwe had the right idea in being so forceful in his warning; yet the only way he could have avoided Edward's watching would have been to never bring it up in the first place.

Edward's thoughts turned toward more questions. He had no idea what the ritual would entail. He had not a clue what lay in store for him outside the hut. He didn't bother reflecting on it. He would soon find out.

He paused at the doorway and gripped the bamboo. It dug into his skin. He weighed the consequences of satiating his curiosity, then shrugged them off. He just wouldn't get caught. That was that.

Before Edward could even roll off the balls of his feet to poke his head outside, the air filled up with a low, hair-raising drone. The sound seemed everywhere, as though without source or reason. He could feel it.

The ritual. It had begun.

Edward couldn't help but fear for Mahanta. Many of the primitive initiation rites he'd studied were none too pleasant for the initiate. Edward liked the young man. He was different than the rest of the Onge. He had an ear sharp for all things Western and a head full of questions.

Edward hoped that difference wouldn't result in consequences for Mahanta during the ceremony.

The droning enervated Edward. He tried to place the sound, momentarily drained of all his enthusiasm to sneak out. He steeled himself to push on along the course that his curiosity had pointed. He poked his head out. No guards.

He slipped outside. The sound became more localized to his ears. It was coming from the bonfire area. Edward crept around his hut and peeked in that direction.

A fire blazed higher than he'd ever seen at the camp. Edward could tell a sizeable crowd had gathered. He could view its fringes even from his dismal vantage point. It must have been half the tribe.

He knew he could risk getting closer. He didn't see anyone around. The camp felt abnormally still. If the tribe had their vision burned out by the fire, they wouldn't be able to see his spying. He cursed to himself using his favorite Onge curse: *"Niet wan-wan."* Fools die fools.

Edward crept to the next closest tent, and then another, edging as closely as he dared to the gathering. All the dwellings were empty. Everyone was at the fire.

It was the medicine man who was droning. Edward could see him clearly, twisting and contorting on the ground, his chant incongruously monotonous. The crowd watched raptly. Their long flickering shadows stretched behind them as though to reach Edward as they shifted to follow the vagaries of the light. Edward stopped approaching when their shadows met his own.

He heard the witch doctor more distinctly now, bellowing at a monotone which eerily lacked sanity or humanity. Edward had the dim realization that he was awfully close. He suddenly was aware of his heart pounding as though lodged in his ears. He had a fleeting thought which he quickly quelled. *I should go back.*

He peered around the edge of the hut closest to the fire, watching with the one eye he dared expose. They stood in rank and file, every Onge with a weapon in his hand, dressed similarly to Nockwe. There were more than four hundred of them. It must have been all the males in the village. Even the children attended. The light flickered ominously off their dark skin and weapons.

On the far side of the bonfire writhed the medicine man. He lay horizontal on the ground, his erratic gyrations out of sync with the constant, insane chant that came deep from his gut. He may have been in his death throes of a drug - or it may have been all ceremony. The whole village was silent, though, except for this "witch doctor" who would have been committed to an asylum in any Western culture.

Edward's ears started to separate out the sounds of the night. Besides the chant, there was the faint rattle of the medicine man's beads. The birds and the animals of the jungle let out their occasional cry. Over it all he heard his own breathing, his heart racing as though if it ran fast enough he could escape whatever threat the jungle people might throw at him.

Over his own breathing he heard another. A tiny yelp behind him clued his ears to it. He twisted around quietly, Nockwe's poison-tipped spear flashing in his mind's eye.

It was only Mahanta. The young man sat in a hut forty yards away. Edward wondered how he'd heard him. Probably the fear was stretching his perceptions.

He saw Mahanta through the hut's entrance. He sat there alone on a mat with a surgical needle in his hand, his arm straight out. Blood pooled red on the pit of his arm. He'd given himself some sort of shot. Edward wondered if that was a part of the ritual.

The anachronism gave Edward something to ponder, but he filed it away for later. His mind never stopped; fear seemed to work it all the harder.

Mahanta would be leaving that hut soon, and might have the same injunction toward keeping the ritual's secret as Nockwe. Edward saw the young man was breathing hard, staring straight forward. The missionary quickly took cover behind another hut, out of view of Mahanta's path to the gathering. Again, Edward peered out to the fire.

The medicine man's chant grew softer. His body now matched the droning, immobile on the dirt surrounding the fire. An ember blew from the fire onto his arm. It rested there, singing his skin before finally smoldering. He didn't move, and the droning didn't stop. The whole village was absorbed in his performance.

Except Mahanta. Edward peered back around the corner. Mahanta was no longer in the hut. Edward spotted the his shadow shrinking toward the fire. Edward turned back around again.

Mahanta walked stiffly towards the gathering, nearing the now quiet medicine man. The villagers bunched closer to the fire to watch. Their weapons gave them more the aspect of a militia than a religious or communal gathering. Edward wondered what was in store for Mahanta.

Edward heard a sudden shriek of pain. He risked craning his neck out to get a better view. It was early in the morning, but he felt he'd never been more awake in his life. He examined his options. If he sprinted at the first sign of the ceremony ending, he could make it without being spotted. Still, it was too close. He thought again about running back.

He turned his eyes back to the fire and the "stage" it lit. *Niet wan-wan.*

He could clearly see the medicine man, still on the ground. Mahanta stood over him, facing the crowd. To his left, Nockwe brandished a burning staff. He touched the flame to the fleshy arm of the medicine man. The medicine man did not respond in any way.

Nockwe then turned to Mahanta. That's why he shouted. Nockwe touched the staff to Mahanta's flesh. Again, the young man yelped, but did not move. The crowd observed passively. Edward could not be so passive, wincing as though the burn had been to his own flesh. Edward was rooting for him.

Mahanta stared straight ahead to the crowd as again Nockwe touched the staff to the medicine man. Again he touched the staff to Mahanta. This time, Mahanta held fast. No sound came from his lips. He did it with an ease that let Edward know he needn't have yelped either of the other two times if he hadn't wanted to. Edward could imagine the burn growing worse and worse on Mahanta's arm, and still Mahanta didn't react. Finally, the chieftain cast the staff back into the fire. Edward sighed quietly, relieved.

Nockwe grunted and raised his arms, chanting over and over again in an ancient tongue. Edward recognized its Indo-European roots. Man, hunter, killer, peace bringer - something to that effect. He could definitely make out the symmetry in the words. The burn was to burn out something animalistic in the youth, and yet bring out all that was animalistic in the soon-to-be-man.

Nockwe's words stopped. In unison, the tribe lay down their weapons and kneeled. The chieftain nudged the boy towards them. Mahanta walked forward warily. He was looking at their weapons.

Mahanta's concentration was absolute. Edward didn't understand what that look was, then. He would later recognize that this was the moment that would launch Mahanta onto his inevitable path.

Quietly, Mahanta stole to the back of the crowd. From the ground next to a young child, he took a small staff. He circled to the front, between the fire and the crowd, and held up the petty stick, shouting, *"Ley book!"* I am.

The tribesmen were troubled. Whispers circulated through them like an insidious breeze. The younger boys looked wildly about with darting eyes.

They feared for Mahanta.

Mahanta was not supposed to choose a child's staff for this coming-of-age. Edward found himself leaning in, as though the few inches he gained would give him a more microscopic view to what was happening. Forgotten was the need to run.

One of the biggest of the males of the tribe stood up and shouted to Nockwe. He spoke too quickly for Edward to interpret, but it had a tone of indignation. It was matched by several angry cries from the crowd, though no one else stood.

"Do you break the way, Dook?" Nockwe shouted back in Onge. He spoke slowly, so that all could hear. His feet were planted firmly, his composure unperturbed. He would let no man disturb his dominance of the tribe.

"This child breaks the way with his weapon, Chieftain. Does he mock our ways?" The dissident matched Nockwe's pace, speaking more to the crowd than to his ruler. He was playing politics; Dook wanted Nockwe's title.

Before Nockwe could answer, he was stopped by the medicine man, who had quietly risen from his trance during the disturbance and now gripped Nockwe's arm.

"*TAUN!*" he shouted at the top of his lungs. It was a curse Edward had never heard before, directed straight at Dook. It blasted the big man down back to his knees and silenced the other dissidents. The medicine man then whispered in Nockwe's ear.

Nockwe surveyed the crowd. "It is the way. The boy has chosen," he announced. "The boy may choose any weapon to become a man."

"Turn around, boy," rasped the medicine man.

Fear gripped Edward. Despite the intertribal politics, there was something else occurring here. He couldn't quite grasp it. The adrenaline pumping through his veins kept it just out of reach of his mind.

The youth faced the fire now. Edward was long overdue on returning to his hut. His legs wanted to run but he could not turn his head from the scene.

They continued their ritual. "I face the fire," Mahanta shouted.

"I face your life," shouted back the medicine man.

"I face a boy," cried Nockwe.

"We face a boy," shouted the tribe in unison.

Silence. Mahanta acknowledged them by bowing his head. "I am a man," he asserted.

"By whose spear?" returned the medicine man.

"By the tribe's spear," shouted Mahanta.

"What shall you slay?" asked Nockwe.

Silence again. The silence grew too long. Mahanta was breathing heavily. Edward wondered what drug was coursing through his veins. Maybe he'd blanked out.

"What do you slay, child?" coaxed the medicine man.

Mahanta said nothing.

"What do you say, child? Will you slay the hog?" the medicine man asked again.

Mahanta shook his head - no. The tribe grew more agitated. The medicine man quieted them with a small hand motion. His stage presence was impeccable.

Patiently, he asked Mahanta, "Then what shall you slay?"

Mahanta gripped his stick and spoke slowly in the formal version of their tongue. "As it is sung in the psalms of our ancestors, I shall slay the panther as a child, and defying my elders, remain a child immortal."

"Blasphemy!" shouted a man in the crowd. Several joined him and started shouting, their weapons to hand.

"You call yourself a god?" asked the medicine man.

"I call myself a child. And I shall slay a panther tonight with this toy and so become immortal," said Mahanta, defiant.

The medicine man nodded, feinting as though he were just motioning toward Nockwe to get his attention, but with a cat-like grace Edward would have never expected out of the old man, he grabbed Nockwe's spear and in one swooping motion hurled it over the fire at Mahanta.

It was hard for Edward to make out by the firelight at such a distance, but in an instant it seemed that Mahanta's whole body shifted, as though jerked like a rag doll by an unseen hand. The spear flew where he had been just a moment before. Mahanta struck the spear in midair with his staff, shattering it in two. Its splinters flew into the crowd of Onge.

The tribesmen could no longer contain their excitement. Edward could make one of the voices out, one of the younger men who he knew trained under the medicine man. He seemed to be quoting. "He shall shatter the spear of the spirit guide." Others voiced terse agreement.

For only a moment, Mahanta locked eyes with the medicine man. Then, with his tiny staff still gripped in his hand, Mahanta launched into an all-out sprint towards the jungle.

Edward's stomach dropped. Mahanta was running directly at him.

Mahanta flew with an unnatural speed. He wasn't just running - every muscle in his body seemed to be propelling him as though he were clawing up for air along the ground. Some invisible force was pushing him, pulling him toward the jungle, and toward Edward.

Behind Mahanta, most of the tribe started running, their weapons to hand. Edward drew back. They were coming so quickly.

He had a choice to make. He could bolt for it, but surely they'd see him and his long shadows.

Edward frantically edged around the hut, losing his footing in mud. He heard the thundering footsteps of the tribe draw nearer. Mahanta flew by. Edward threw himself into the hut behind which he'd been hiding. He would wait it out.

Edward noticed the walls of this hut didn't come all the way down to the floor. It was a cooking hut. He jumped up onto a bench against the far wall to avoid running the risk of some observant Onge noticing his legs. The shadows of the tribe raced on the floor. Their feet drummed the earth, only yards away.

It would only take one Onge taking pause at the hut to see him through the holes in the bamboo reeds, but they were all in pursuit of Mahanta.

Edward started to get the same feeling he'd had just half an hour before when Nockwe had entered his hut. He might not survive this night.

Through one of the wider gaps in the wall, Edward peeked to see what was happening. The tribe had all raged into the jungle. He didn't know enough to be able to analyze it. Unanswered questions whizzed through his mind. Were they trying to kill Mahanta or just watch him? What was happening? Mahanta ran as though possessed. Perhaps he had overdosed on whatever drug he'd injected in his veins. An insane part of Edward wanted to follow, to run with the tribe as though one of them.

As the pounding of the Onge feet receded towards the nearby jungle, the voice of reason (and terror) triumphed. It was time to return to his hut. He had been fortunate; no need to push his luck. The men were in the jungle. The women seemed to be gone somewhere, too. The whole village was empty. He wouldn't even need to sneak to make it back safely.

He stepped down from the bench and turned toward the doorway.

An Onge stood where only the darkness had been a minute ago. It was Nockwe.

2

Edward clambered back to the bench and tried to pry his way through the gap in the wall, to no avail.

He was trapped. The only way out of the hut, full of holes as it seemed, was through the doorway and through Nockwe.

Nockwe's hand gripped the dagger at his belt. Edward was happy Nockwe's spear had shattered. The chieftain edged toward Edward as he spoke in Onge.

"You are a foolish white man. I told you not to leave the hut."

Edward kept eyeing the sheathed dagger. He felt numb and out of breath.

Nockwe moved closer still. "You will pay a fool's gamble to feed your curiosity."

Here was a shimmer of hope. Nockwe was still talking. As long as Nockwe was talking, he was not dead. Edward abandoned all pretense of not knowing Onge. "I heard shouts. I thought there might have been violence."

"You left the hut!" shouted Nockwe.

"I feared for my life."

Nockwe shifted his feet and checked his back. When he addressed Edward again, he spoke quickly and softly. "You were right to fear so. You are a good white man but a stupid one."

Edward was barely able to keep pace translating in his mind. Onge was definitely not second nature to him yet.

"There is nothing you could gain," said Nockwe, "and everything you could lose. This we call the fool's gamble. By the laws of the tribe you will die."

Edward could not press back any further to the wall. He scanned the room for weapons, anything that could help him. He had nothing but his bare hands to defend himself from Nockwe. Edward waited for him to make his move.

Nockwe's move never came. "I'll not be the one to kill you," he said. "You are a good white man - you see my peoples' hardships and you help. But you are victim of your curiosity. If the tribe learns what you saw, either I or someone else will have to end your life."

Edward started breathing again, sagging from the wall. Nockwe would bend the rules so long as there were no witnesses.

"What is happening?" Edward asked.

Nockwe shrugged after considering his question. "You just saw a coming of age."

"But he didn't ask for a hog. He was supposed to ask for a hog?" asked Edward.

"But he asked for a panther."

"Yes, a panther. Why?"

"I don't know. There is a legend…"

"With a panther and a child's staff?"

"You came before the yelling."

Edward smiled weakly. "I am a very stupid white man."

Nockwe grinned. "You speak very good Onge for being such a stupid white man. There is a legend, it must be what Mahanta is thinking. But it is only a fable. No boy can kill a panther with a toy. No man can even find a panther to kill. The panther finds and kills him. This is the way of panthers and men."

"He took a drug," Edward said.

Nockwe furrowed his eyebrows and searched Edward's eyes. Finally Nockwe nodded, accepting the truth in his statement. "What sort?" he asked.

"I thought you'd know."

Nockwe shook his head. "There is no drug or potion for the ceremony. Nothing to dull the senses. Even with the hog half-dead and drugged we do not want to lose any of our youth to an accident."

"It was by some sort of…umm…infusion," said Edward. He had to use the Onge cooking term; they had no medical vocabulary.

"Perhaps that explains it." Nockwe's eyes glossed over momentarily. He looked disheartened.

A cry reached them from the jungle. Nockwe whipped back into action. "You will follow me, white man," he instructed, "and stay very close if you want to live through the night. I am no threat, but the tribe is. And I am a threat in the presence of the tribe." He gripped Edward's shoulder. "You are a friend to my people, but they are no friend of yours. So remember when I am your friend and when I am not. Come with me."

"Should I just go back to my hut?" Edward asked. At that moment, his hut was very appealing.

"The hut is not safe for you there. You were right to fear for your life in the hut, if that is true. But only because of what is now occurring."

Nockwe backed toward the entrance.

"Follow me, white man," he said in English to Edward. "Stay close."

Edward numbly followed. Nockwe's English was better than he had before pretended. *And I thought I had Nockwe fooled.* "Where are we going?" Edward asked.

"To the jungle." There would be no arguing with him. He was already moving out the doorway. "Perhaps we can help young Mahanta survive the night," he said quietly. They heard another shout from the jungle. "We must run."

Edward plunged into the jungle, trying to keep up with Nockwe. Edward had never dared travel the jungle at night.

Nockwe wasn't running so much as swimming through the jungle, leaping across crevasses and darting between minute openings in the foliage with ease and fluidity. He somehow always found footing despite the irregular undergrowth, and Edward had a hard time emulating him. The missionary was in good shape, but nowhere near the physical prowess of the head of the Onge tribe.

As he sprinted deeper into the jungle, Edward's need to keep up with Nockwe grew. If he lost his guide, he had no way back to the village. Nockwe changed direction unpredictably, and Edward's lungs heaved the humid air until they felt ready to collapse.

Nockwe stopped suddenly, but Edward didn't see him in time. He slammed into the chieftain. Nockwe's firm hands grasped him and kept him from falling headlong. "Shteck!" whispered Nockwe. It was the Onge injunction for silence.

Edward strained his ears over his own desperate breathing. Far in the distance he heard the shouting and running of the villagers.

Edward and Nockwe twisted their heads back around. An animal was shrieking not far from them. Edward scanned the trees. At any moment it might drop on him.

"There," said Nockwe. "The panther." Edward was relieved to see Nockwe point in the distance. It had like it was right there.

An Onge battle cry drowned out the last of the roar. It sounded like Mahanta.

"Quickly," urged Nockwe. He rushed toward Mahanta, away from the mob of villagers closing in behind them. Edward had to fight his every impulse in order to follow. His only comfort was that there would be only one panther, but hundreds of angry Onge in the opposite direction and thousands of jungle animals should he simply flee into the darkness.

They broke into a clearing. At the far end of the open space was a huge, ancient tree, its branches arching down to kiss its far-reaching roots. Mahanta and the panther danced back and forth before it, silhouetted by the moon.

The panther was furious, yowling, jabbering, hissing and scratching, pouncing at Mahanta. Mahanta bore the stick in his hand and pounded the panther's skull every time it made a pass at him.

The young man moved as though he were some sort of animal, himself

- something far more wild and threatening than the jungle cat. Edward had never seen a human being move like he did. The panther struck with an inescapable power and agility, and yet here was this boy who dodged it easily.

Neither Nockwe nor Edward advanced closer than the edge of the clearing. The chieftain muttered a curse.

Edward wrenched his eyes from the fight to look at Nockwe. His moonlit eyes watched the fight, but Edward could tell by his frozen pupils that he was thinking, not watching. Unexpectedly, Nockwe wrenched his head to the right as though he were a deer reacting to the crack of a rifle. "DOWN," he whispered furiously in English, shoving Edward into the grass.

Edward soon saw that Nockwe had good reason for his abruptness. The sharp pain of Nockwe's rough handling faded into the back of Edward's mind as he tuned his ears to the soft sounds of hundreds of footsteps nearby. The tribe had reached the clearing, too. Peeking up from the grass, he saw the villagers exit the jungle here and there. They cautiously kept to its edge, just like Nockwe.

Edward turned his eyes back to the roaring panther and the quiet youth. The panther was further enraged and had lost all caution in its pouncing. As soon as it landed it launched into the air again, trying to reach Mahanta. It may as well have been pawing at its shadow.

Mahanta only struck the occasional blow as he dodged the cat. He kept glancing at the tribe gathering at the edge of the clearing. He wasn't looking for help.

Seems like he wants an audience. Edward dismissed the thought as soon as it came to him. Mahanta was fighting a real panther. This was life or death, and though he fought with a child's toy, it was no game. Surely he didn't care whether or not there was a crowd. Surely by now whatever drug-induced delusions of grandeur he had were shattered by the necessities of survival.

Edward thought about the injection Mahanta had taken. This is a drug-induced insanity. *It must be stopped.* Mahanta's drug might have been an effective upper, but it was only a matter of time before that panther tore him limb from limb.

Much to Edward's amazement, no member of the tribe moved to intervene, not even Nockwe.

"Is there anything we can do?" asked Edward emphatically from the grass.

"Not if you wish to live," whispered Nockwe. "You can't even be seen here. And no Onge can intercede in the coming of age. It would be death."

"It's death right now! That boy will die! He's not in his senses!"

"Be as that may, there is nothing that can be done." He sounded resolute, but his shadowy face was slack and his eyes looked empty. Edward knew Nockwe wanted to save the boy. Nockwe's power was simply not absolute; he could not break with the Onge tradition.

There's too much dissent in the tribe for Nockwe to make a move like that. Edward had seen the politics at the campfire. "Please, help him," Edward pleaded.

Nockwe did not answer. His eyes were riveted on Mahanta.

Mahanta looked back to the crowd. The panther had tired and was circling again, growling at its pray. Mahanta yelled in the formal Onge tongue, "You shall die, panther, and so shall my earthly flesh! No mortal Mahanta leaves here tonight!" He pulled his staff to the ready.

The panther pounced as if to answer, swinging for him with its huge paws. Mahanta deftly side-stepped and brought his staff down with both hands. The staff shattered on the panther's skull.

It wobbled for a moment, giving Mahanta enough time for a fatal blow. He jabbed the splintered remains of his staff at the panther's face.

The cat flinched back, however, before Mahanta could drive his weapon in. It struck back, swiping Mahanta's torso with its wicked claws. It was the first hit the panther had gotten in all night, and it was a vicious one. Edward cringed as Mahanta dropped. He wouldn't be coming up from that one.

From the grass, Edward could no longer see Mahanta. The panther dove, disappearing from Edward's view as well. It sounded like the two were struggling.

Edward's desire to run was overshadowed by an impulse to go jump into the fray and help Mahanta. He craned his ear as though the extra six inches would give him some insight as to what was happening.

The noises vanished. The clearing was quiet as the moon. The night felt robed in an unnatural calm.

The native figures looked like statues all around the clearing edge. Edward watched the faces of the nearest from his hiding place. Their hopefulness slowly gave way to disappointment as the silence reigned. Silence was the way of a panther, not a man.

Then came a cry.

First, soft, then stronger - a victorious, human cry.

Mahanta's figure surged up from the grass, hefting the carcass of the panther over his head.

"*T'ley'to'ni,*" cried Nockwe. Literally it meant, "Death God," but he was certainly using it as a curse. Edward cursed, as well. Though he was glad to see Mahanta alive, he did not feel relieved. The shock overrode any sense of that. The wiry young man was shaking the panther over his head like a trophy. Edward's scientific mind was not willing to absorb it all. He doubted his own perceptions, as a magician might watching another illusionist's tricks.

Nockwe muttered, "He lives. He shall be a god."

Mahanta's fulfilled a prophecy... Edward wondered what Nockwe meant by "god".

"What does this boy hope to do?" Nockwe asked himself, vocalizing Edward's own thoughts. The words echoed between Edward's ears.

To the left of Edward came an angry Onge curse. Edward jerked his head in that direction. No more than twenty yards away, an older Onge was screaming and pointing directly at him. The thin grass did little to hide Edward from that angle of view. "Nockwe!" shouted the native. "Behind you! The white man sneaks behind you!"

Nockwe was startled, but it only took him an instant to regain his composure. The last thing Edward remembered seeing was Nockwe's face. He looked sorry. His foot crashed into Edward's head. It happened so fast that the missionary could hardly perceive the motion.

Edward was unconscious before he hit the ground.

CRAIG GEHRING

3

"Tell me the story," Edward croaked. His head spun. He could not remember how to ask, "What happened?"

"What story?" asked Tomy, the teenage Onge who sat at his side.

"Tell me the story of what was and is," said Edward.

He squinted his eyes to take in the rest of his surroundings. He lay in a corner of the largest hut he had ever seen. There was no hut like it in the village. It was simply colossal by all Onge standards. He tried to crane his neck to take in the entire scene, but a sharp pain thwarted him.

He lay propped up in a bed of straw on the dirt floor. Only the chief of the village slept on such a bed as this.

His head throbbed as though it might hemorrhage or explode at any minute. Some sort of demon was climbing back and forth along his optic nerves and scalding him to his core. The pain sharpened further as he came to full awareness.

What happened? Just tell me.

Tomy leaned in to examine Edward closely. The boy looked tired, as though he had been watching Edward for quite some time. His eyes were wide.

Tomy's stare spurred Edward to start a self-inventory. Aside from the sharp pain along his nerves and his immobility, his throat and mouth felt parched. As he waited for his attendant to formulate an answer, he caught a water bowl in his peripheral vision. He deliberately looked over at it.

God, my eyes burn, too.

"Water. Drink. You drank nothing for a sun and moon." Tomy grabbed the bowl and enthusiastically pressed it against Edward's mouth. Edward sipped suspiciously. No Onge would ever attend a white man in such a way.

Then again, Edward was suspicious of even being alive. By all logic, he should be dead. Instead, it appeared he was resting in a chieftain's bed attended by an Onge in a monumental hut. His predicament defied all reasoning.

Edward felt a frantic urge to get up, to leave his bed, to somehow escape, but he couldn't even sit up. He felt trapped in his pain-wracked skin.

He forced himself to calm down and took a few minutes to drink, the cool water's soothing action on his throat temporarily distracting his mind's probing.

Gradually, the events of the night came back to him, like bits of flotsam netted from a river. He remembered it all. *Mahanta, the drug, the variance in the coming of age. The panther.*

A muscle in his head cramped that he didn't know he had.

Nockwe's foot. *I remember now.*

He reviewed each piece of the puzzle in his mind. He was still missing quite a bit of jigsaw. Once he ran out of the past to examine, he looked over the present.

Such odd surroundings. He hadn't yet ruled out delusion.

Next to the bed was a sitting mat made of a velvety fabric that probably represented a tenth of the tribe's total wealth. It must have come from their underground cache.

He pulled his head up slightly. It hurt tremendously but he needed to see.

Far across the hut was some sort of chair. *A throne?* It certainly had a grandeur that seemed other-worldly in an Onge setting. Its wood was freshly carved and lined with red fabric. The roof of the hut actually arched to some degree over the chair area. Decorative strings with shiny metal and beads hung from the ceiling down to the floor, framing the "throne."

He rested his head back on the bed. It hurt too much to keep it up.

Edward's delusion hypothesis couldn't overcome the fact that in the final analysis, the straw felt real and the space looked real. His head and body ached realistically. These factors taken together lent credence to his alternate hypothesis that he had not the foggiest clue what was going on. The mystery ached nearly as bad as his injuries.

He shifted his head for comfort, waiting for the merciless throbbing in his skull to ease before once more addressing the boy. Tomy still hadn't answered up.

"Story," Edward gently prompted him.

The boy had been staring at him the whole time. Edward hoped the reason for Tomy's rapt attention wasn't because Edward's brain was exposed or something else equally gruesome.

"Nockwe kicked you," said the boy slowly. *Yes, the flashing foot.* Edward grimaced and then immediately regretted that he did so. His attitude had provided new muscles to join in the aching.

"Yes, yes…" prodded Edward. It even pained him to vibrate his own vocal chords. Speaking was a necessary evil.

"A lot of people kicked and hit you. Medicine man and Dook wanted to roast you." *But I'm here.* "Manassa said no."

"Who is Manassa?" asked Edward.

The boy scrunched his eyebrows. He sighed, then started his story over again as though to a child. "Mahanta had his *ret'nal'u* two nights past. You sneaked to watch it, you silly white man. But only he didn't kill the pig. He left the village to kill a panther, and Mahanta died."

He died? Edward's mind scanned again through the night. *He died?* There Mahanta stood before his mind's eye, hefting the panther over his head. Edward would never forget that moment. He saw it as clearly as if he were still there, hiding in the grass. The incident was unbelievable but certainly a reality.

"What happened when I passed out?" Edward asked.

"I just told you," said Tomy, obviously frustrated. Before Edward could say anything else, Tomy tapped his forehead with his palm. "Oh! I forgot!

Manassa told me to get Bri'ley'na as soon as you wake, if you do." He ran out of the hut.

Edward attempted to further assess the damage to his weary body without moving. He didn't want to stir up the pain again.

He had no visible wounds, save for some scratches from the jungle brush and syringe marks in his arm. He dared not touch his head. His legs felt numb, presumably from lying in the same position all day and night. *Sun and moon.* He gave them a try and got no response.

He would need to shift his body up to get his circulation going, but he didn't want to risk that without assistance. It had been hard enough just lifting his head to an upright position. It felt like he'd had his head amputated, used for a football game, and then screwed back on.

What is this hut? Manassa's? Who is this man?

Edward speculated that Manassa was an elder from outlying tribe. In Edward's other missions, there were always respected outsiders coming in and out. These primitive opinion leaders had always been his key to getting any work done. Being roamers and travelers, they were more open to new ideas. Often they'd already been introduced to Christianity, and were at least familiar with the concept of missionaries and Western advances.

Unlike the Onge, any travelers' great-grandparents and entire descendancy didn't all live and die within a thousand yards of an old tree. *Perhaps this Manassa is such a traveler. Perhaps he can help me.*

Immediately Edward dismissed his own thoughts. It was pointless speculation, as his position on the island was untenable. Even with the support of this outsider, Nockwe had to follow the laws of the tribe. *As evidenced by my aching head.* If he couldn't bend the rules for Mahanta, he certainly couldn't do so for a white man. Both the medicine man and Nockwe's main adversary wanted Edward dead. The best Edward could hope for would be a return to Sri Lanka, and from there back to London.

He kept at examining his surroundings as though the dust motes floating near the rafters of the hut might suddenly give him answers.

There was nothing else he could divine by looking. Tomy had not yet returned.

For the second time in less than a week, Edward prayed. This time he started with one his father had drilled into him from the first day he could say the words.

Our Father, who art in heaven, hallowed be Thy name. Thy kingdom come, Thy will be done, on Earth as it is in heaven. Give us this day our daily bread, and forgive us our trespasses, as we forgive those who trespass against us. And lead us not into temptation, but deliver us from evil. Amen.

Then Edward added:

I hope somehow Mahanta's still alive. And if he isn't, I'm sure you're taking care of him. It's a shame, though.

Whenever Edward did really pray, he just talked to God. He didn't even throw in an "amen" at the end.

"You're crying." A female's soft voice, in Onge.

"Hmm?" Edward mumbled. He opened his eyes. A woman stood over him. He recognized her at once as Nockwe's young wife, Bri'ley'na.

"Water?" she asked.

"No, Tomy helped me with that," he answered.

Bri'ley'na was twenty-five years old. Edward had never seen an Onge woman with hair even slightly cared for, but hers was washed and combed that day. Her thick black hair ran straight down the sides of her dark face and swept back and forth gently as she moved. She was full-figured and quite beautiful, by any standards. He suddenly felt excruciatingly aware that she was topless. It must have been something about her hair.

"What happened?" Edward asked, keeping his eyes on her face. He ignored the tears that had collected on his cheeks. He didn't want to wipe them and make the pain worse again.

"Nockwe kicked you. Manassa saved you." Her voice carried a kind tone. Her eyes assessed his injuries. It seemed Bri'ley'na actually cared how Edward was doing.

I must look terrible if I'm getting sympathy from an Onge woman. Their society was patriarchal; so was American society, and that didn't mean anything in either case. The Onge village ran on the hardened backs of the women.

Here was a woman who didn't seem so hardened, and yet he knew that she was probably the toughest of them all. Edward had heard that one fool challenged Nockwe after he had become chieftain. She had killed the man personally rather than have her husband be troubled with the duel. *They're quite a match, Nockwe and she.* She ran the village work crews from sun up to sun down as the chieftain's wife.

"Yes, but what happened to Mahanta?" Edward asked.

"Mahanta died," she said.

I've heard this before. "Yes, but how?" he asked.

"You have many questions, Ed-ward." She peered at him for approval on her pronunciation. He nodded with his eyes and she grinned slightly. "Now you must sleep. You must rest and you must heal."

"But I have so many questions," he insisted.

"And so does Manassa. But first you must be well." She knelt down on the ground beside him. "Your skull seems broken. Nockwe kicked you hard, but I am told two others got in blows and almost killed you. My husband stopped them." He heard her open a box. "Manassa told me to give this to you. This is your last shot. He showed me how to do it. It will heal you."

Edward glanced down as far as he could manage. In his lower periphery vision he saw her fiddling with a syringe.

"What is that?" he asked. *I'm not going to let them inject mud into my veins or something.*

Her warm hands pulled his arm open to expose the vein. She answered with a sing-song voice. "Nectar of the gods, that only Manassa and his chosen may drink. Magic medicine, he said."

A doctor. Perhaps this Manassa is not a tribesman at all. No wonder I'm still alive. "Is Manassa a doctor?" he asked. *Maybe he has painkillers...*

She looked at him quizzically for a moment and then gave him the injection. It hurt; her nursing skills left much to be desired. Edward wondered why Manassa hadn't administered the medicine himself.

"Now, Manassa told me to tell you this, in these exact words." She breathed in deep and looked up, reciting mechanically what he had told her. "Something strange is about to occur. Don't do anything except fix your head. Fix your head. Fix every part of your head. Fix your body and don't move your body. You will have the power to heal your body but if you move your body you may die."

Edward's stomach turned somersaults. This was not a doctor; more like another "medicine man". For all he knew, she might have injected peyote or worse. Certainly something was happening. He felt as though he were swimming at the bottom of the ocean, with all its crushing pressure bearing down, and every time he stroked in one direction he was spun completely around.

He was not losing consciousness, but it was certainly being altered.

"Just fix your head." She said again. "Just fix your head."

The last time she said that, it took her a full two minutes. It was at the end of these two minutes, as she turned to walk away in slow motion, that Edward noticed something was wrong inside of him.

The rushing sensation stopped, as though he were plunging off a cliff and had frozen in mid-air at the onset of free fall.

Disconnect. Disconnection.

He felt a peace that he had achieved only once before. Three weeks into the arduous retreat he'd taken to qualify as a Jesuit, he had sat upon a mountain top from one sunrise to the next. He'd achieved a total serenity, a detachment from this world. He had not hungered or tired. He'd felt at one with the universe.

His mentor had called it "being with God". He knew of other faiths that had terms for the same thing. It was this experience that most Jesuits shared, in the tradition of their patron saint, Ignatious, which caused their order to be more liberal than most of their Catholic brethren.

The sensation he felt now (or rather, the lack of it) was far stronger than anything he'd experienced on the mountaintop. *Total disconnect.*

Life is. I am.

Perception was perception, which had its own realities and significances and no particular emotional connotation unless he chose to have it. Detached, he could view his surroundings far more clearly.

The awareness dawned on him that, he had total control of his senses. His perceptions churned through his mind like a clear, unstoppable river. He could draw from it as he chose. *A flood of sensation. And nothing. As I choose.*

His perceptions and memories seemed without limit. Experimentally, he stretched his hearing. He heard an Onge wife arguing her husband into gathering more firewood. They were in another hut.

He shut off his hearing entirely. The world turned silent. He was mute. He turned it on again.

He sensed Bri'ley'na had left the giant hut.

Edward wanted to know what had happened to him. Perhaps in this strange, heightened state of awareness he could reach an answer without having to rely on the cryptic Onge.

When he began to examine his memory, Edward was startled to discover that he knew with certainty the whole path of his life. He could dive into his past and pull up a full recollection of what he'd witnessed - every sight, sound and sensation instantly available.

A Christmas kiss. Callista. He re-experienced it as though he were living it. The fireplace. The music playing. Her warmth.

He rapidly flicked through a dozen more memories. All were shockingly complete. What was more, he could just pull up data.

What was the name of my first grade teacher?

The answer flashed into his mind the instant he formed the question.

He picked a random number. *Element number 64?*

Gadolinium. He'd never memorized the periodic table before. His mind had pulled its response from a distant memory of the chart.

He closed his eyes. He started calculating. His mind leaped to associations which had never occurred to him five minutes before. Huge chunks of his data, his education, his memory blew into view to assist him in evaluation. He rapidly inspected old conclusions and faulty evaluations, blew them out like so many cobwebs. He could see everything from his schooling, and yet could know without looking at any of it.

One of the first mysteries he'd been working on since he'd awakened came to light in little more than a glance. *Manassa. Mahanta. Mahanta's words to the crowd. "No mortal Mahanta leaves here tonight." The Onge root of Manassa: 'mana' - of Polynesian origin, meaning 'powerful, magical, of gods', and 'sa' - Onge for 'boy, child'. Mahanta's words: "As it is sung in the psalms of our ancestors, I shall slay the panther as a child, and defying my elders, remain a child immortal." The hut. The "throne."*

Mahanta died. Manassa lives. They are the same - Manassa is the boy now deified.

In those minutes he reached many other conclusions, resolving the past, the present, and what might lay in store. Much of it might have perturbed him if he weren't so detached. The emotion connected to the facts with which he calculated had distorted and blocked them from use.

Much needed to be contemplated further, but at present there was an immediate threat to his survival. He wondered at how he'd been able to go so far off on a tangent. He had to secure his own survival, not experiment with his mind.

Mahanta. My life is in the hands of this young man. Edward assessed his chances at escape. Mahanta could not be predicted, and Edward's condition was more than questionable.

The young man took this drug, and so killed the panther to become a god in the eyes of his people. He is a powerful threat. Edward sorted through every encounter he'd had with Mahanta in his months at the village.

In retrospect, it was no wonder he'd been so inquisitive, yet so reserved, and why there'd been such strangeness about him. He must have been planning this for a long time.

Observation: Mahanta gave me this drug.

Evaluation: If he had reason to fear me, he would not.

Conclusion: He has a purpose for me, so he will not kill me yet or permit me be killed.

With that matter put to rest, at least for the immediate present, Edward worried over what intentions the Onge had for him since they knew he'd spied on their ceremony.

He remembered Nockwe's injunction: "If the tribe learns what you saw, either I or someone else will have to end your life." Edward wondered now if there were any teeth left to that threat.

Considering this hut, it seems Mahanta has established control. The whole tribe must have worked day and night to erect this "temple". As long as I am useful to him, I have no threats to worry about.

Edward had no idea what that use might be.

He turned his attention to his injury, realizing that he had subconsciously shut off the pain coming from his head to aid his concentration.

He deliberately turned the perception of pain back on in full. The devil took out his pitchfork again and began wreaking havoc on his brain and the nerves along his body. He was amazed at how much control he had over his own perceptions, even the undesirable ones.

Edward could sense every part of his body - every gland, every organ, every function. He noticed his pulse was racing. He could detect the subtle rush of blood along his veins, the pressure that forced the oxygen-laden cells to all his organs.

He slowed his heart rate as easily as he might consciously slow his breathing. He had once seen a medicine man do the same. The witch doctor had even stopped circulation in his hand for a time, but it had taken much hypnosis and to-do.

Edward just monitored his heart rate at will. He knew that if he so desired, he could take conscious command of every function of his body, automatic or otherwise.

What was this drug in his system? What was this trance he'd entered into?

It was too real for him to think he was dreaming or delusional. It was the most real moment of his life.

There was a task he had to tend to before he wasted any more time. He remembered the simple words of Bri'ley'na. *"Fix your head."*

Edward explored his injury without moving. He could sense it. His body knew what was happening. There seemed to be a near-fracture in his skull that was giving him the trouble. The bone was weak and the tissue bruised. Blood pooled in places it shouldn't. The bone would weaken further. His mind knew what was wrong.

He sensed an energy near the injury, one that he couldn't touch. It seemed to have its own perceptions connected to it, neurons that kept firing off the same signal.

He picked up what it was broadcasting. *The impact of the kick. Nockwe kicked me and then…nothing.* There was something there. There were other kicks. He kept prying, and finally it flew into view of his consciousness.

The damaged cells had recorded their attacker. They were just energy waves, playing over and over again from the nerve bundle. His mind translated them into something he could make sense out of.

Nockwe shouts. Then others. The impact. More impacts. Nockwe says to get away, to leave him be, that he is dead, and if not he will be tried.

The pain, the voices. Mahanta's voice.

The pain subsided noticeably. Connected nerve bundles were helping it discharge as he played the energy of his attention across the damaged area.

Finally, the nerves stopped sending out their distress signal.

Fascinating.

Edward's glandular system had tried to go into motion to heal the fracture, but the hormones and blood cells never reached the injured area. The misfiring nerves had kept telling his body over and over again that he was still being injured. Edward got the glands going again.

He remembered back to his classes in medicine. The Jesuits were so well-trained. There were certain healing conditions one tried to create in a body. Regular heart rate, regular breathing, increased circulation. Reduced pain. High protein intake. The first four he enforced directly on his body by will alone. The last he substituted by working his stomach glands out of starvation mode. It might deplete his store of resources but he needed his head mobile and functional. He needed to heal.

And of course, the last healing condition was a given. Sleep. He directed his body to it and instantly he was out.

4

Doctor Callista Knowles treated her last patient of the day. He was a small native boy whose father had offered a chicken in exchange for medical care.

She had declined the payment. Callista was a doctor, not a farmer, and in the three years she had practiced in the port city of Lisbaad, natives paying anything at all had been few and far between. She made her way with a grant from St. Mary's and the occasional paying foreigner who found his way into her clinic from the docks.

The two islanders had knocked on her door after hours. Callista had locked up more than half an hour earlier, but she could tell that the man must have trekked from an outlying area.

The boy was in no shape to walk; his father must have carried him most of the way. The man's legs trembled. His body had sagged with relief when Callista opened the door.

She put her hand on the boy's head. She had stopped using thermometers after the first month in Lisbaad, unless it was a paying patient who would expect it. The back of her palm did just as well. The boy was running a fever, but not too bad. His father looked at her expectantly. She smiled to reassure him.

She checked the boy's eyes, mouth, and ears. The boy coughed. She checked his lungs with her stethoscope. She made breathing motions to him and got him to mimic her. She didn't like what she heard.

"His lungs are sick," she told the father in Tamil. "He is hot, he has a fever." She went to her medicine closet and pulled out the last of her antibiotics. There would be another shipment in a couple days. Until then the island would have to cope. She'd be sure to point out the deficiency to the next inspector from St. Mary's. "You are a farmer?" she asked the father.

The man nodded.

"You are not to let him work for two weeks. Every day you are to give him one of these, until they are all gone. Do not save them. They will go bad. Do exactly as I say."

The man nodded.

"What did I say?" she asked.

"No work, these every day," said the father. Tamil was obviously not his first or even second language. On this island, everyone spoke a bit of everything, though. He pointed at the medicine bottle full of pills from the clinic's dispensary.

She nodded. "Very good."

"No work?" asked the little boy in much better Tamil than her father. "And candy every day? Yippee!" He rocked back and forth on the exam table with all the enthusiasm he could muster. He coughed again.

"Not candy, medicine. Only one each day. It doesn't taste good. And no running around and playing, either. Rest."

The boy sagged his shoulders. She couldn't suppress her smile. He would make it, and she needn't worry.

She said to the father, "Come back in three months. Free. Duiyon will make you an appointment."

Another person knocked at the door. "Excuse me," she said. "Please follow me back to the reception area. Duiyon will be back from her errands in a few minutes."

She checked the front door. It was James.

"Dr. Seacrest," she shouted through the door. "We're closed. If it's treatment you seek you'll have to come another time."

"Just need to borrow some sugar, neighbor," he shouted back. She opened the door let him inside. James was about fifteen years older than her, in his early forties. He was wiry yet handsome and walked with quiet aloofness. She knew the majority of his sex appeal was due to the fact that he obviously didn't give a shit about anything. Not her sort of guy - but he certainly caught her eye, today. He'd just had a haircut, and something about the way he'd done it reminded her...*Oh, stop it.*

The two doctors had the distinction of being the only two whites of their profession on the island. "How can I help you?" she asked. "I'm out of sugar, as well as everything else in the dispensary. I have some water, but it will evaporate soon. And they just got my last antibiotic." She filed charts, making sure he saw that she wasn't wasting any time in getting out of there.

"Actually I just wanted to borrow some of your time. I have reason to celebrate, and wanted to take you out to dinner," said Seacrest boldly.

"Well, I appreciate your offer, James, I really do..."

"Why don't you take me up on it just once, Dr. Knowles? It's my birthday."

"It was your birthday seven months ago."

"This is my real birthday. I've grown older," he said.

"James, will you ever give up?" she asked.

"Hmmm..." he said. She walked down the hall to the exam rooms. She changed the paper towels running across the beds and sanitized. As she sprayed she thought about Seacrest. She got a feeling about him that made her want to keep her distance. A lot of had to do with the mystery as to how he ended up in Lisbaad. It was something he wouldn't talk about.

Of course, it's still a mystery to me how I ended up in Lisbaad...

She had to admit there was a feeling she got about every guy that made her want to keep her distance.

Dinner sounded nice, though. It was something she rarely was able to treat herself to. Seacrest, in his Corvette and infinitely deep pockets, was more than capable of delivering a fine dining experience.

When she walked back into the reception room, James was crouched near the natives, muttering with them. He stood up when she walked in.

"What are you up to?" she asked with cocked eyebrow.

"Apparently, Mr. Guin here had to carry his son eight miles to reach this clinic. It will be another eight miles before they get to sleep." He paused.

"Mmhmm?" she prodded.

"I have made them an offer," said Seacrest.

"And what is that?" asked Callista.

"I will drive them in my glorious candy apple red quad cab '95 Corvette with all leather interior all the way to their farm, if you will agree to accompany me and then let me take you out to dinner."

He smiled gamely. He knew he had won. She sighed and looked at the little boy. She envisioned his eyes lighting up as he took what was most likely the first car ride of his life. Probably he wouldn't even need the pills after that.

I do it for the children...he does look handsome today...and ten, fifteen years is not all that much difference on this island...it's just a date...

5

The pain had changed. Edward sensed that his body had made definite progress on the head injury, but the torture along his nerve channels had grown much worse. It felt as though every neuron in his body were generating charge, ripping up and down his body like electric fire and ice.

The feeling of disconnection was gone. Instead, he felt much too connected to his body.

He heard a din of voices nearby, hundreds of voices. Some sort of crowd. They were muttering, shouting, displeased.

He felt trapped, and for an instant he fought the impulse to jump up and flee. He checked himself. Sudden motion would undo every bit of healing he'd done.

According to the reasoning he'd conducted before he'd fallen asleep, running would serve no purpose and could actually estrange Mahanta, the only reason Edward was still living.

That logic, however, seemed hazy at best. He didn't feel like he could process again everything he'd gone through before the sleep. Just the thought overwhelmed him. He couldn't bring back into recall the concatenation of evaluations that had led him to that conclusion.

I guess I could...very slowly...

He picked it all over in his mind as best he could. The pain dispersed his concentration. The salient points stood out. *Manassa is Mahanta. Mahanta, for now, is a friend.*

His mind drifted to the drug that Bri'ley'na had injected into his veins.

And I had worried it was mud. A dream he had buried a decade ago resurfaced.

Edward stands in Father's study. Father is kneeling, praying on his rosary. Thomas has just left the night before. "Are you sad, Edward?" asks Father.

"No, sir." But his voice is cracking.

"It's fine to miss your brother."

"I do miss him."

"Let's prayer together."

"I don't want to pray tonight, father."

"That's when we need to the most - when we don't wish to."

"I don't want to go off like Thomas, father."

Father chuckles. "Then what do you want to do?

"I want to learn about science, father. I want to learn about electricity, biology, chemistry. I can't stop reading about all of it. I want to make a difference."

"You will be a Jesuit, then, the most learned of the priests. You won't be a Franciscan like your brother Thomas. You'll be a Jesuit like Allen."

I don't want to be a priest, father. I don't want to be like either of them.

That part was never said.

Edward had held hope. After Edward had won a scholarship to Oxford, his father had let him attend for his bachelors "to prepare him for the priesthood." All while he was in school, he'd held hope, though, that his course would change.

As he'd neared graduation, the pressure had mounted. *Father. Then brothers. And then Cali - a different sort of pressure, and a final one.* It left him with a terrible question: had those dreams ever been real? Though he held them so hard, had they fled?

They had. Now, after his experience with this mysterious substance, the dreams rushed back to him in full.

He knew that under its influence, with the inhuman mind that it gave him, he could solve mysteries that had plagued humankind for centuries.

That substance is not of God. The voice of his father. Edward ignored it.

It's a drug, Edward, his cautious side protested. He quickly quelled it.

I don't know what it is. Whatever it is, I need to learn more.

"Edward." Edward opened his eyes. Mahanta sat with his legs crossed on his velvet pad.

"Manassa," answered Edward with what might have passed for a smile. He noticed his throat didn't croak so much this time.

"We shall name me something Western in time," Mahanta said thoughtfully in English. Clearly Mahanta felt comfortable in Edward's company.

Edward said nothing but took note of this. Mahanta was hinting at something that Edward wasn't awake enough to decipher.

"How is your head?" Mahanta asked.

"Better and worse. My nerves…"

"It is the *lleychta*, the nectar - the unfortunate side effect of its trance."

Edward could hear a growing din of Onge voices outside the hut. They were getting loud enough to contribute to the aching in his head.

"It hurt before I was given it," said Edward.

"I tried to give it to you twice, while you were out, when it looked like you wouldn't make it. But it doesn't work while you are knocked out. I didn't know," he said. "I've never been knocked out and given it to myself before."

Edward couldn't help but chuckle at this. He was awarded immediately by a fresh throbbing radiating from his spine out to his toes and fingers

"I will get some eucalyptus paste to help with the pain. It soothes the nerves after the liquid," said Mahanta.

"I could definitely use some soothing. What was that stuff? What did you put in me? And in you?" Edward stuttered trying to get out all his questions at once.

Mahanta smiled warmly. "I have many questions for you, too. All that in time." The young man sighed as he stood up. "First, there is a challenge we must face. Can you sit?"

"I don't know." Edward hated the idea, but there was urgency in Mahanta's voice.

"Let's try," said Mahanta. He helped Edward up into a sitting position. The motion was all Edward could bear.

"Quiet!" whispered Mahanta. Edward realized he had screamed. "Hurts?" Mahanta asked.

"Yes. I can't take it. I need to lie down."

"Can you stand?" asked Mahanta

"Oh, God, no," said Edward.

The crowd outside kept shouting. They were getting loud enough for Edward to make out some of the words. *Manassa. White man.*

"Your 'no' is not a sufficient answer today," said Mahanta.

"What is this crowd?"

"They want to kill you."

Oh, God.

"You do not recognize their living god. This is a holy house, this hut, consecrated to me and those I command. It should be safe for you so long as I deem it, but unholy men might creep in the dark of night and kill you despite my commandments. Such is the force of our traditions." This he said quickly, in the rolling poetry of traditional Onge. The older tongue was easier for Edward to follow, being closer to its Indo-European roots.

"What must we do?" asked Edward.

"I have a question for you, Jesuit." *A question that you obviously don't want to ask.* There was pain in Mahanta's eyes.

"Yes?"

"Would your lord Jesus desire you to spit on his face if it eased your suffering?"

Edward thought it over. There was an awful hole in his stomach as he started to see where this was going. "Yes."

"Today you must spit and ease your suffering." Mahanta waited for Edward to prompt him further, but the priest said nothing.

"If you desire to live today, you must renounce your God and bow to me,

48

proclaiming me the only living god on Earth, with the power to change the destiny of nations. It must be said this way." Again he said this in traditional Onge, flatly. The prospect didn't excite Mahanta one bit - in fact, it seemed to disgust him. Edward was feeling nauseated, himself.

Mahanta continued matter-of-factly. "I will announce that I have healed you with my powers, that you have come to see the light and that you are now my servant, higher than all Onge for you are the only mortal who may sleep in my house. I have calculated this in trance. This is the only path I see in which you may survive. Nockwe has grown ill and can no longer help protect you. Dook gains power by the day. It will only be a matter of time before tradition kills you. Perhaps today." This was no argument. Just the facts.

Edward turned his head to vomit beside the bed. His body spasmed in pain as he retched. This didn't faze Mahanta at all; rather, it was as though he'd expected it.

"Of course, your God will still live and be your God. I am no god at all, merely a...scientist." He said this last word measuredly, in English. There was no Onge word for it. "This is all just a matter of survival. I know this is happening fast, but we have no other options at this point. I'm glad you finally woke up when you did. Are you ready?"

Edward knew he had no choice but to be ready. Whether Mahanta's logic was correct or not was inconsequential. Whether or not his intentions were pure did not matter. If Mahanta told him to eat manure Edward would have to comply. Edward was too weak physically to defy his only protector. He did not want to die. He didn't feel that God wanted him to die, either.

Edward heard one man's voice ring out clearly over the wild hubbub outside. "Give us the white man!" He was followed by an approving roar.

God, please forgive me. Edward had prayed more in one week than he had in a year. "Yes, I'm ready."

Mahanta nodded. "It is important, Edward, that during your brief demonstration to the tribe, that you look completely healthy. Is that understood?" Edward nodded. "I can't give you any more of the nectar. You've had three injections in less than two moons. I've never had to experience the degree of pain that I know you now feel." There was a touch of compassion in his tone that Edward somehow found reassuring. "Let us stand."

49

Edward couldn't help but scream again, though this time he was well aware of it. Once moving, he found it helped to stay moving. He wobbled back and forth, his vision almost seared out by the pain.

"Breathe more quickly. Increase your heart rate. Release your adrenal glands...get angry...Don't look it, though." advised Mahanta.

Oddly, Edward found that he could follow the commands, not nearly as thoroughly as he would have been able to while in that trance, but he started to feel his heart rate go up and the pain ease a bit. It was still unbearable.

"Are you okay?" asked Mahanta.

Edward did not speak, but almost swooned. Mahanta propped him up.

"You will need to speak loud and clear out there," said the Onge. "You will need to look healed. And you will need to stand tall, and then bow to me."

Edward breathed in deep and wiped the tears out of his eyes. He let out a long, frustrated groan. "Let's go," he muttered.

He leaned against Mahanta, shuffling all the way to the entrance of the hut. Bamboo reeds hung from the arch of the door by strings to make a rigid sort of drape. Mahanta deposited Edward to lean against the wall just inside and walked out to the crowd.

6

The tribe stopped their shouting. They had long awaited this hour to hear the wisdom of their Manassa. They knelt before him, the white man momentarily forgotten.

Already, their god had conjured the clouds; the rains had come for two days just as he had foretold. He had, of course, slain the panther. He had defeated the medicine man, even though the medicine man had cheated and attacked Manassa unarmed upon his triumphant return. Manassa had even healed a child, Tomy, of demons.

Every day, for a short time, Manassa talked to his people.

The tribesman Tien, on his knees, pushed his way closer to Manassa. He had a mission that would fail if he did get near.

Even if Tien's deed meant his death it would be for the greater good of the tribe and his god. He was to slay the white man on sight. If the white man didn't come out, Tien was to wait in the night and assassinate him as he slept.

Others were agitating the crowd to draw out the white man. Tien was to wait at the front of the crowd, his dagger in hand. But the crowd was thick, thicker than any other day. Tien could not get up to the front; the people there were jealous and kept pushing him back. They refused to be far from Manassa. They had waited all day to be near Him.

"MY PEOPLE!" shouted Manassa in the traditional Onge tongue he favored. My great god, thought Tien. He had been one to see Manassa fight the panther, and again fight the medicine man. Earlier, he'd seen Manassa shatter the medicine man's spear. He had no doubt in his mind that this boy was the immortal of their legends.

"Manassa!" shouted the crowd in unison, Tien along with them. He was several rows back. Now that everyone was kneeling it was difficult edging closer.

"YOU ARE THE CHOSEN!" shouted Manassa.

"As are you, our god!" said the tribe.

"Hear me today, my people. A mighty miracle is at hand. Here today is the first shudder of a powerful earthquake. Here is the first branch bent by an unstoppable typhoon. Here is our first advance to the high throne to which the Onge are destined." Tien had never learned traditional Onge. He did not understand what Manassa was saying. He would hear the story later, from Dook or another. He could not help but be excited, though, by the tone of his god's words, by the rustling enthusiasm of the tribe all around him.

Dook had explained it all to him. All was as had been prophesied for generation upon generation. Their living god would lead the tribe to become the chieftains over all chieftains…

Manassa continued. "I told you that past the horizon, where the sun sets, lies a land ruled by the white man, a land of untold riches and plenty. Though we know of them, they know not of us. We are but a speck to them, a termite, an ant. They know not that their living god walks the earth today. They fear not the Chosen Tribe.

"But today, Manassa has made the white man his slave, has made the white man to recognize the living god. For today, the white man, the Jesus-man-no-more, Edward Styles, is healed!" He dramatically pulled aside the bamboo reeds. The white man exited the temple.

The priest stood resolutely, every muscle in his body tense. There was no sign of his head injury. Tien had seen Edward's body in the clearing after the panther fight. There was no way he could be standing so soon; no human could recover so quickly. *White demon. He is here to work his witchcraft on our god.* He wished he knew what Manassa was saying. It would help him kill this demon.

Tien felt a fluttering in his stomach, the same that he got while on the hunt. A part of him wished the white man had never shown himself. He did not want to have to perform. *I must not fail.* Dook had promised to kill him if he failed. Tien gripped his knife's reassuring handle. To succeed was glory.

"I am healed!" shouted Edward, also in traditional Onge. "I am grateful eternally. I renounce my God and my ways." Edward took the cross hanging from his neck and broke it off its necklace. He threw it to the ground. "Manassa, you are my god, the only living god on earth, with the power to change nations."

Tien slid the dagger from its sheath. Odd the priest was throwing down his necklace. Perhaps he was working some kind of spell. He was always wearing that strange cross. *Why is Manassa permitting him to do his magic?*

Tien launched through the rows of onlookers. They resisted his surge instinctively but he pushed through. Finally, he was in the open, stumbling forward, the white man within his reach. He leapt to plunge his knife into the kneeling priest's back.

In a flash, Manassa interposed himself in front of the white man. Tien couldn't stop his momentum. Manassa chopped the knife out of Tien's hand before it reached him. Oh, gods, thought Tien. *I attacked our god!*

"TIEN!!!" shouted Manassa.

Tien collapsed on the ground, trembling. He sensed the eyes of the Onge upon him.

Manassa loomed over him. Tien felt his shadow. It would be nothing for Manassa to shove the dropped dagger into his head. He'd seen what Manassa had done to the panther.

"My child!" shouted Manassa. "Think you a dagger can stop a god?" It was in that old Onge tongue, again. Tien risked looking up at him. Manassa narrowed his eyes.

"I..." Tien mumbled. He looked back down at the ground. "I don't know what you're saying, my lord," he mumbled in vulgar Onge.

"My child," Manassa said, matching his dialect. The god sized up Tien and the silent crowd. "You didn't hear my words, unmindful of the tongue of our ancestors. Others have heard my words, however, and still they disobey. For them there will be no mercy." Manassa's eyes locked with Dook's, but only for a second. "I thank you for your service and your heart, but this white man recognizes me now as his god."

Manassa glanced over at the white man. He was shaking heavily. Perhaps he'd gone into terror over the assassination attempt.

"The white man is now my chosen servant," continued Manassa. "Let it be known that he is higher than all mortals, for he is the first of foreign lands to recognize the true living god, and he shall be the only mortal to ever sleep in my temple. So it is said, so it is. The words of Manassa." He said the last in traditional Onge. Every word was memorized by the old women to be added to the oral history.

Manassa forcefully grabbed the white man and practically threw him into the hut. Edward was trembling all over. Apparently, the incident had given him quite a fright. *Our god does not permit weakness.*

"LONG LIVE OUR TRIBE!" shouted Manassa, retreating back into the hut.

"ETERNAL IS OUR LIVING GOD!" chanted the tribe. They stood. Tien plunged into the crowd. He had to get away.

Tien made it only ten yards before Dook seized him by the shoulders and threw him to the ground once more.

Tien cried out, holding his hands before him begging for mercy. "It was the will of the god."

Dook spit on him and growled. "Perhaps. But that foreigner will be dead along with the other, despite your cowardice. I will be chieftain of the living god, and your idiocy won't stop me." Dook kicked him and walked away.

Tien noticed the boy Tomy walking past. Had he been listening? Tien dismissed it. He was just a boy.

Tien pulled himself up. It was not yet noon, and it had already been far too long a day.

7

James ordered wine. Callista asked for water. *Well, at least I've got her here, finally.*

This had been his life's work for close to a year. At least it had kept his mind occupied. He had developed much more unsavory hobbies in his earlier years. "Callista-courting" was the most therapeutic of the vices he'd indulged in so far.

Not only was she completely out of his league; she knew it, without even an inkling of his shady past.

They were seated at a table for two in a restaurant that James had chosen months earlier. The lighting was low, and the noise level sufficient to allow for intimacy without having to speak too loudly. The sea-drenched breeze wafting in from the outside dining area reminded him of the Mediterranean. She reminded him of the Mediterranean. He missed it.

"I can't believe you brought them all the way to their farm! You bottomed out your car five times!" she laughed. "The roads were terrible."

"A promise is a promise," he said nonchalantly. He'd need to get a mechanic to look at his car in the morning, but it was worth it to impress her. She had already impressed him.

She had the thin, chiseled elegance that he admired in Americans, but there was a posture and certainty in her that led him to believe she'd traveled. "You're an American from England, aren't you?" he asked.

"You're an Australian from Melbourne," she countered. It wasn't a question.

"Actually, from a little bit north of the city. Born in Sydney, though. How'd you know?" He was surprised. She'd figured him at least as well as he'd managed to figure her.

She shrugged. "Lucky guess. I was born in New Jersey. Left there by the time I was six for London."

"Does it show in my accent?" asked Seacrest, still stuck on her deduction. "I've spent a good deal of time abroad. Wouldn't think it was so obvious, my accent. Is it obvious?"

"It just shows. I knew a man from Melbourne. My father worked at the American Embassy in London. I practically grew up there. Met all kinds of people from all sorts of places." She sipped her water. He sipped his wine.

"Have you travelled much?"

"Not as much as I'd like. We stayed pretty rooted in England. I even ended up going to school there."

"Well, how do you like *this* island?" he asked. "Good change of pace?"

"Well, it's what I asked for," she said.

"What do you mean?" he asked.

"I was looking to do something like this. For me it was a good opportunity, strange as that may sound. What about you?"

I hate it. I can't wait to get off this ridiculous rock. I'd rather drown in my own piss than stay here another year. "Well, I'm here right now, so I may as well make the most of it." He sipped his wine again. He needed to change the subject. That was all he could tell her. One more question and he'd really have to start lying. He shifted in his seat and smiled. "Anyway, tell me, why is it so hard to get a date with Dr. Knowles?"

She laughed.

"Are you married with five illegitimate children and three adopted Chinese babies?" he asked quite seriously.

She laughed again. "No." She smiled. "Is this a date, Dr. Seacrest?" she asked, matching his serious tone.

He smiled. *Can't get anything past this one.* "I'm paying, so it's a date. And your purse is locked in my 'vette, so you can't do anything about it." He gauged her response. She was making a decision.

"Well, I guess it's official," she said. "You're on a date, and I'm a hostage." The waiter put the appetizer on their table.

Toughie. "You're lucky. Usually I take my hostages to rundown bars. You're more in the 'distinguished captive' category."

She looked at the candle in the middle of the table and watched the dance of the flame. She didn't look up at him as she spoke. "You know, James, I appreciate you taking me out to dinner."

He'd known this about her. She hadn't done this in a while. *She's got a long story.* He had decided he wanted her anyway, even though he knew he'd be competing with a ghost. The challenge suited him. He'd just have to take things a lot slower with her than he was used to.

I guess I've got a thing for the good Dr. Knowles. "Well, Callista, I appreciate you joining me. I hope maybe we can do it again."

She looked up at him and smiled. Whatever had shadowed her face a moment before was gone. "Well, all you have to do is lock my purse in your Corvette and, rest assured, I'll follow you to the end of my days."

8

Edward could not sleep.

For one, he hurt too much. He was exhausted by pain past the point of rest.

But that's not it. He was thinking.

Since he'd had the trance, he could not stop thinking.

He was thinking about the periodic table in just that moment. He saw it projected in his mind's eye on the dark ceiling of the temple.

Seconds before that, he was thinking about some other scientific possibility. In a few minutes he would think of another.

For now he was thinking about proteins. There was a pattern with them. He'd glimpsed them in trance while his life's knowledge had flashed before his eyes. It had come to him when he'd thought of Gadolinium. There was something to a pattern with the proteins, some sort of periodic table of proteins. He'd never seen a pattern before; he didn't think anyone had seen it before.

For the first time in six years, one month, and seven days, he did not regret becoming a Jesuit missionary.

Then again, he wasn't really a Jesuit missionary anymore. He felt new and whole.

He'd just faked renouncing his God and declaring a boy his soul's ruler, and yet he'd never felt more free. He felt he was finally doing what God had meant him for.

He hoped Mahanta would trust him with the substance again. He felt certain he would. *He needs me for something.*

And I need him.

He closed his eyes and did not sleep. Protein molecules danced on his eyelids. He almost had it, and yet it eluded him.

9

It was a date, thought Callista as she got into her car behind the clinic. It was around 10:00 p.m.

After three years in Lisbaad, she thought she would have gotten used to the nights. It was no London. Since her first day here, darkness had taken on new meanings and new depths. She recalled the chilling night her headlights had both burned out, and she had to struggle home along the pockmarked road with only the diffused light of the cloud covered moon to guide her. She'd eventually driven back to the clinic and slept the night there.

She saw James's hand wave out of the Corvette's window as he pulled onto the road. She started her car.

A dark body flickered past her headlights. Dark skin and a loincloth. A woman with something in her arms.

The woman was gibbering loudly. She pounded on Callista's window. The doctor didn't understand a word the woman was saying.

Callista looked for Seacrest, but he'd already left. She screamed for him on reflex. She realized with a touch of panic that the woman had probably waited for the Corvette to leave.

She checked the door's lock. Fortunately it was secure.

The woman kept pounding the windshield and shouting. She was frantic.

Callista shouted to her, "Get away!" through the window. The woman did not stop. Callista tried the five dialects she knew besides Tamil. She got no response.

Callista put the car in drive. She decided to try to make a break for it.

The woman screamed even more loudly. She ran in front of the car's headlights. Callista finally saw her clearly. She had a limp body in her arms. She looked no older than 25, her long black hair framing her face. She looked half Indian, half Chinese, with dark skin, nearly black. Now wonder Callista hadn't seen her.

Callista had her hand over the horn, planning to force her way past this native, but stopped when she saw the body.

The woman was crying hysterically. She gripped the hood of Callista's car to steady herself.

She was holding a little boy, younger than the native who she'd treated earlier. *Must be her son*, thought Callista. He had the same complexion as his mother.

For Callista, there was little choice at this point. The woman had stopped shouting. She was leaning against the car hood with one arm around her son as she took gulping, arrhythmic breaths. He tears sparkled down her dark face.

Oh, God. Callista wrestled with the door lock and stepped out of the car. She approached the woman carefully. The woman looked at Dr. Knowles, but did not show any signs of relief. She showed the doctor the boy.

He was limp, and some saliva had foamed out of his mouth. He was dead or close to it.

Callista moved with all the efficiency of an ER doctor, grabbing the woman's arm and escorting her through the back door of the clinic. "Come this way," she said in Tamil. She knew the woman probably didn't understand her, but the voice tone was important. Callista left the car running; there wasn't time.

Once in the exam room, Knowles touched the woman's shoulder and made eye contact. She breathed deeply, in and out. She got the native to do the same. Callista needed her to calm down.

"Do you understand me?" asked Callista in Tamil. "What language do you speak?" The woman looked at her blankly, moving her lips as though trying to work out the words. No comprehension.

Callista gently took the child's limp form into her arms and laid him on the exam table. He was dressed in a loincloth and wrapped in an off-white homespun. Callista watched the slight rise and fall of his chest. She checked his pulse. It was far too low.

All the while Callista made her exam, the boy's mother hovered. The mother could not look at him for more than a second; she could not look away from him for more than a second. She was perpetually touching him and releasing him, gulping back her tears only to let them loose again.

Callista opened the boy's eyelids and flashed a light in his pupils. He was out cold.

On a hunch, Callista pulled out a needle from the cabinet in the room. The woman reacted violently to the glint of steel, throwing her body between her and the child.

Callista held out her hand, refusing to react. She demonstrated breathing deeply again. The mother calmed herself, and Callista edged past her to the boy. She pricked his finger and tested the blood. The results were conclusive almost instantly.

He's in a diabetic coma.

Callista pointed at the child, then made a sleeping motion, then pointed at her wristwatch with an upturned eyebrow and a shrug. The woman didn't understand. Callista needed to know how long he'd been out. She sighed. It was irrelevant, anyway. The treatment would be the same.

Callista made a "stay here" motion. The mother nodded. Callista sprinted down the hall to the medicine closet. She pulled out the IV equipment and hauled everything back to the room.

The woman was stroking her son's hair. Her tears splashed his face. She was still trying to choke back her sobs.

Callista hooked up the IV. The woman restrained herself from another reaction to protect her son. She was terrified, though, whimpering and moaning.

Knowles checked the boy's vitals every half hour.

It was an exhausting night. The three never left the room. Knowles sat in her swivel stool, watching the boy breathe and the mother hover. At any moment, with his blood sugar that low, he could go into cardiac arrest. She had to be ready to resuscitate him the instant she didn't see those little lungs rise and fall.

The woman caressed his face and brushed his hair. She kept muttering to herself in a foreign dialect.

Callista felt an empty edge as the adrenaline drained from her body. It would be easy to fall asleep now, were there not a little native boy half-dead on her exam table. Tonight would not be a question of what would be nice or comfortable, but rather a question of what is necessary.

The doctor had no one to relieve her. She would stay with the boy until he was no longer critical. Time was not a factor. In the little exam room, with the door closed and the mother pacing, the world seemed timeless.

Callista kept counting breaths. She forced herself to stop looking at her watch.

At six in the morning, the boy's chest stopped.

Callista was shocked. She launched out of her swivel chair to the boy. His blood sugar had bounced to a livable range. As the night gave way to morning, Callista had been sure of recovery.

The mother panicked at Callista's sudden motion. She gasped and rushed to her son's side.

Before Callista could reach him, The boy took a deep, grasping breath. His eyes popped open. He tried to roll to his side.

The woman grabbed her son and hugged him fiercely. She kept squeezing him, crying and yelling aloud. The boy didn't say anything, but tried to squeeze her back.

He looked around the room. He saw Callista and pulled back. The woman glanced from her son to see what he was reacting to, then muttered to him soothingly.

He looked at her dazedly, then back up to Callista. He smiled a weak, toothy grin. He hugged his mother again.

Callista couldn't help but smile. She was so tired her bones ached, but she still felt the rush. *That boy is alive.* The little family was smiling now. The mother still hadn't stopped crying. She held her forehead to her son's forehead. *This is why I do medicine.*

After a while, the native woman nodded at Callista. They did not share a language, but no words were necessary. Callista got a pillow and propped it under the boy's head, motioning that he should go back to sleep.

The little boy started snoring quietly. The woman hugged Callista. Callista hugged her back. The woman started crying once more. She cried hysterically. Callista didn't let her go from their embrace until she had cried it all out.

Though Callista had never had a child, she knew exactly how the mother felt.

10

Once Edward finally slept, it was difficult for him to pull out of it. He would return to consciousness for only moments at a time. *Tomy putting a cup to his mouth. A woman feeding him stew.*

The Onge "god" was waiting at his side when Edward finally came to.

Edward tried to pull himself up. Mahanta held a steady hand to his chest and didn't let him. "Relax," said Mahanta. "There's no need to rush."

Edward took the advice. He felt like he had a bad hangover. "I feel a lot better," he said.

"That's good," said Mahanta.

"We need to talk," said Edward.

Mahanta smiled. "You've been out cold for three days, and you want to talk."

Edward looked startled. "Your English…"

Mahanta smiled more widely. "I've been practicing."

The drug…of course…

Mahanta explained unnecessarily, "I've read your books a few times and practiced while you were out. I thought I'd learn something from your medical texts that I could use to help you recover."

"Yeah? Did it help?"

Mahanta shrugged. "It helped my English, at least…" Now it was Edward's turn to smile. "Is the pain gone?" asked Mahanta.

"Pretty much. I've got a headache, but I've had worse hangovers." Mahanta cocked an eyebrow. "I wasn't always a priest, you know."

Mahanta nodded. "And I wasn't always a god…" The humor was lost on Edward - the incident a few days ago was too fresh and too abhorrent.

"Am I safe now?" asked Edward.

"As safe as I am," answered Mahanta. "Our ruse worked wonders on the attitude of the tribe towards the white man."

"So what is this substance that you gave me?" asked Edward.

"Well, in terms like your medical books, it tears down some sort of subconscious barrier. It lets you use your entire mind, your brain, your nervous system, all of it."

"And in your terms?" asked Edward.

"In my terms, it allows for the attainment of *infinite mind*, oneness of mind, body, and soul."

"What does it come from? How did you find it?"

"My tribe has been using a particular hallucinogenic plant sap for centuries. I learned a bit of chemistry from your white predecessor here. I distilled the sap. Blind luck."

"It's the discovery of the millenium," said Edward. Mahanta was silent. "What? What's the matter?"

"Nothing. You have many questions and I don't wish to over-excite you. But yes, it could change our world. That's why I need your help."

That's why you let me live, thought Edward. *But why?*

Edward sat up. He was surprised how relatively easy it was to do so. "My help? Why my help?" he asked.

"You are a Jesuit, aren't you?" asked Mahanta.

"Yes. Why, do you think the Catholic Church can help you?"

"No, but you can. You are a Jesuit, so you are well-educated. And you are well-read besides. I need a fellow scientist. I cannot research alone."

Edward could not help but laugh in disbelief. "Alone? We need a team of scientists. We need to bring this discovery to the scientific community. This needs to get researched…it will change the face of science…"

"No, Edward," said Mahanta.

"What do you mean, 'no'?" Edward asked, looking up at Mahanta's stern face.

Mahanta shouted an order to man near the entrance of the temple. He left. Edward and Mahanta were alone in the hut.

"Edward Styles, I did not want to discuss this with you yet until you were fully awake with a meal in your stomach, but I guess now is as good a time as any."

Edward just watched him. He didn't know what was going to happen. He glanced at the doorway. It was a long way off to make a dash for it.

"I am sure you have mulled over the scientific ramifications of this drug. Probably you realize them far more than I do, since you've been in a university and I only have books. But have you given any attention to the social and political effects this will have on society?"

"Sure," said Edward. "It will revolutionize everything."

"Edward, think." Mahanta started at him intently, as though he were again fighting a panther.

"I thought. What do you mean?"

Mahanta sighed. "Perhaps you might have a better mind for science, but I apparently have a better knack for survival patterns. All we do here, every day, is survive. Survival of the fittest."

That got Edward thinking. "You think…" he started.

"Once someone knows about this drug, that knowledge will get to someone else. That will leak to someone else. Eventually someone who recognizes its value will expend the necessary effort to obtain it. And that will mean everybody who knew about it is dead. It's a simple equation, Edward, one that I'm surprised you haven't already arrived at."

Edward was tongue-tied. He wanted to deny the truth of what Mahanta said. Deep down, however, he knew. This discovery was like a billion dollars in a suitcase. Who could you trust with it?

Only this is worth trillions.

"Well, what do you propose, then?" asked Edward.

"It is not a matter of my proposal, right now. I wish to have you on my team, to help me research this drug. I will trust you with it, within reason. And you must trust me, within reason. But first, before all of this, you must come to decide that this is what you want. You have some hard decisions to make, Edward. You must make them tonight."

"Like what?"

"You've sworn an oath of allegiance to your Jesuit General. Not even your pope can supersede that. But this project must. You've sworn yourself to a regimen of prayer and meditation. For that we have no time. You've sworn to abide by a Bible and commandments that may have no place in my jungle world and in our scientific method. If you agree to start this project with me, not even God himself will be able to get you out of it until it's done."

"Until what is done?" asked Edward.

"That's the question you should ask yourself. You must sort out what you want done, and whether it's worth it. It's your choice. Good night, Edward." Mahanta walked out of the hut.

Edward lay back down on his pallet to think.

II

Where is that idiot going? thought Dook as he watched Tien creep from hut to hut.

No moon lit the village that night. Were Dook not a hunter, he wouldn't have been able to spot Tien at all.

Dook didn't trust him. He spied on Tien from the outlying brush. Surely Tien was up to no good. Dook hadn't directed him to do anything since the last debacle.

Idiots are not to be trusted.

Tien approached the chief's hut. Its larger size and little flag demarked it from the rest.

Dook debated with himself. *Either Tien is ambitious and wants to assassinate Nockwe as amends for his errors, or else he has turned and wishes to join my enemy. I'll break his neck either way. Maybe tonight. Let's see what he does.*

Tien slumped to the bamboo door of the hut, and knocked gently. Only the chieftain had a door.

If it's a murder he's after, Tien makes the worst and most polite murderer I've ever seen, thought Dook.

Tien glanced furtively behind him. Dook resisted the urge to duck. There was no way he could be seen in the brush, but the movement might have given him away.

Getting no answer, Tien knocked again, fidgeted more. Dook could tell he was getting spooked.

Tien knocked one more time. He started to lurk away. The door opened slowly, and Tien jumped up nearly a foot as he turned back in surprise.

"Tien?" It was the voice of Nockwe.

Maybe I should kill them both now and frame Tien…But Nockwe is awake, and in his own home…I only have my dagger tonight. Who knows what traps Nockwe has in wait…

There was the matter of Nockwe's wife, too, nearly as fearsome an adversary as Nockwe, himself.

Tien nodded in answer to Nockwe.

"Come in, Tien," beckoned the chieftain. Tien entered the hut.

Dook was shocked. Tien was low class. Dook would have never let Tien into his own hut.

The door closed behind Tien. The long lance of light from the hut's candles folded back into the dwelling. Dook ran to a perch beneath the window opening of the hut where he could hear their conversation. Tien spoke in hushed tones, but Nockwe answered him loudly.

"Nockwe, I am here to warn you. Dook…"

"You put your life in danger by your presence here, Tien," said Nockwe. He coughed. Though obviously sick, he still sounded commanding.

Maybe I was right to wait.

"Still, I am loyal," insisted Tien. "Dook wishes to kill you. You and the white man. By challenge if you grow sicker. By other means if he must. But he wants your flag."

Nockwe wheezed and coughed louder. He said nothing.

"I will challenge him to protect you," said Tien.

"He will kill you," replied Nockwe without hesitation. "Thank you for your loyalty, but do not waste your life."

"I can match him," said Tien. "He must be matched. I see now that he doesn't care about anything but himself…"

Justifying your incompetence…

"At first we were friends…"

Until you showed you were just like the rest of them.

"He will not let anyone match him," interrupted Nockwe. "That's the problem. You will never have an even fight."

The chieftain is wise in this - and this only. A snake can tell a snake, I guess…

"Thank you for your loyalty," said Nockwe. "It will be remembered, Tien." Footsteps. Nockwe was trying to usher him out, but Tien would not go.

Fool.

"Chieftain, our tribe has not gone through the hunger in many seasons," said Tien. "Water has been plentiful, and disease has not taken any of my family. Your reign has changed the lot of our people. Only a demon would challenge you, no man, because even if he's stronger than you physically, you are the better ruler."

Dook heard another wheezing cough.

"Promise me, Tien," said Nockwe, "that you'll not challenge Dook."

"Nock-"

"Promise me!" Nockwe' shouted.

"I promise." Tien sounded subdued, but truthful. They exchanged farewells briefly and soon Tien left the hut to slink off to his own home.

That traitorous Tien! I'll kill him in his sleep, the fool. What rule of Nockwe? Nockwe's a self-serving, pompous weakling, a white-lover who kills the tribe with every day of his rule.

Dook hated Tien. He crouched pondering of ways to kill him slowly and agonizingly.

Before Dook left, he listened to the chieftain cough. He heard mucous come up, more coughing, and finally wheezing before the settling of hay. More coughing. It seemed that Nockwe had been fronting with his voice; that the simple physical exertion of his encounter with Tien had actually taken quite a toll.

Dook took note of this. He adjusted his plans accordingly.

12

Mahanta found Edward pacing near his throne. The guards told him that Edward was still up and hadn't yet left the temple.

The priest was following the walls, absent-mindedly trailing his fingers along the bamboo reeds and straw.

Mahanta watched him for a while before finally joining him.

"I take it you haven't decided," said Mahanta.

Edward looked up at him, then returned his attention to the walls. He did not stop his pacing. "I have."

Mahanta did not prompt but rather just kept walking alongside him. "Your mind is heavy."

Edward did not acknowledge him.

Mahanta tried again. "It would be a difficult thing for a priest to do, what I ask. But you are not a priest, I think."

"You read my journals, didn't you?" asked Edward. It wasn't really a question.

Mahanta was caught off-guard. In some ways Edward had a mind much more agile than his own. He would have to be careful with him. "Yes," Mahanta fumbled, flat-footed. "A reasonable precaution, you understand."

Mahanta studied Edward's face. Edward's nostrils flared slightly, and his cheeks reddened. He did not, however, stop his pacing. "A reasonable precaution," echoed Edward stoically.

"You know, a priest would not join me, but a scientist, a scientist could," said Mahanta.

"Or a traitor. Or a liar," said Edward.

"My friend," said Mahanta. "You are both a traitor and a liar already." Edward did not respond, so Mahanta continued. "You are a traitor to yourself - a priest who gave up all his own desires and aptitudes to become one. You robbed yourself of your own life. You are already the greatest of traitors."

"And a liar?" asked Edward, slightly amused.

"A liar because you keep the girl in your heart, though you've sworn celibacy. You are a most admirable liar and traitor."

Edward pursed his lips to say something, but then held back.

"Yes?" asked Mahanta.

Edward changed the subject. "You trust me, Mahanta?"

"No."

"What happens if I don't like where this is going?"

"You'll need to trust your own abilities," said Mahanta

"You'll try to kill me if I quit, if I disagree with you," said Edward. Mahanta was again startled at both his foresight and his frankness.

"A matter of circumstances," said Mahanta. "Certainly, though, if it seems you plan to leak knowledge of this substance, or imperil my own survival, well, you will be threatened. And I would only expect the same from you."

Edward nodded. "I don't trust you either," said Edward.

"A solid foundation for friendship," said Mahanta. He laughed. Edward didn't. "Let's put it this way. Are you really willing to just walk away now?"

Edward stopped his pacing. He locked eyes with Mahanta.

"I'm in, if you promise to tell me everything. No secrets," said Edward.

"Naïve, Edward," said Mahanta. "An empty promise from an Onge." He sighed. "I promise to tell you what I tell you. I'm sure you'll find out everything there is to know whether I tell you or not."

Mahanta extended his hand to Edward. Edward accepted it. They shook.

"My god!"

The pair turned to face the source of the exclamation. It was Tomy, bursting through the entrance of the temple.

13

Tomy was thirteen years old. He was the messenger of the living god. In four years he would go through his trial, just as Mahanta had, but he would come out a man, not a child eternal.

Until then, he was a child in the eyes of the tribe, just like his master.

He remembered Manassa's words every time he doubted himself. Manassa had a way of saying things so poetically.

You are a child like me. Do not slight my age with your doubts. I have said you can do it, so it can be done. It must be done. It is as I have foreseen.

You have the protection of your god's foresight, and you are your god's eyes and ears.

You will be remembered not for your might but for your brilliance, Tomy; not for your speeches but for your ability to hear.

You are my messenger, and you will not fail me.

Tomy would not fail his master, the Onge living god.

Manassa had fulfilled all the prophecies. Tomy was grateful to serve him. He was grateful to live in the most hopeful, prideful days of Onge history.

Tomy saw that Manassa was not alone in the temple. Manassa was speaking with the white man. Tomy stopped on a dime when he saw his lord had company. He almost tripped over himself.

Manassa beckoned. Tomy, with more decorum and no more shouting, walked to the pair.

I must remember the protocol. I must never speak unless recognized. I must never shout. Manassa might not care about my manners while it's just the two of us, but I must always follow the protocols in company.

I must always follow the protocols anyway - never know who might be watching.

Tomy knelt and looked at the ground. He waited for Manassa to acknowledge him.

"Tomy," said Manassa.

"My lord," said Tomy.

"You have news." It wasn't a question.

"Yes, my lord," said Tomy. He tried to slow his breathing. He hadn't realized he'd gotten so worked up. In contrast, Manassa was emotionless, which somehow made it even more difficult for Tomy to calm himself.

Tomy looked up at the white man. He seemed disinterested, but he was not leaving.

Manassa answered his messenger's unspoken question. "Edward Styles is on our side, Tomy. He has agreed to help us. You may speak to me in his presence."

"Yes, master," said Tomy. Still, he was suspicious.

Manassa continued addressing Tomy. "You wish to tell me that you've spied on Dook, and know he intends to make a move soon."

Tomy's jaw dropped. He refrained from asking, "How did you know?" Any knew the answer. Tomy tried to find words. "He--I watched him--he spied on Nockwe, my lord."

"Yes," said Manassa, nodding. "And you spied on him."

"Tien went into Nockwe's house. At first I thought he'd try to kill him. But Tien was warning Nockwe about Dook. All the while Dook listened at the window," said Tomy quickly. He realized he'd started looking up at Manassa's face, and again turned his gaze to the dirt floor of the temple.

"Yes," said Manassa.

"There is more. Dook heard our chieftain coughing. Nockwe is ill, far worse than we've suspected. I think Dook knows, too. He may risk a challenge soon," said Tomy.

"It won't be any risk," said Manassa. "Not to Dook. Not with Nockwe's illness. Dook plans something, though. He would rather not challenge Nockwe directly. The chief is too popular. He is smart. He has something else in mind."

"Yes, my lord."

"Search Dook's hut."

"I have, my lord," said Tomy.

"And?"

"Poison," said Tomy. "He's stored up some special poisons. Nothing else out of the ordinary."

"You have done well, Tomy. Though I fear there is nothing yet we can do to help our chieftain."

"Surely, my lord, you are the living god. All things are possible," said Tomy.

"So they are, my messenger, so they are." Manassa crouched close to him. "But even I cannot stop the jungle flower from wilting, or add one more hour to the setting of the sun. Nockwe's sun may very well be setting. We must prepare for all futures and so guide our own."

"Yes, my lord." The idea of Nockwe being killed saddened Tomy. Nockwe was a hero of the tribe. His people compared him to Le'ton, the savior of centuries past who led the tribe out of the Sickness.

"It will be a tragedy and a setback if Dook murders Nockwe. Nockwe is a great chieftain," said Manassa.

Tomy momentarily toyed with the idea of murdering Dook. It was not beyond question. Yet Tomy had never taken another man's life, and there were too many unknowns. He decided that he would do so only if his master wished it.

There were other matters, matters in town that he knew he could not talk about with the white man there. So he remained in his place and said no more.

"Who is Dook?" asked the white man.

"Dook is the man who tried to have you killed," answered Manassa.

The white man looked directly at Manassa when he spoke to him. Tomy was afraid the white man might be punished for the sacrilege, but it didn't seem Manassa cared at all. Tomy cared more than Manassa.

"And Tien is the one who tried to stab me?" asked Edward.

"Yes," answered Manassa.

"Why can't we warn Nockwe?" asked Edward.

"Nockwe already knows," said Manassa. "And furthermore, once Dook makes his challenge, it will be up to Nockwe to survive. There is no way around the most basic laws of our tribe. Again, we must be ready."

"For what?" asked Edward.

"We'll discuss everything much further. The time has come for that. But suffice to say that if Nockwe is killed and Dook becomes chieftain, there will be no order in the tribe. My plans could be set back several months. I am a religious figure, not an administrator," said Manassa.

Manassa turned to Tomy. "Furthermore," Manassa continued, "Nockwe is a friend. He does not deserve to die. Tomy, you have my leave."

Tomy looked up to Manassa. The god nodded. There was still much to discuss, but it could wait until the white man was otherwise disposed.

Tomy was learning many things under his master, not the least of which was that there were various degrees of friends.

14

"Look at that tree," said Mahanta. "In the trance, you would know how many leaves flutter in its branches."

In the morning, Mahanta had taken Edward to the "holy clearing." The dawning sun bore through the thick mist of the jungle.

"Hmm," said Edward, noncommittally.

"You will see. You will be in the trance again, soon, if you so wish. The thing to understand about this is that you already know how many leaves flutter in that tree," continued Mahanta.

"Is that so?"

"If your mind did not know how many leaves were in the tree, it could not process them at all. How much harder do you think is it for your brain to capture the entire sensory message of that tree? A number is simple. And some people do it already - your medical texts call them idiot savants."

Edward nodded grudgingly. "You must have read an older text - that's an old name - but yes, to a smaller degree than counting the leaves on that tree, I'll admit that's true."

"My theory is that the substance, the lleychta, which bring about the - the trance -"

"The nirvana effect," interrupted Edward.

Mahanta stewed that one over. He nodded finally. "Yes, that's a good English name for it, yes. The nirvana effect. So when a mind is under the... nirvana effect...it isn't doing anything that it can't already do. There are just certain abilities of the mind which are apparently repressed in everyday life. The drug seems to take away those repressions."

"What's been repressing it?" asked Edward. Mahanta's lip curled slightly. "I'm just playing devil's advocate."

"Devil's what?"

"Devil's advocate. I'm just testing your theory," explained Edward.

Mahanta nodded. "Well, devil, this god hasn't taken his theory that far. And neither have your scientists, either. We could label it, call it subconscious barriers, call it what you will, but that would only be a label. I know of no structure to it, just an idea and my own experience. It just seems that there is a cap on my mind's abilities, and whenever I am under the - the nirvana effect, that cap is lifted."

"Well, I've certainly experienced that, too."

"It seems there are certainly hidden portions of the mind that are under one's full control during the trance."

"Like the body control," said Edward. "I was able to make my body heal, shut off pain. It even seemed I could experience my neurons to some degree."

Mahanta nodded. "I've had the same experience. And are you able to control your other sense channels during the trance?"

Edward nodded. "I can hear farther."

"And individual conversations in a crowd?" said Mahanta.

"It seems impossible, but yes," said Edward.

"Well, your mind has always been perceiving it - your mind perceives every voice in a crowd. Why can't it be aware of each voice?"

"It's just impossible," insisted Edward.

"Well, apparently it's not. And I've been able to trace much phenomena of the nirvana effect to previously observed phenomena."

"Like what?"

"There are cases on record of extended hearing, of near super-natural sight, of uncanny calculation. There are cases who have seen the exact future in their dreams - déjà vu - and who have accomplished physically impossible acts under moments of stress. It would seem hardly an assumption to postulate that the drug does not add mental abilities, but rather reveals them."

Edward mulled it over. He could not help but notice how Mahanta had adapted to the style of communication found in Edward's scientific texts. It was as though the native had absorbed the books. "It sounds like a correct assumption to me," Edward finally said. "You see the future in the trance?"

Mahanta shrugged. "I can predict. It is akin to seeing. I am interested to see what you can do. Since I have been the only human being to experience the trance, I do not know if all such experiences are uniform. Your description of the trance matches mine to a large extent, but it may be that not all minds work the same."

"That doesn't sound particularly scientific," said Edward.

"Just an observation. Observation is absolute science. We can only draw conclusions once we have more observation," said Mahanta. The Onge sat on the grass near the giant tree in the clearing.

"Time slowing down?" asked Edward, as though the question rushed out before he could even formulate it into a complete thought.

"I don't know why," said Mahanta simply.

"I thought that perhaps it's just the effect of so much more sense data coming into the brain. Things appear to be moving more slowly when in actual fact time is clipping along at normal speed."

Mahanta nodded. "I thought something on the same order."

"So what is your plan?" asked Edward, taking his seat.

"Much of it is planned, but much of it isn't. I wish to go West. I want to leave this place. I want to eventually announce my discovery, in a place and time that will not result in destruction. I will do so in a way that benefits me, my tribe, and all humanity. I will be no martyr to science. In your history books, science has more martyrs than religion, it seems."

Edward nodded. Mahanta's plans seemed reasonable. "And what is in store for me?" he asked.

"Having tasted it, you have a right to the lleychta as much as I do. You'll be able to set your own destiny, and we may or may not remain friends in the end. For now we are friends, and we will help one another."

Edward observed from an anthropological viewpoint how pragmatic the Onge really were about matters of alliance and survival. The only assurance of honesty and loyalty from an Onge was strength. It was a game Edward had never played, but saw that he would quickly need to learn.

"Why all this 'god' stuff?" asked Edward.

Mahanta nodded as though he'd been awaiting the question. "Power. Control. Influence. I need it all. Religion is the only way I'll be able to alter the culture of my people. I will modernize my tribe by gaining enough influence to reinterpret the oral tradition that so far has kept us bound to the mud."

Edward's priest side objected on moral grounds to Mahanta's abuse of religion. The scholarly side could not help but agree with him, though.

"I know what you are thinking," said Mahanta. He laughed. "You are thinking, 'This young man is not a god.'"

Edward laughed, too.

Mahanta continued, "You are right - to you, I am not. To the West, I am not. To a Christian, or a Jew, or Muslim, or any monotheist, I am not. But to my people, I am. I have fulfilled their prophecies. I am what they have always wanted. And I will lead them to civilization and freedom. You cannot slight me or my manipulations for that. If you do, you are not who I think you are."

"We are an odd couple," said Edward. "If anyone were to write a book about this, they could title it, 'The Priest and the Heretic.'"

"Or 'The God and the White Devil'," said Mahanta. "In any event, my status has given me control of the tribe's resources. Already they have begun to harvest the substance per my instructions. The Onge are at our disposal to carry forward the research of this substance as far as we can before we need to leave."

"What do you plan to research about it?" asked Edward.

"That is up for discussion," said Mahanta. This surprised Edward. "I have some ideas, but I wanted to give you all the facts that I have on the nirvana effect, the plant sap it comes from, everything, and have you trance on it before we set on a course of investigation. We can discuss it all as we walk back to the temple. If you're willing, I'll inject you with the substance again."

Edward nodded. He was more than willing.

15

"Concentrate this time upon unlocking your mind, and upon the mysteries of this substance," urged Mahanta. He pulled a syringe from a medical pack at his side. He drew a clear liquid from a penicillin vial. The medicine had obviously been replaced by the drug.

Edward had no reservation. The after-pain was inevitable. He knew he would be facing that many times further in his research. And obviously, Mahanta had survived many doses. To Edward's scientific mind, there was nothing to fear.

The native wasted no time in injecting Edward. The drug took effect almost instantly. Edward noted there must have been outward signs of the lleychta going to work, because Mahanta was nodding with approval.

Edward closed his eyes. It helped the trance. *I can't waste time; every micro-second counts.* He reviewed all the facts. Indeed, he reviewed *all of them.*

His whole education flew into view, sorted by relevance, probable veracity, and importance.

It was as though his mental filing system had transformed from a mere "date and place" tabbing to a sophisticated cross-indexed catalog in a blink of his mind's eye.

Every fact could be reached, as he might reach every drop of water in a lake, and yet the important facts stood out brilliantly. His whole education was at his fingertips, ready for access at a speed far faster and a relevance far more refined than any internet search. He briefly indulged in wondering at the capacities of his mind. *How much data is actually there? Is some of it delusion?*

All of it? He had to keep in mind that he was still under the influence of a drug, no matter how wonderful that drug might seem.

Perhaps this was what Mahanta meant by "unlocking his mind". Its function was certainly enhanced, and all in what was perhaps ten minutes in real time. He wondered if the effect would last after the trance. Already, he had more control of his body than he'd ever had before his first trance. He wondered if it would be the same with his education.

Edward turned off his hearing, and most of his other perceptions as well in order to aid his concentration. A dull sense of touch remained, and of course automatic control of body function. *Focus.* It was all too tempting to venture down the rambling paths of speculation. He had a job to do.

The vital data surrounding the substance were few. He examined them all. Mahanta had done well relaying everything he'd encountered so far.

The substance came from the sap of a tree that for all Mahanta or Edward knew was found only on this island.

Edward verified this by ransacking his memories. Towards the end of his schooling, he had flipped page by page through a botany book which catalogued every known form of exotic tree in the Eastern world. It had been a particularly boring day in Botany and he'd kept the appearance of business by looking at all the pictures.

In his mind's eye, the memory hung suspended in front of him and played like a 3-D movie with full sound and fifty other perceptions. As he examined the recall, he felt like he was back in Botany. He even felt the boredom.

He found he could slow the memory down or even stop it. This surprised him, but seemed natural enough. He had plenty of memories in his past that hung suspended like that in one crucial moment, though he'd never thought to press the "rewind" or "fast forward" buttons.

He could freeze the "playing" of the memory at each flip of the page and study its contents. In such a wise he re-examined every page of the book.

No picture matched. No description matched. The plant, indeed, was a totally unknown mutation apparently populating only this island.

Edward's concentration flitted back to the rest of his conversation with Mahanta on the way back to the temple. The plant's sap had long been used by Onge medicine men as a hallucinogenic. Mahanta became curious after he saw the medicine man smoke it and then catch a fly between his fingers as easily as he might catch a ball. Mahanta wondered how such a substance could make an old man so agile.

Mahanta later learned the art of distillation from an earlier missionary and subsequently distilled the sap. He found that it contained a hallucinogenic compound separate and apart from the substance which produced the nirvana effect. When he drank the distilled substance, he received a watered down version of the effect - heightened senses, bodily control, a sort of numbed version of the full-blown trance.

Mahanta got the idea of injection from the last doctor that had visited the village, a non-denominational whom the Jesuits had set up to start a clinic. The clinic failed, but not before the doctor taught an interested youth some first aid procedures and what medicine he could grasp, including vaccination and the administration of penicillin.

Injected in the blood stream, the full effects of the liquid were realized.

The after-pain. What is it?

Edward's mind scanned again through his whole education and experience, and threw out some possibilities.

A side effect - naturally. Sensory overload? Shock? Dehydration?

It could be one or a combination of all three.

Perhaps it's from the chemicals in the sap. Perhaps they aren't all distilled out.

The answer, at least in part, came to him in a flash of certainty.

Nerve damage. That was it.

He sensed it not so much from his past but rather from a searching examination of the present condition of his body. There was a terrific amount of output coming from his brain, a terrific amount of electricity being handled. His nerves couldn't handle it. They were like the muscles broken down during a hard workout – only nerves don't heal like muscles.

He sensed his nerves were diffusing the charge as best they could, but it was still too much.

It hurt, actually. The perception was too much and caused a definite pain.

In trance, he was able to shut it off and ignore it. After trance, he would no longer be able to. Thus, the after-pain.

He scanned the memories of his body's recovery from the three injections. Somehow, his body had known to rebuild the nerves. The pain receded day by day as the nerves rebuilt. They were not conditioned, now, into greater strength. They were a bit weaker, if anything.

The after-pain was the damage caused by *too much perception* - too much current along the nerve channels.

His first hunch, sensory overload, was right, but not in the sense he'd originally meant. He was thinking psychologically, not in the raw electronics of the human body.

Is this substance lethal? Damaging?

He worried over the problem, but could find no answer. He needed more data. Certainly, his nerves weren't back to normal, yet. Prolonged use could possibly damage his nerves beyond his ability to heal.

Any way out of the after-pain?

This question, he knew, was what should be his first line of research. Its solution would permit much more trance time.

The problem had many facets. He worked all of them. Two simple answers stood above the rest that flooded his mind.

The nerves must grow stronger. Or the impact of the nirvana effect must be lessened.

A thousand solutions flashed to him. He picked out the best few, keeping in mind that he wouldn't be trancing during most of whatever conditioning he planned. Pain shut-off would not really be an option. He rolled to his next question.

What is my plan? And Mahanta's plan...is it true? Can Mahanta be trusted?

And perhaps a more relevant question: *Can I trust myself?*

Tapping. Something was tapping Edward's cheek. He opened his eyes. Mahanta was slapping his face *hard*. It felt like a gentle nudge each time. Edward instantly turned his present-time perceptions back on. His face stung like hell. His arm, too; Mahanta must have pinched him there to no avail.

"Do you hear it?" asked Mahanta.

Of course he did. As soon as his perceptions were running a wealth of data came rushing to him.

A fight. A challenge. The busy hubbub, the shouts as clear as though he were in the thick of it.

"What's happening? I can't tell from here outside of trance."

Tien. Dook. Edward heard their names murmured, rippling through the crowd.

"A challenge," Edward answered. "Dook has challenged Tien. They are fighting now. The crowd surrounds them."

"Dook challenged Tien?" asked Mahanta. "I would have thought the reverse."

Edward furrowed his brow. It was not easy picking out single voices in the crowd, but he could do it. He got his answer from a conversation to a newcomer. "Dook challenges that Tien insulted your honor and conspired with Nockwe to challenge *you.*"

"Nockwe?"

"Yes. I believe he is there," said Edward. He did not hear Nockwe's voice, but rather heard a pocket of quiet in one area of the crowd.

"Dook lies, of course," said Mahanta. "He is making his move. We must hurry."

Mahanta sprinted out of the hut. Edward followed him. It was the first time Edward tried to run while in trance, and it was a bit like first learning to walk. He was too aware of his body, so that the curling of his feet and the pumping of his leg muscles seemed unnatural and the cause of study. He rapidly got the hang of it, and after a dozen steps was catching up with Mahanta. In the trance Edward was able to perfectly place his feet and push forward. He remembered Mahanta's inhuman sprinting into the woods, as though a rocket were strapped to his back

The conflict was only fifty yards from the temple. A hundred tribesmen circled and watched.

Edward studied every one of them. He observed their stances, the way they seemed slack, almost grief-stricken when they looked at Tien. Those with their eyes on Dook had an angry tension about them. A handful had various other reactions. Edward noted those down as possible allies of Dook. It was apparent that the majority of the tribe wanted Tien to live.

Edward and Mahanta pushed through the crowd toward the edge of the ring of natives. Edward examined these possible members of Dook's cabal. They looked nervous, but by all signs, none of them were intending to cheat for Dook. They were only spectators today.

A woman was crying hysterically, as were a few babies.

Dook and Tien circled one another warily. No one had struck, yet. Dook had a knife in either hand, while Tien had only one long dagger. It was the same he'd tried to use on Edward just a day before.

Edward spotted that no ally was needed to cheat for Dook. Dook had already done his dirty work. Tien's skin was a shade of green, and he shook almost imperceptibly. Not just nerves.

"Dook poisoned him," Edward muttered to Mahanta.

Mahanta cursed and spit.

A tribesman standing next to them jerked his head up in Mahanta's direction. Recognition dawned. The man backed five feet and knelt at the same time, exclaiming, "Manassa!" He collided into several people as he moved.

The crowd diverted from the fight for a moment. They knelt, murmuring their god's name. The nearest to their Manassa had a similar reaction as the first man, shocked that they had not given their god the deserved respect as he'd approached. They quickly restored a healthy distance from Manassa and his white servant.

Both Dook and Tien glanced at the disturbance, but neither stopped circling.

Dook lunged at Tien just as he returned his attention to the fight, but Tien managed to sidestep the blow in the nick of time and follow up with a lick of his own. He drew blood on Dook's dark arm.

Weakened by the poison, Tien couldn't follow through like he needed. Dook quickly regained the initiative, swinging low to gash Tien's shin with his left-handed knife. Tien tripped backward, crying out in surprise.

Dook charged in to make the kill. Tien was too slow in getting up. Several members of the tribe cried out.

"At'tan! At'tan!" a deep, booming voice broke over the din. Dook stopped his charge quickly, as though he'd been expecting an interruption. He looked up and then smiled. Edward followed the path of his eyes to Nockwe, who looked tired more than anything else. Dook sheathed his knives and walked away from Tien to the far end of the circle.

"Nockwe intercedes," explained Mahana.

"Dook was planning this all along!" whispered Edward.

"See!" shouted Dook to the tribe. "See with your own eyes! Nockwe and Tien work together to try to kill our god." Murmurs rippled through the crowd. They did not believe his words, but there were doubts. The Onge way was one of unwavering suspicion.

"No mortal can kill our mighty god," said Nockwe, slowly, using the same deliberate pace he'd used before to address the crowd.

"And yet you are fool enough to try," said Dook.

"Your tongue is full of lies, Dook, but it will soon be cut out," said Nockwe.

Dook beckoned him with his hand and once again pulled out both daggers. He was making quite a show. Nockwe pulled out his own dagger, and they began to circle.

Edward now studied Nockwe. He could tell that Nockwe was moving heavily. He was not in the same shape he'd been in when guiding Edward through the jungle. He looked weary and flat-footed.

Edward was no student of war, but knew that the wrong time to be tired was with a maniac circling you with bloody daggers in his hands.

Nockwe attacked repeatedly, striking at the snakelike Dook. The chieftain's aggression stretched to the point of incaution.

"Nockwe moves quickly. He must not feel he can withstand a drawn-out battle," commented Mahanta unnecessarily.

Dook refused to engage him. He dodged back at every strike, refraining from taking the easy opportunities presented by Nockwe's over-extension.

By their shouts, Edward knew the crowd was rooting for Nockwe. They wanted him to live. Yet as the battle petered on, as Nockwe's step further lost its spring, the natives tired as well. They took on the aspect of a crowd watching an inevitable train wreck.

Mahanta's explanation during their last talk echoed in Edward's mind. *If Dook becomes chieftain, he will not long remain so. There will be many hungering for his blood, and many that would seek to take his place. This is a wild variable that could result in both of our deaths and the loss of this discovery. The turmoil that will attain in the tribe will prevent any work from being done as chalk lines are drawn and neighbor fears neighbor until a new ruler rises. I do not have the brute force to bring such a people in line without my chieftain. Under trance I am near invincible, but I am not under trance at all hours of the day and night.*

Unless something drastic happened, Dook would kill Nockwe and become chieftain. Dook will be chieftain today. That calculation was a certainty in Edward's mind. Already, Nockwe had stopped his lunging, had stopped even his circling, and instead just rotated in place as Dook worked around him, looking for an opening. Dook wasn't worn at all, despite the bleeding from his left arm, and he looked ready to make his kill. Nockwe coughed spasmodically.

Dook finally leaned to make his first strike. Nockwe feigned to the left, and then swung his body savagely to the right. Dook missed him, but Nockwe caught Dook's left arm near the first gash and again drew blood. Dook cried out and swung again, but Nockwe ducked his blow and kicked out with all his force, landing his foot squarely into Dook's abdomen. The smaller man flew backwards and landed in the dirt.

All eyes were on Dook as he flew, but then went rapidly back to Nockwe. The chieftain hadn't gotten up from his flying kick. Instead, he trembled on the ground.

Nockwe strained to lift himself, only to collapse again. Dook was back onto his feet, grabbing his daggers from the ground. His lips curled into a savage smile. The illness had finally overcome Nockwe, as the poison had overcome Tien. Still hunched over from the blow to his stomach, Dook swaggered as best he could to the chieftain. His time had come to claim Nockwe's flag.

Nockwe managed to roll himself up to his hands and knees and made a grab for his dagger in the dirt.

It was to no avail. Dook idly kicked Nockwe in the head. Dook was showboating. The dagger flew back out of Nockwe's hands as he collapsed again the ground. He pushed the dirt, struggling to get back up. His muscles trembled but would not move him.

Dook laughed, checking out the horrified crowd. He wasn't getting the response he wanted, but he was certainly enjoying himself.

Dook grabbed Nockwe by the hair. "Stand up!" he shouted as he yanked Nockwe into a standing position. Nockwe used the momentum to lunge at Dook, but to no avail. Dook simply threw him by the hair back into the dirt.

Dook wielded his knife once more to finish the job.

"At'tan! At'tan!"

Edward had made an instantaneous calculation of hundreds of factors. Much of his calculation involved the future and his survival chances. The course he chose had many possible dead-ends, most of them immediately, but he felt he had to choose it. He would not have Nockwe's blood on his hands. Nockwe had spared Edward's life.

Mahanta is not able to help - he's no match for Dook physically. Only one person had a chance at interceding successfully for Nockwe. It was the only person under trance.

Under the nirvana effect, the present was crisp and real to Edward. The past was just as definite. He could move his consciousness to any moment of it.

He could move his consciousness to the future, as well, and calculate. It was much less real. It lay across many paths, many probabilities. Most real was the present and the few seconds leading from it. Less real lay the infinitude of survival patterns or deaths that lay ahead of Edward and his allies. Many portals led to his goals, his dreams, and survival. Few doors were open past this encounter.

And still, Edward yelled the words of intercession.

Mahanta turned abruptly to Edward in shock.

Dook froze. Nockwe craned his neck up to see his benefactor. The hundred voices of the crowd all started jabbering at once. Edward could pick out every single one. "The white man intercedes! He'll surely die. Thank the gods. Nockwe might live. He can't do that. That's Manassa's slave."

Mahanta grabbed his arm. "You're still trancing?" Edward nodded slightly. "That's no assurance of victory. And the trance will end any time now. You were meditating for a while before I disturbed you."

Tell me something I don't know.

Mahanta slid a long dagger into his hand. The Jesuit gripped the handle. Smooth, well-sanded wood gave some weight to the slender, sharp blade. "These fights are to the death," cautioned Mahanta. "Don't be a forgiving priest, or you'll end up the sacrifice."

Edward knew that outside of the nirvana effect, he would have difficulty delivering the fatal blow. He had never killed a man, and never wanted to. He shoved those thoughts away, along with the fear. The truth of the matter was that if Dook killed Nockwe, his own life was on the line. This was strictly self-defense from here on out; kill or be killed.

Dook had made one long glance at Edward to size him up, but now refused to look at him. Instead, Dook spoke slowly, directly to Manassa, with one knee on the ground.

"My lord, with all respect to your white magic servant, only a man of the tribe may participate in a challenge." Nockwe writhed on the ground beside Dook, coughing.

Mahanta surveyed the crowd. All eyes were on their living god, now. Mahanta matched Dook's pacing. "So it was said by our ancestors, that the living god shall have all manner of creatures as his warriors. His servants shall number the thousands, of every race and nation of earth. My servant fights in my stead."

A harsh murmuring rippled through the crowd, chased by silence. The silence was golden to Edward. It seemed to shock Dook to his very core. Dook obviously hadn't foreseen this eventuality. He had been stopped by his own living god at the moment of his greatest triumph.

Dook clanged his daggers. Edward advanced into the middle of the dirt, then immediately drew back into the crowd, reshaping their arena so that Nockwe was now on the ground behind the audience. Bri'ley'na rushed to the side of the fallen chieftain and began to attend to him.

Edward noticed the after-pain was starting to edge into his consciousness. He shoved it out of his mind, to the same place he'd moved the fear. In its place, he heightened his senses and pumped adrenaline throughout his body to prepare for the exertion to come. He knew he would not have much time, just like Nockwe and Tien hadn't had much time. In mere minutes, the nirvana effect would be gone, and he would just be a puny white priest battling an animalistic primitive who lived by the hunt and the kill.

Dook tested him quickly, jabbing gamely after they circled once. Edward saw the vector of the knife, saw that it would miss him, and refused to react, Dook's swing falling mere inches from his body. The priest then swung his own dagger at the Onge, but Dook's natural reaction time was far better than Edward's. Dook feigned a sidestep, then swung under Edward's blow, coming up with a knife aimed directly at Edward's abdomen.

Edward perceived every motion, every possibility. It was as though he were fighting the entire battle in slow motion, where he perceived one hundred seconds for Dook's one. But he knew that even if the trance held out, there was a great chance he would not survive this encounter. The trance seemed to not be enough.

Edward had new data now, data that might have kept him from ever stepping into the ring a minute ago. He hadn't seen Dook fighting an able opponent. No wonder Mahanta had looked so incredulous. Dook was just so much more physically able than Edward was. The native was a killing machine.

As Edward read Dook's jab, he twisted his body backwards into the air. It was the only way out of the blow. His foot caught Dook's wrist as he flew. The dagger went flying out of the Onge's hand, but Dook still had another, and Edward didn't land on his feet in the follow-through. Instead, he had to roll away and back up.

In that moment Dook was already back on top of him, swinging furiously to press his advantage. Dook had the initiative.

Edward was able to read each of Dook's moves at its onset, at the first tension of the first muscle of his arms or legs. Every ripple of muscle foretold a change in direction. Edward knew exactly where Dook's weapon was flying and exactly where his own body was in relation to it, as though he were fighting in an almost infinite slow motion. Still, it taxed Edward to the limit of his abilities just to keep the dagger out of his gut.

The surrounding Onge crowd was silent, totally absorbed. They seemed awe-struck, watching as each of Dook's swings drew a little closer, as the white man kept up his impossible dodges.

Edward was unable to counterattack. Dook would inevitably hit him if he didn't *do something*.

Dook made a long lance at him. Edward stumbled back to avoid the dagger to his chest. He heard Mahanta instinctively cry out. The tribe shouted, too.

Dook was about to pounce on him. Edward knew he needed the initiative, just one minute in which he had control of the fight. He probably only had a minute left.

Edward let loose a bloodcurdling war cry. It was enough to make Dook flinch. As Edward stumbled backward, he planted his left foot and pushed off to hurl his knife through the air at Dook's head. Dook ducked it, as Edward had foreseen, but lost his eye contact with the priest. That was all the distraction Edward needed.

Edward dove, grasping Dook's weapon. Dook tried to swing, but at the close distance Edward could feel every tension in Dook's body. In the trance, Dook was an open book to Edward. Edward moved *simultaneously* with him in a deadly dance that kept the Onge from ever getting in a blow.

Edward worked Dook's arm around in an expert pattern…he'd seen it once…somewhere…something in his mind urged him through the motions. Edward leapt to Dook's left, then behind him, all with the primitive's arm in tow. Finally, Edward wrenched Dook's arm around in a complete circle using both hands, and Dook flipped, his back slamming into the ground.

Edward wrenched the dagger out of Dook's hand. The Onge was defenseless, his arms flying up far too slowly to stop Edward's inevitable killing blow.

Stop! With a gut-wrenching twist on Edward's nerves, the trance ended. He could not kill a man. He would try to give him mercy.

No, he'll kill me! Kill him! It was only a moment of hesitation, but that was all Dook needed to reach Edward's wrist and deflect the blow.

Dook kicked and rolled, and now it was Dook with the knife, Dook on top of Edward, Dook driving down his blade toward Edward's throat.

Edward could no longer break apart the perceptions. The slow motion of the battle rushed into a fast forward.

As the knife rushed down, Edward thought of Callista. In the end he gripped her in his mind's eye as though he might take her with him to the hereafter if he held hard enough.

Thud. Dook's body jerked to Edward's side as though yanked by unseen strings. For a moment Edward did not react. Where Dook had loomed, there was only sky. The dagger had fallen away.

Edward scampered up. Dook had a long spear running out of his temple. Blood rushed from his skull and mingled with the muddy ground. Tien lay awkwardly on the ground nearby, his right hand still gripping the spear's handle. He had lunged with spear in hand and collapsed once he'd hit his target.

"Get him, get Tien, kill him! He's broken the law!" The tribe shouted in uproar. The Onge surged into the ring and gathered around Tien and Dook. Edward slid through the crowd away from the scene, momentarily forgotten.

A couple of the younger men grabbed Tien and started to drag him away. Tien's woman shrieked.

Mahanta burst into the center of the crowd. The tribe backed away. The Onge god examined the bodies. Both were dead. Tien's tongue lolled out, his body limp, his face frozen in a determined scowl. His veins looked green, his skin pale.

"He's dead. The gods killed him for his law-breaking. He's dead," Edward heard the Onge muttering.

"He lives!" shouted Manassa. The tribe quieted, stepping back even further to give their god a wide berth. Mahanta continued in the traditional tongue of the Onge. "He lives on with the fallen as a hero, for Dook poisoned him before he ever was challenged."

"Poisoned....he was poisoned...Dook poisoned him..." murmured the tribe.

"Dook was to punish the whole tribe in his lawlessness. He would have been the end of our customs. He would have been the end of our tribe. Let this be known as the day that Tien, son of A'lan, saved our tribe from the traitor. Let it be known. These are the words of Manassa."

Mahanta abruptly left the circle without even waiting for his tribe's response.

16

Edward followed Mahanta in lock step. They soon reached the temple. No one had followed them. The tribe was absorbed with handling the bodies of the two fallen.

"Tien will be properly buried. Dook will be dragged into the woods," Mahanta said matter-of-factly as they entered the hut. Edward feigned an interested glance. The pain had started. "The after-effects?" asked Mahanta.

"Not as bad as before," answered Edward.

"You had him. The trance ended as you were striking." It was not a question. Edward nodded. "That was stupid."

Edward shrugged.

"Is that all you have to say, white man?" asked Mahanta. He was downright hot. His fists were in knots. "I can understand your logic - you were the most likely to defeat Dook between you and me. If Nockwe died, Dook might finish what he had started through Tien and have you killed...but still..."

"Actually, that thought never occurred to me," said Edward.

Mahanta glowered . Edward was only inciting the Onge's rage.

"Nockwe spared my life that night at the coming-of-age. I felt it was only right to help him. I like him," explained Edward. He chuckled.

"You *like* him?! You did that because you *like* him?!" shouted Mahanta. He tugged at his hair, his voice filling up the temple.

Edward felt frustrated. Mahanta had no right to talk to him like that, Onge god or no. "You know, there is such a thing as honor," said Edward. "There is such a thing as doing the right thing."

"The right thing?" echoed Mahanta. He sighed and looked at the ground. He started laughing. At first, it was just a chuckle, but soon the rage melted into mirth. He lost his breath before finally settling down. Edward watched him incredulously.

"You Christian martyr..." muttered Mahanta at length between chuckles. "Well, it worked this time. Maybe I should study your knight-like methods."

Edward was disarmed by Mahanta's change in mood. "Maybe you shouldn't," said Edward. "I almost got slaughtered."

"You were certain, weren't you, that you could beat him," said Mahanta.

Edward shook his head 'no', then reconsidered. "Yeah, I guess I was. And then I was very certain I was going to lose," he said. "So I had to change the game and re-take the advantage. Then I was very sure I was going to beat him again. Then the trance wore off," added Edward.

Mahanta nodded. "I call it trance certainty."

"Trance certainty?" Edward repeated.

"It's a phenomenon I've encountered. I've observed a great magnification in the emotions of *certainty* and confidence while I've been under trance."

"Hmmm..." said Edward, thinking over his own experience.

"Apparently, since a mind under trance has a great ability to *cause* the future, the mind tends to feel certainty about *any* course one decides to take. Even minute probabilities can seem great certainties while in trance."

"It's a false certainty," said Edward.

"Well, not necessarily false at all. For example, let us say it was a little more right to you than wrong to jump into that fight. Well, even this slight differential in rightness and wrongness becomes a dead certainty in trance," said Mahanta.

Edward nodded. "I see."

"It's key not to use one's understanding in normal life to entirely evaluate data and conclusions while under trance. Trance has a different feel and feedback than normal life."

"Kind of like a blind man who gets his vision restored might react incorrectly to various sights for a while," said Edward.

"Yes, kind of like that. But don't get me wrong. It seems that certainty has a great value. Certainty seems to me to be necessary for successful action."

They talked all night, mulling over Edward's experience with the substance, comparing notes. They resisted the urge to philosophize, and stuck mainly to the facts and details of what Edward had learned while under trance and how Mahanta's trances differed. They agreed on working on reducing the after-pain as a primary research goal, and Edward threw out some of his ideas.

But when he finally lay down on his pallet, Edward could not stop mulling over Mahanta's initial rage and condescension.

There was another side to Mahanta that Mahanta did not want seen by the likes of Edward. Edward decided to protect himself from that side. Mahanta had given good advice. The only way he could trust Mahanta was to not trust him at all.

Before he finally slept, he ripped the back page out of his journal and wrote a note. He rolled it into a tube. He scratched the bottom of the wooden crucifix hanging from his hut. He then carried the tube to the southernmost free-standing tree in the village and buried the tube three feet deep three feet south of the trunk. He was sure he was not followed. That was important, since it was his only "card in the hole," literally and figuratively.

It was an old Jesuit trick.

17

Dr. James Seacrest was knocking on her door. Callista was watching him through the peephole. Behind him she could see a red, distorted blob that could only be the cherry apple '95 Corvette that he'd bottomed out repeatedly in an effort to gain a date with her.

She made the mistake of pressing up against the door to get a better look out the peephole. The deadbolt clicked against the jamb.

"Callista?" asked Seacrest. "Are you there?" He squinted a bit.

Oh, God, I don't want to do this right now. After Friday night, she'd avoided him. He'd called several times. She didn't answer or call back. He'd showed up to the clinic twice. She'd had Duiyon tell him that Dr. Knowles was still seeing patients.

Watching that boy come back to life, watching that mother die and then resurrect all in the span of an eternal night, had touched a raw nerve. It was a desperation, a rush, an affinity that she hadn't felt since her college years before med school.

She still missed the man she'd almost married eight years ago. She had dated, of course, and tried to forget him. She'd buried her regrets in the middle of a nowhere called Lisbaad.

And yet it had resurfaced, as it always did. She shouldn't have expected anything else.

Ridiculous. She chose this one particular island so she might have a chance to relive her past. And yet she tried to bury it. *Ridiculous.*

She was right to bury, to forget. She had to assume he would never come;

she had to get on with her life. The many voices of her friends, her family and herself all told her that.

She'd keep things going with Seacrest. He was a handsome man, a doctor, older than her, but still in his prime. *No reason to stop.* It might come to something. It might come to the new start she so hoped for.

She would ruin it, though, if she saw him before she got her head straight.

She couldn't think of anything to answer him. He'd heard her. She couldn't avoid him anymore. She saw him pace a bit on the porch. *He probably feels like a fool.*

"Coming!" cried Callista, as though she'd just heard him. "Just a minute!"

She sat down on the bench in her foyer and composed her thoughts. She breathed and thought. She wiped a tear off her face.

You're coming apart at the seams, Callista. It's just a boy out there. You're acting like a traumatized wacko. You are Doctor Callista Knowles, not Cali, Oxford undergrad with a melting heart. Pull yourself together.

She saw *him*, though, in her mind's eye. He wouldn't bury, not yet. So she just tucked him into a corner of her mind and stood up. She opened the door.

Seacrest had flowers behind his back. He showed them to her. She smiled, but it took her too long to do so. She saw him reset his stance. It wasn't a look she was used to from the typically over-confident Seacrest.

"Hello, Callista," said Seacrest, gently passing her the flowers.

"Hello, James," said Callista. "And thank you."

"No problem," said James. He examined her face, then fiddled with his pockets a bit. He seemed to be deliberating on something - something he'd seen in her eyes. He sighed quietly and smiled. "Thank you for the lovely evening Friday night. It was very good for my soul."

She smiled back at him weakly. "You have a soul?" she muttered.

"Occasionally." He smiled. She could tell it was only for her benefit. His body was a lot slacker than it had been just a second ago. Excitement had been replaced by something almost fatherly. "I want to let you know that whenever you'd like, I'd love to enjoy another dinner with you. And if that's never, I'll understand."

Her smile faltered. *He knows!* In that moment she felt exposed, and yet safe. She nodded unconsciously. "Thank you, James."

"Thank you," he said. He tilted his hat. With his accent, it was almost ridiculous. She didn't laugh, though. It was actually quite attractive. He looked at her meaningfully. "Goodbye, Callista," said James. He turned to leave.

"Goodbye, James." She leaned against the door frame as he drove off.

Oh, Edward.

18

Lila had requested an audience with him three times. Manassa had never granted it.

When he walked into his quarters she was on his bed.

She studied his face to gauge his reaction. He smiled.

"I'm not going to even ask you how you got in here," he said.

"Your secret exit is also a secret entrance. You should guard it."

"Then it wouldn't be a secret," he said. He could not resist talking to her. Or looking at her. She wore a loincloth but she may as well have been completely naked on his bed.

"What is this I am laying on?" she asked.

"The English call it a 'mattress'. It's a bed."

She giggled. "You did it. You're a god, and you sleep on a 'mittress'."

Manassa stifled a laugh at the mispronunciation. *I wish.*

"You'll need to leave," he said. "You're married."

"I don't want to be married anymore."

"That's too bad," said Manassa. He walked to his desk.

"Can't you do something?" she asked.

"It's the laws of the tribe."

"But they say you can do anything. You've done miracles. You appear out of the air…"

Manassa started working at his desk.

"Mahanta...I miss you, Mahanta. I'm sorry I married. He's so old and gross. My family needed it. I'm sorry." She was crying. "I miss you. Please, help me. You don't have to marry me. I could just be your..."

"'Mattress'?" he asked without looking at her.

"What?" she asked.

He chuckled. He turned around in his chair. She was standing up pleading beside his bed.

He missed her, too. And the idea of her in bed with her husband made his blood boil.

"I swore I'd marry you," said Manassa. "And you married another. This was an unforgivable sin." She held her breath. "But that was against Mahanta. Mahanta is no more. I am Manassa, and no Onge can sin unforgivably against me."

She sighed.

"I will have you," he said. "But in order for me to have you, you must follow what I say exactly. Understand?"

"I understand," she said.

19

"It's ham and rice in banana leaf," explained Nockwe as he served Edward his wrap. It felt warm in Edward's hands, but not too warm.

Bri'ley'na and the three children sat on the floor with them. They all ate quietly, Bri'ley'na occasionally chirping to one of the children to stay seated or to go fetch some seasoning.

Nockwe coughed repeatedly. The coughs rocked his whole body. Still, he sounded better. Once he recovered from the fit, he smiled wearily at Edward.

"Is there anything Western medicine can do for me, Edward Styles?" asked Nockwe.

"We could remove your lungs," said Edward.

Nockwe frowned at him. Edward laughed.

"A joke," said Edward.

Nockwe's eyebrows went through contortions. He still looked quite serious; Edward hoped he hadn't affronted the chieftain. Then Nockwe burst into laughter. Bri'ley'na asked Nockwe something very rapidly in Onge. Nockwe responded just as quickly. She started laughing, too.

"What?" asked Edward.

"You have a very strange sense of humor, white man," said Bri'ley'na. She laughed more. She told the children to go play outside the hut.

"Actually," said Edward, "there is very little we could do for a cough. We have cough drops. It can keep your throat from being so sore."

"How do I get this 'cough drops'?" asked Nockwe.

"Go to a corner store in Lisbaad."

"I might just do that," said Nockwe. "Even though it breaks every code of my tribe."

"Better to break that little code and live, I say," said Edward.

"Now you sound like Manassa," said Nockwe.

Bri'ley'na quietly took her leave from the two men.

"What's that?" asked Edward.

"Nothing," said Nockwe, quickly. Still, Edward leaned for an answer, so Nockwe said, dismissively, "Manassa is the bringer of change."

"He is? He breaks your codes?" asked Edward. His interest was piqued.

Nockwe shrugged. He coughed again. "He is interpreter of the code. The prophecies say that he 'shall bring all the words of our traditions to new meaning, to new light.'"

"What does he say about medicine?"

"Our law says that no potions of foreigners be allowed in our bodies."

"Mmhmm?" Edward prompted.

"Manassa says that all the Earth belongs to the Onge - that now that Manassa has come, there is no foreigner."

"That's what Manassa says?" asked Edward. He couldn't hide his reaction. His pulse was racing, his breath evacuated into the jungle night.

Carefully, Nockwe answered, "That's what Manassa says in his sermons." He spoke more guardedly. Edward took his time to form the right question, something that would let Nockwe feel comfortable once more. Edward realized he needed to know a lot more than he knew.

Nockwe spoke before the words came to Edward. His brow furrowed and he talked slowly, with the same rhythm he usually reserved for crowds. "Edward, have you ever attended one of the sermons of Manassa?" asked Nockwe.

"No," said Edward.

Nockwe looked into the candlelight. He had another question, and Edward just waited for it. Finally, Nockwe asked, "White man, what do you view as your role here?"

"I..." Edward started. "I am the servant of Manassa. I am here to perform accomplish his will," lied Edward.

Nockwe scowled. He leaned very close to Edward, and whispered in his ear. "That is all well, since the eyes and ears of Manassa are everywhere. But tell me how you truly see your role. I owe you my life; I will not betray you."

Edward nodded. He thought of Tomy. It was likely that he was crouching outside, just as Dook had spied on Tien's conversation with the chieftain.

Should I talk to him? Edward trusted Nockwe, far more than he trusted anyone else in the tribe. Why shouldn't he? Edward whispered back, "I am researching..."

"*Lleychta?*" asked Nockwe.

"Yes."

Nockwe drew in a breath and considered once more the candle. He seemed to be meditating. Edward's eyes drifted to the walls of the hut. They were adorned from top to bottom with skins and various artifacts inherited from the Onge chieftains of ages past. Edward did not really see them. He was just letting Nockwe think.

Finally, the chieftain whispered in the formal Onge tongue, "White man, I will tell you the story of Manassa, the same way it is told our children, and was told to me, and was told to my ancestors for hundreds of years. I do this for you. You say I saved your life, and you were only paying a debt, but my debt is greater than yours, now. If I did not owe such a debt, I would not help you. I would not tell you the story, for doing so is truly a disservice to my tribe, and a disservice to Manassa, who empowers our tribe. Still, I will tell you."

Edward rocked back and waited for Nockwe to begin.

The chieftain spoke smoothly. It was a familiar tale to Nockwe, told in all its flowery phrases.

"We are a people of many, many gods, but three are higher than all. The first god is the creator, maker of heaven and Earth. He became the Earth and the stars that we might have life. He only lives through us, through the beasts of the jungle, through the trees and streams, even through the mud. He sacrificed his life as a seed for all of our world."

Edward was already, familiar with the Onge pantheon, but listened carefully.

"The second god is the all-seeing, all-knowing god of now. He is the Watcher. He is the Taker. He is the guardian of the Onge. He keeps us on the island, to keep us strong, to keep by our codes, to wait for the sign.

"The third god is just born. He is the immortal child. When the first god sowed this Earth with life, he planted a seed of immortality, that one day he might be reborn as himself. And the second god watched over the seed, guarding it until the proper day had passed. And when it passed, the third god was born, the child eternal, Manassa.

"Manassa leads us, his chosen people, to reclaim the Earth he seeded with his life. For just as the greatest of Onge must be the chieftain, so must the greatest people of Earth be the chieftain of Earth."

Surely Mahanta did not buy into this claptrap. Edward nodded.

"Has my god Manassa told you of this?" asked Nockwe.

Edward said, "Yes," for the benefit of any eavesdroppers, but shook his head decidedly, "No."

Nockwe sighed. He leaned in close to Edward once more and whispered. "Mahanta became Manassa because of the signs. He fulfilled the prophecy. But there are more prophecies. Ruling the white man is one of them, including ruling you. That pretense has already been achieved. But there are many more. And if Manassa does not fulfill the prophecies, he is not Manassa. He is not the child immortal."

"Then what is he?" whispered Edward.

"Dead," said Nockwe. He then leaned back. He watched Edward meaningfully as he finished his story, "Like a Chinese rocket, Manassa shoots us to our fortune, our future." He slowly enunciated his last sentences. *"Like an Onge arrow, our path is set and unwavering. Once fired, no man can divert it, not even he who let it loose."*

Nockwe rose. Edward stood with him. Nockwe led him to the exit of the hut by his arm. The chieftain whispered in parting, "There is a saying with my people. It goes: the foolish man, facing the panther, dives into its waiting mouth. Goodbye, Edward."

20

For the first time, Edward turned his attention to the future while under trance. Half his trance he spent in the future. The other half, he spent in Mahanta's private quarters, behind the throne in the temple.

The future was a haze of probabilities. It arced along many channels. He found that it was already calculated to some degree. He did not have the think about it so much as view it. It had already been subconsciously, furiously computed.

The future hinged on the single question: "Who to trust?" From there, it branched out to many more questions, chief among them: "What did Nockwe mean, exactly?", "What does Mahanta really intend?", and "What the hell am I doing?"

If Nockwe was being entirely truthful, then Mahanta's course was set. He was not "Mahanta, the scientist." He was "Manassa, the Onge god," manipulating Edward in order that he might fulfill prophecies and aggrandize himself.

Or else Nockwe sought to undermine Mahanta, and take power for himself. It would not be the first time an Onge chieftain used subterfuge to maintain control. To lose power was death for him and possibly his family as well. It was an unreasonable assumption to think that Nockwe was truly on Manassa's side.

It was an unreasonable assumption to think that Nockwe was truly on Edward's side. Honor or no, he was an Onge first and foremost.

He would not have told Edward what he did if it did not benefit himself or the tribe.

The whole *honor* bit was just to sell it to Edward.

Edward had the feeling of a man playing chess who suddenly makes the unhappy discovery that he's a pawn, sitting on a giant chess board absorbed in the little chess board on his lap.

What was Nockwe trying to do?

Instead of thinking about it, Edward just viewed all of the possibilities that led from the facts. The facts were that Mahanta hadn't told Nockwe what Edward was up to. The facts were that Mahanta and Nockwe were involved in a game that Edward did not yet understand. The facts were that everyone was playing a game except him. He was just a pawn.

From where he sat, each of the possibilities were just as plausible. He lacked data. He needed data before he lost the trance.

Again, he had to steal the initiative, just like in his duel with Dook. The time had come to play the only card he had.

Edward stood up from his bed of straw. He walked briskly behind the throne to Mahanta's personal chambers. He was not surprised to see a candle still burning and Mahanta hunched over his desk.

Mahanta turned abruptly, but his posture remained natural and his face relaxed. Still, Edward noticed the nigh-imperceptible clenching of Mahanta's back muscles in fright, the minute surprise that told Edward he had Mahanta off balance. Mahanta hadn't been expecting Edward to make a move so suddenly, but had been expecting a move.

Edward knew with a trance certainty that Tomy had indeed spied, and perhaps had done better than Nockwe and Edward suspected he could have.

"Edward," said Mahanta. "Can't sleep?" Mahanta was watching Edward's eyes. He was looking for the trance, and found it there.

"No, I'm very awake, Mahanta," said Edward with a casual smile.

"Can I help you?" asked Mahanta.

"I wanted to tell you that I'll be leaving for Lisbaad immediately," said Edward.

Mahanta was shocked. Edward could never have known he was shocked outside of trance. Mahanta's eyebrows quivered. His pupils dilated a fraction of an inch, but in perfect reaction to the end of Edward's sentence as it struck home. It took time for Mahanta to respond. Edward waited, not elucidating further.

"But why?" asked Mahanta carefully.

"I have business to attend to," said Edward.

"I see." Edward could see Mahanta thinking. He could almost articulate the thoughts whirring behind Mahanta's eyes. "I trust you don't believe in Onge mythology," said Mahanta.

"As much as you do," said Edward quickly.

"I trust you don't use Onge mythology to guide your life's decisions."

"I've got my own mythology for that," retorted Edward. *He did spy, and openly admits it.*

"What brings you to Lisbaad, then?" asked Mahanta.

"My researches, of course," said Edward. "What else could bring me to Lisbaad?"

Mahanta was silent.

"I need equipment to continue my researches, and the advice of a doctor," continued Edward.

"Tomy can get you what you need," said Mahanta.

"Tomy can do nothing of the sort. And I am sure he is already indisposed," Edward said. Mahanta's eyes froze. He sought to make them divulge nothing. But even in their immobility they spoke volumes to Edward while in trance. "What is more," Edward continued, "if a letter isn't received by the Lisbaad church within three days with my signature and code, there will be a team of Jesuits here searching for me. While I was injured, I neglected to send my usual note through the traders."

Mahanta's voice took an odd, cold tone that was hard to read. *He knows I'm peering into his soul right now.* "That would be unfortunate," said Mahanta.

"You see, it's a peculiar thing, but I am very sure that such a team would be able to divine what is happening here, either by God's direct revelation, or various other means, whether I'm here or not. It would be quite unfortunate if you or your people learned firsthand why the Jesuits' leader is called a General or why we're known as Soldiers of Christ."

Mahanta got the point.

"It would be quite unfortunate for me, too," said Edward. "I have many hopes. Good night, Mahanta. Do not do something foolish just because I have some leverage. You could hardly expect that I wouldn't figure something out. I'm just following your advice to the letter. I will return in ten days, hopefully with some good news. I will not share our secret unless you make me. Even now, if I were to die suddenly, it is arranged that that secret be shared with a group that shouldn't have it. That would be unfortunate for me, unfortunate for you, and unfortunate for humanity."

Mahanta just watched him and said nothing. Edward moved towards the exit. He saw Mahanta relax almost imperceptibly out of the corner of his eye. It was the exact moment Edward had been waiting for. Edward turned and said, "I do not fault your desire to have the Onge rule the Earth."

Edward watched Mahanta's eyes. Mahanta answered, "I have no such desire."

Mahanta spoke truth. Edward was convinced of it. There was no way Mahanta could lie in front of him. Not one minute reaction could slip by Edward's awareness. Mahanta was answering with total honesty.

Which only led Edward to more questions. But there was something more important than the questions and the answers, and that was precious *initiative*. It was his, for a fleeting moment, and he would not lose it. Clueless, with no idea who to trust, and no sure way out of the maze, his only defense was to be unpredictable.

He left for Lisbaad by foot in the dead of night.

21

Never tell a lie to a Seer. It was an axiom Mahanta had developed in his philosophical study of the drug. It had served him well tonight.

The white Seer sees too much. He sees further than me in some things. He is blind in other areas. He is a fool and brilliant all at once.

So am I, I suppose.

Manassa wrote in his journal:

The Seer sees what he sees. He believes what he sees is all, yet he sees little. And knowing this, still he so believes.

"So it is written." He chuckled. Such a maxim gave him an advantage over another Seer, unless that other Seer had also so calculated.

As a matter of fact, any random arbitrary he threw into his calculations would give him some advantage over another Seer, whether it was wise or not. It could be "Only attack on Tuesdays," and he could throw off the other's calculations.

All this was hypothetical, for only two Seers walked the earth. Eventually, Manassa knew, there would be only one Seer.

He cursed himself for being so stupid as to involve the white man.

He could help me with the after-pain. It is my only stumbling block.

On the other hand, he could slow everything down.

Manassa had meditated in trance for several hours after Edward had so abruptly left the village. He had to find his course after the unexpected turn of events. Manassa did not foresee any way that Edward could stop him, even if Edward completely turned on him from the moment he set foot in Lisbaad. *I'll give him some rope and see if he can fix the after-pain.*

It was obvious that Edward was still with him, still wanted the substance. Otherwise Edward would have simply left without a confrontation.

Manassa walked out the temple's secret exit, directly from his quarters through a hole dug out of the ground. It let out at the edge of the jungle. He walked toward the clearing with the ancient tree where he'd slain the panther. He'd trapped it in a cage a few weeks before the coming of age and released it for the "show".

It was time. Usually, Tomy would accompany him for such an occasion, but his messenger was out on other business. *I'll need more messengers.*

Manassa reached his destination as the morning mist finished evaporating. He peered out the edge of the clearing and saw several hundred of his Onge gathered. There would be more. Manassa had requested the presence of every man, woman and child, which would amount to well over a thousand. It would be the largest assembly they'd had in living memory. Even the most important of rituals did not involve *everybody.*

Manassa watched his people, unheeded. Their attention was scattered. The hunters of the tribe, particularly, seemed jittery. They did not like sitting in the clear like that for any reason. They knew what happened to animals that did so. The rest of the villagers were involved in conversation, bored, but not rushing to return to their toils in the midday heat.

Manassa bided his time, thinking over his speech. Finally the crowd swelled to the desired size. A couple priests of Manassa's inner circle sounded gongs at the rear of the assembly. The Onge turned their heads to see their god arrive.

Manassa took that moment to scamper into the clearing and up the tree. He perched on a branch he'd chosen the day before. It supported his weight, and the whole mob would be able to see him easily.

"MY PEOPLE!!!" Manassa shouted to the backs of a thousand heads. They all jerked around to see him. A thrilled buzz swept through the crowd. He felt its electricity. He was in his second trance in less than twelve hours. He would need to rest for several days after this, but his performance here was crucial.

Under the trance, he could hear and process every word spoken by every one of his Onge. He knew this crowd more than any performer had ever known his crowd. "Manassa, he appears…he is truly a god…look, he's in the tree…look!…Manassa!" they murmured to one another nervously.

Mannassa let his cry ring out again. "MY PEOPLE!!!" He projected his voice so that its echo permeated the air all the way to the trees of the jungle, so that it reached the ears of every Onge in his village.

The mob stirred as one. "Manassa!" they sang out in unison. That shout, given at every one of Manassa's public appearances, never sounded as it did that day. Triumph rang in their voices. Their god exuded a wave of exhileration, and the Onge rode it willingly.

Manassa knew in that instant that he had succeeded. He had created his image. Now it was time.

"YOU ARE THE CHOSEN!" Manassa shouted out from the tree top.

"AS ARE YOU, OUR LIVING GOD!!!" They didn't stop yelling after that. They shouted and clapped furiously, stomping and singing. The youth cut loose from their parents and ran to one another, jumping and pointing in excitement. They cried out his name. Manassa felt the tree sway with all the stomping and shaking on the ground.

It was an interminable time before the Onge began to notice that their leader had said nothing further, but rather stood patiently in his tree watching over his people. One by one, the exultation of the Onge settled into rapt attention.

Manassa took in the eyes of every one of his villagers. Every face would guide his speech. He would change the very fabric of Onge culture in this moment.

When Manassa started speaking again, his voice was calm and clear. He modulated his volume until the last person at the back of the clearing, standing in the path, could hear him perfectly, but no more. He wasn't yelling. He didn't even sound like he was making a speech. He was sharing a deeply personal communication with his people. "My people, beloved, I have brought you here today, on the grounds where I shed my mortal skin, that I might share with you my vision."

He heard some of the villagers say, "Tell us…Tell us…Tell us your vision." Their wide eyes, their bated breath, spoke more loudly to Manassa.

"I was born with a vision," he continued. "It is a godly vision. Yet it is a vision that I am sure you have seen, too. Every Onge has a touch of holiness in him; else we would not be guarded by the Watcher, else I would not have grown here as the seed of our Creator.

"In this god-sent future, I saw myself at the throne, I saw myself chieftain." He saw nods of agreement, a couple uncomfortable glances to Nockwe, who was standing near the front of the crowd. They had all had that vision, even the women, Manassa was sure. It was in their upbringing.

Manassa pressed on: "But I was not myself in this dream; I was the tribe. And the tribe I ruled was not this tribe, but rather all the tribes of the earth and sea." The crowd was silent, now. He read their faces. They dared not hope; though they knew the prophecies of Manassa, they dared not hope.

Manassa shifted in the trees. "I knew it was a godly vision, for it was one that any mortal would have rejected. You, my people, rejected it, though you've seen it yourselves countless times. You look at the people of other lands, with their powerful weapons and incomprehensible culture. The greatest of you felt threatened and ineffective; the weakest of you felt inferior. All of you are forgiven for forgetting what it means to be Onge. Mortal vessels cannot hold immortal treasure."

Manassa let his voice begin a slow crescendo. "But now is the time for me, the Onge child-eternal, to give you back the treasure you dreamed of but let slip from your grasp!"

They were nodding agreement. The younger men were sold. Still, he knew he'd have to win the elders. He had to win everybody. "How could a thousand men, women and children come to lead the world?" asked Manassa. "How could we have prosperity, and never starve, and never be sick, and never die?" Murmuring erupted in the crowd. Excitement bubbled over, even amongst the older men. It was another of the prophecies of Manassa.

Manassa let the buzz lull before he continued. "I ask you another question, far more relevant. *HOW COULD WE NOT!?*" He shouted, giving the crowd permission to go wild. They did so.

"It is this god's vision. So it shall come to pass," he said, but no one could hear him. It was a long time before he could speak again.

When he did so, he spoke a little quieter, so that the Onge in the back had to quiet and strain their ears. "My people, our heroes of old all had powers and abilities. Some called down lightning to defeat their adversaries. Others rode chariots from the heavens. We will need such a weapon.

"My Onge, I have provided it to you: I have called down a nectar from the heavens that makes us *invincible* to our foes. This is my greatest miracle, one that will take us to our destiny."

There was quite a din of back and forth discussion in the crowd. They'd lost all discipline in their ecstasy, though they had no idea yet what he meant.

Manassa had made sure a small circle in front of the tree remained clear. One of Manassa's inner circle of priests stepped into the ring. He was experiencing "the lightness" - what Manassa called the effects of drinking the substance, rather than injecting it. The priest walked to a basket in the center of the ring.

"Behold, I have blessed my loyal priest with the nectar!" shouted Manassa. The priest pulled the top off the basket. Six birds flew out. They scattered in the air. Another man stepped into the ring and handed the priest a semi-automatic rifle.

The priest pulled the weapon up and spun in a circle. He squeezed out six shots from the rifle as he did so. Many of the Onge were taken aback at the loud spit of the gun - very few had seen such a weapon fired before.

All six of the birds dropped nearly simultaneously. Each had been an impossible shot on the fly. For a moment, not a soul was breathing in the clearing. Then absolute pandemonium broke loose. The crowd was in uproar.

Manassa bellowed at the top of his lungs, riding the wave of their exultation, "BEHOLD, THE POWER OF THE NECTAR! THE POWER OF MY MIRACLE, MY GIFT TO YOU, MY PEOPLE!!!!!" The Onge jumped up and down, screaming blessings and curses. They settled into a chant.

"Manassa! Manassa! Manassa!"

Their god could not help but smile. For the first time in living memory, his people were excited, happy, empowered.

Manassa had planned another demonstration, but he'd save that for later. He could not get them into a higher foment than this. "JOIN ME IN MY VISION!" he screamed.

They roared back at him once more. "Manassa! Manassa! Manassa!"

Manassa jumped down from his perch, flipping from branch to branch and finally reaching the ground. Behind the tree, no one could see him leave.

When Manassa returned to his temple, not a soul was in the village. And yet, he could hear his people's voices shouting in unison all the way from the clearing.

"Manassa! Manassa! Manassa!"

22

Edward hiked to the port town of Lisbaad, the only "civilized" district on the island. Lisbaad had a small church run by two Jesuits, and a few Catholic nuns instructed a school, so once he arrived Edward took no chances with the main streets and cloaked his head.

The roads were narrow, made for carts, but a few cars kicked up dust here and there.

Aside from the occasional anachronism, the town was a full century behind Western civilization. For Edward, who had lived with the Onge for months, it was a mighty advance.

He arrived late at night and purchased board at a run-down inn on the southern outskirts of the town. Of course, everything was run-down, not just the inn.

A few merchant seamen manned the bar, each sipping on something unhealthily brown. Edward asked the small Oriental innkeeper for a room. The man led Edward up the stairs and unlocked a creaky door.

The innkeeper showed him around. The wire frame under the mattress had stray springs falling out, and the room stunk of mold, but to Edward it was quite an upgrade from his straw pallet. *Not that it matters.* Edward's mind was fixated on what the future held, not on the inconveniences of the present.

In any event, Edward had never much cared for material things. *Knowledge, on the other hand...*

"You come from the south?" the old man asked in Tamil, which Edward

127

fortunately understood.

"I do. I have a question for you," said Edward.

"What is that?" The man stroked the wispy white hairs that languished on his chin.

"If I were sick, where would I go?"

"To the doctor," answered the little old man.

"Well, yes." Edward smiled. "But where in this town would I go?"

"To the east end. You are white, so you would see the white woman. She has the clinic. You wouldn't want to see the brown man."

"No?"

"No." The man did not elaborate any further on that point. "She charges whites," he continued, "but you have rupees, so she would help you."

"Thank you."

"What is your illness?" The old man's eyebrows furrowed. He actually cared. Edward stifled a laugh.

"I appreciate your concern," Edward answered. He ushered the innkeeper out.

Once alone, Edward took a deep breath, checked the room and locked the door. He lay down on the mattress. It sunk in the middle and felt divinely comfortable. *A room all to myself.* He slept deeply for the first time in weeks.

23

Nockwe sat behind the closed door of his hut, staring into the fire pit. The chief's hut was one of the few dwellings with its own cooking fire. His wife stood behind him, also watching writhing of the flames. He had her stand behind him so she could be there and yet not distract him from his meditations. His three children were sleeping in the bedroom, which was only divided off by some bamboo hanging from the ceiling of the house. His second children and second wives lived elsewhere. He was responsible for the three families of the men he'd slain.

The chanting of his people played over and over in his mind. *Manassa! Manassa! Manassa!* He did not yet know what to think of it. It was something new, something he was ill-prepared for.

In all his time as chieftain, he'd operated on the rule that if something was surviving, only change could destroy it. Only change could improve it, this was true, but all too often one was disappointed.

This boy is change.

Nockwe had not yet made a judgment on what that change meant.

This boy fulfilled the prophecies of our forefathers. He is a leader, and inspires the people. These things are good.

Nockwe had never seen his people so spirited. They were so *proud.*

But to where does he lead us?

In all things the chieftain serves the tribe. It was a line from their oral history he often repeated to himself. It said tribe, not god. No matter what religious significance Mahanta assumed, Nockwe would always serve the tribe first.

Nockwe did not like to think about such things. He wished he could do as everyone else and simply follow Manassa.

The white man had been right. It had been a drug.

Nockwe's mind drifted to other things...to the white man who had saved his life, whom Nockwe had tipped off against his own better judgment. Nockwe was certain that Mahanta would not let the white man live a season. As soon as the white man was no longer useful, he would be sent to death to rejoin the Earth. Such was the way of the Onge in times as these.

It feels like war times. Is war upon us?

Nockwe stood up and rubbed his head with his hands. He wiped these matters out of his mind. It was too late at night to be dwelling on such things.

Nockwe felt fortunate that his cough had left him Saturday morning. He had fallen asleep while in the lightness after supervising a training session, and when he awoke he felt like he had never been ill. Disease had always left him quickly once he broke it. All that was left was some tiredness.

His young wife came to him, rubbing his back and his shoulders. He felt her warm skin against his. It was a different, richer sort of warm than the fire. She pressed against his bare back and held him. He sighed. His muscles relaxed along the exhale of his breath.

I will be ever watchful. But I must stop thinking. I am a chieftain, not a medicine man nor a philosopher.

"Is something wrong, Nockwe?" asked his wife.

"No, my guardian. There are only thoughts, shadows. There is nothing wrong." He closed his eyes and concentrated on her skin. "Bri," he said, turning around to face her. He kissed her forehead. He said her name again. "Bri'ley'na." It meant literally "Bright Sky."

She took his face in her hands and looked up at him. Her rich chocolate eyes conveyed her concern. "I worry about this Manassa. You may kill me for saying it, but still I worry."

He kissed her forehead in an effort to soothe her but said nothing. He did not want to betray his own doubts. She would be able to hear it in his voice.

She pulled back again slightly, more agitated. "You have always lived for the tribe," she said. "I don't know if this is Manassa's way, too. Something else may be driving him."

He told her what he had told himself. "I'll be watchful, Bri." He stroked the long, flowing hair along the side of her face. "I will be careful. I will always serve the tribe."

"And I will be careful for you. And I will always serve you," she said. He smiled.

She pulled him to her gently and kissed his mouth.

24

Manassa stood at his "throne". It was a joke to him, his chair, but it had the effect he needed on his Onge. One day he would need a throne that would impress more than just a tribe of primitives, but also popes and kings.

One day very soon I'll need more to impress my Onge.

Tomy knelt facing him to his left, Nockwe to his right. The boy stifled a yawn. It was still several hours until daybreak.

"You were awake when I sent for you," commented Manassa to Nockwe.

"I was," acknowledged Nockwe.

"Much on your mind?" asked Manassa.

"A chieftain's mind must never sleep," answered Nockwe.

"Please stand and report," said Manassa.

Tomy took his turn first, as had been the tradition since this temple had first been erected. Nockwe was the only member of the tribe who ranked higher than Manassa's messenger, and that was only within these walls. Outside the hut, even Nockwe had to feign lending his ear to the boy.

"Internally, the Onge as a whole are excited. They talk of nothing but your sermon at the clearing, the gun and the birds. They are ready to do your bidding. There remains only a small knot of dissenters." Tomy paused for a moment.

Manassa nodded, giving his consent. Tomy tilted his head to signify his understanding. Nockwe missed it, still looking intently at the ground as was protocol.

The young man continued his report. "Externally, we have secured seven vehicles, some guns. I have not been to town for two days. Our ears are slow here, in the village. There is no phone, no way to get a message across. I am working on this."

We must move. This is no place for a headquarters, thought Manassa.

"You are to go to town. You are to do as we planned," Manassa instructed.

Tomy nodded. He would follow the directions to the letter. "Nockwe will soon have our army ready. When it is ready, so must the village must be ready, and so must Lisbaad be ready. Lisbaad is in your hands, Tomy. Goodbye."

"Yes, lord." Tomy turned to leave.

"My messenger," said Manassa.

"Yes, my lord," said Tomy, turning back.

"I need intelligence in regards to Liang."

"You will have it," said Tomy. This was what made Manassa keep Tomy as his messenger. Tomy did not know who Liang was. Tomy would not ask him. Tomy refused to add one single thought to Manassa's workload - he would rather work without sleep than trouble his god with a single clarification.

Still, it would be foolish to unnecessarily overstrain his messenger. Manassa took the time to explain: "Liang is a big figure in the Sri Lankan underworld. He practically owns Lisbaad, and controls all of the trade to, from, and through the island," said Manassa. "I must know more, for I wish for the tribe to enjoy some of his vast resources and consideration. This much I already know. I leave the rest to you."

"Yes, lord," said Tomy. He bowed, then maintained his position, head downturned.

"You may go, now. Do not fail me."

Tomy left the hut.

"An amazing young man," said Manassa. It was a comment that Nockwe did not answer. He had not yet been recognized by the throne.

This amused Manassa. It had been quite easy to revive the old traditions. There was a time when the Onge were more than a mere speck on the map. Their economic model of hunting had given them some fine warriors, and at one time in the distant past their "empire" had actually stretched through Sri Lanka to the southern tip of the Indian mainland. At that time, the Onge had advanced into a centralized feudalism, complete with roughshod court. Manassa drew on their history to show his people their future. Nockwe seemed to know his ancient role and played the part ably enough.

"Nockwe," said Manassa. "Give me your brief."

"Yes, lord," said Nockwe. He turned his eyes up to face his people's god. "All goes as you have foreseen. The gardens are full now with the nectar plants. We have two hundred fifty-six plants. We have twenty liters of the sap and are now producing five liters per day. The replanting experiment continues, with favorable results and four of five surviving thus far. Your personal lab will be complete tonight as an adjunct to the temple, accessible from your sleeping quarters." The chieftain effortlessly rattled off the facts.

"Very well." Manassa was impressed with Nockwe's easy command of the numbers. Manassa knew it was Nockwe's administrative talents, not his skill with the spear, which had made him so popular with the people. Unfortunately, the Onge method of choosing rulers eliminated all but the warriors. For the first time in over a century, a warrior-administrator had the helm. "Continue," prompted Manassa.

"We have fifty warriors trained in the lightness and battle-ready. We have twenty-five more under training, and four hundred more warriors ready to begin training at your command. At this rate, it will take three months."

"For every ten warriors you have trained, you may train four more at once. You must be done in a month. Time is an enemy far worse than any potential dissent," said Manassa.

"As you wish, my lord," acknowledged Nockwe with a respectful nod.

Manassa did not want any more trainees armed with the lightness than he felt he could control. "Continue," said Manassa.

"The inner circle is also fully formed. I recommend that you assign Lock to lead it."

"Lock?" asked Manassa.

"The late Tien's brother. He would do an admirable job, and could report to you. Though he was trained under the medicine man, he is most loyal."

Manassa didn't hesitate. "You will do it," said Manassa. "You will lead my inner circle of priests." Manassa gauged Nockwe's reaction. The chieftain's face remained placid, but even outside the trance Manassa sensed with much conflict behind Nockwe's near-black eyes. "Do you not wish to do so?"

"My lord…" Nockwe breathed deeply and gathered his thoughts. "It is not that I do not wish to. It is the ultimate in opportunity…I wish only to serve you and the tribe. It is only that I fear that I should fail you if I were to stretch myself too thin. To run the tribe in the coming months will become a formidable challenge in and of itself. Your security and your vision are of course the tribe's most important assets. And the tribe is key to your vision coming true. I feel I cannot ably handle all of it."

Manassa sat down in his throne. Nockwe knelt. "You will do it. You will have assistants, you will organize it, but you will do it. I have foreseen it," said Manassa.

Nockwe must gain a religious significance to the people, or he will become worthless to me. His wise words will fall upon deaf ears; a single priest of my inner circle will hold more sway than the great chieftain.

Nockwe acquiesced after consideration. He did a good job of burying his frustration. "Yes, lord," said Nockwe. "As you wish."

"Please see to it. And continue your brief."

"The tribe is 1,163 -" said Nockwe.

"I thought it 1,162."

"We had a birth," said Nockwe.

"Very well. We need more of those. Encourage it whatever way you can."

"Yes, lord. We have food stores for three months. As your messenger reported, we have guns right now for only twenty warriors. We have seven cars, with a total capacity of thirty-five soldiers. Two are larger vehicles, vans."

"This must be remedied immediately," said Manassa. *I need more resources.* "Tomy is working on it, but now you must remedy it as well. There is no use in training our warriors with weapons they don't have, or educating them in the culture of the West without giving them the swordpoint that won Westerners their culture. We must have at least five hundred guns, at minimum. Two thousand of different types would be best, but not necessary at this time. Small handguns all the way up to semi-automatic rifles. Armor if you can find it. These are things we'll need to find in Sri Lanka. There are only so many of these on the island."

Manassa paced a bit, then leaned against the arm of his throne. "Start a forward post in Sri Lanka," Manassa ordered.

"Yes, lord."

"Is there anything else you have to report?" asked Manassa.

"Not at this time, my lord."

"Very well. I have a question for you, then," said Manassa. Nockwe's body tensed. *Yes, he senses it.* "You helped Edward, you warned him." It wasn't really a question.

Nockwe's tired eyes shot wide, but he did not otherwise move. He was speechless.

"In all things the chieftain serves the tribe," said Manassa. "I do not think you served the tribe in this. Are you no longer chieftain?"

Nockwe's mouth opened and closed. There was nothing he could say.

"Explain your motives, Nockwe."

"In all things I do serve the tribe. But this was not out of service, but of honor. I am a loyal man. I felt that since he saved my life, I should at least give him warning."

"Warning of what?"

Nockwe locked eyes with Manassa. "Of his impending death."

Manassa could not deny it, so he didn't take it up anymore. "Tell me, Nockwe, do you owe favors to any more outsiders? Does your honor call you to help any more white men?"

Nockwe maintained his composure. "An important question, Manassa. My debt with Edward is discharged. I only serve the tribe and have always served the tribe."

"You realize you may have created quite a setback," said Manassa.

"I did not think that I did anything that you did not already foresee and plan for."

Actually, Manassa hadn't seen it. The idea that Nockwe would do such a thing was totally foreign to him. Manassa toyed again with the idea of getting rid of Nockwe. He'd been working it over in his mind for the past day.

I am spread too thin, already. The chieftain is smart, loyal. By his actions, he is unique in that he does not buy into my godhood, and yet does not neglect my power. He does serve the tribe; in this he's utterly predictable. I understand what he did with Edward.

Manassa's thoughts turned to the opposite end of the spectrum. Perhaps he could awaken Nockwe with the drug, as he had done with Edward. *I could trust him more than that white man. That white man has too many crazy ideas in his head, ideas I didn't even know about until after I gave him the drug. I had not yet grown up, that week ago.*

Manassa's tired mind drifted briefly back to his decision with Edward. It had indeed been a stupid mistake, but one he would let ride. In ten more days, Edward might have the cure for the after-pain. If not, maybe Manassa could eventually come up with it himself. Manassa just didn't have the time; he'd have to study, he'd have to work on it, and there was so much more he needed to accomplish. It would just waste precious trances, and he had to make every single one of them count. Just with the power of the drug in its present form he had much too small an infrastructure and organization. There was hardly any reason he should spend his own time working on the drug's improvement.

At first, Manassa had considered just giving Edward the lightness by administering the substance orally. He may have died, then, though, and not been able to work on the after-pain.

With the after-pain gone, I really would be more the god…right now, all my motions limited by just one trance a day…so long as Edward doesn't turn on me, it's worth the risk.

"Are there not more Edwards? Do you want me to get you another?" asked Nockwe.

Manassa remembered he was still in audience with Nockwe, a very tense Nockwe who thought he might meet death in this confrontation. He felt so *disconnected* recently, his mind shifting into and out of the problems and threats at hand. The present held so little threat compared to the future. Manassa was in the present and he was not. He dismissed Nockwe's query with a wave of his hand. He'd made his decision. "Edward still works for me. If he stops, I can put others in his place. It is your loyalty that I need much more than a white man's research. I feel after talking to you tonight that I have it. I have a question for you, though. Why do you wish to see my vision through?" asked Manassa.

"You are the living god, Manassa," said Nockwe. Manassa looked around the hut, ensuring they were alone.

"Don't give me this *kcleyp*," said the living god, using a choice Onge expletive. "It is important that everyone else believe that, this is true. But you don't. There is no need for you to. You may never say this to another being, nor even speak like this to me outside of this temple, even when alone, but you and I both know I am no living god."

Nockwe's face was again frozen. He looked more threatened than before. Manassa could tell the chief did not know how to react. *Good.*

Manassa continued. "Except, of course, to the degree that I can exalt our tribe. And in that sense, you could be a living god, too. I would be not a god but a madman to believe otherwise."

Nockwe knelt. "My god, I do not -"

"Nockwe! Stop it! Get up! Stop it! Say it. Say 'Manassa is Mahanta, and neither are living gods, except by their deeds.' And quit all this religious *kcleyp* when we meet in seclusion. Say it!"

"Manassa is Mahanta," Nockwe began to say, carefully. Every muscle in his body appeared tense, as though he might flee the temple at any second. He stopped.

"SAY IT!!!" screamed Manassa.

"And neither are living gods, except by their deeds," Nockwe finished quietly.

Manassa let a silence ride the air between them before he spoke again. "It is a cruel trick, our legends, to deny men their opportunity at godhood, their opportunity to become heroes, by painting anyone with real power as coming down from the heavens or being born of hell," said Manassa.

Manassa stepped down close and rested his hands on Nockwe's shoulders. "Nockwe, if I am ever recorded in our oral histories as a living god, so will you be. We need religion on our side, to keep our men and women disciplined and their morale high. But we would be fools, as the generals of our army, to think of it as anything more than that. The only divinities we have on our sides are our wits, made in the Great Thinker's image, and our able bodies, which were ultimately created by He who is Unmoved. Things will only go right when you make them to go right, not because you have me on your side."

"Yes, my lord," said Nockwe.

"Yes, my chieftain," echoed Manassa, imitating the form with a familiar smile. "Now answer this question, without your *kcleyp*. Why do you wish to see my vision through?"

"For the good of the tribe, my lord. It is the natural order of things. Just as the most fit must rule the tribe, so it is with the world. With this nectar of yours, the tribe can soon be the most fit. Our tribe deserves prosperity.

Manassa nodded. "And who do you serve?"

"The tribe."

"Very good." Manassa clapped him on the shoulder and hid his disappointment with an encouraging smile. Nockwe was not yet ready to become awakened. Manassa could not afford his loyalty.

25

The sun awakened Edward. *Too late.* He started, but remained in bed to gather his thoughts. He had wanted to be rested when he began his work in Lisbaad, but more importantly he wanted to do his work in the early morning while his face would not be seen or remembered in the harsh shadows of the dawning light.

Edward lifted himself up and examined the streets below. Morning was in earnest in Lisbaad, and the calls of the street vendors at a nearby market drifted into his room.

He looked at his room. He hadn't yet seen it in the light. It was a true dump. Rays of sunlight were actually visible from all the dust mites caroming through the air. The curtains were molded around the edges, and the carpet was hardly a carpet anymore, but rather fuzz growing out of the cement floor. *And all this is still splendid compared to the squalor of the Onge. That's what you get when you don't trade and don't modernize.*

The lingering after-pain was almost gone. The long hike and good night's rest had effectively cleared his head.

Edward checked his pack for his medical kit. The syringes of "penicillin" were still in place. Not a drop of the substance could go missing. Even a tiny particle in the wrong person's hands could spread like a plague of chaos and warfare around the world. Someone getting the whole kit would be disastrous. Edward scarce could contemplate it - except in trance, he had.

He replayed those possible futures in his mind. *A corporate mogul using it for economic monopoly and subjugation; a new Hitler with a weapon that will let him win; a new "freedom" that results in almost everyone a slave. Or the most likely course: anarchy and destruction as the current power structure is toppled, followed by all of the above.*

All if it falls into the wrong hands.

And who could possibly have the "right hands"?

That was a question he couldn't answer. He certainly didn't feel that he had the right hands. *What to do with such a substance?* It was the holy grail of medicine, of enlightenment. With it discoveries could be made to bring mankind to a whole new level of survival and happiness. He was sure that many mysteries of the sciences and humanities would be solved in relatively short order.

And yet, in its raw form introduced to the planet at large, Edward foresaw only destruction.

Even in the hands of only two men, the future was hazy and full of dangerous possibilities. Mahanta was a wild variable in Edward's trance calculations. Edward could not predict him because he had the trance, too.

Certainly, Mahanta sought power. *And yet he swore that he didn't want the Onge to rule the Earth.* Edward was sure he wasn't lying.

Edward paced to the mirror over the room's dirty sink and examined his own dark brown eyes. In a matter of only days, his life had completely changed vectors. Not only was he accelerating exponentially, he was also beginning to align all his decisions and thoughts along the path of this drug and its effects. *The nirvana effect.*

It was as though he were a railway engineer on a runaway locomotive, and the longer he remained aboard, the faster the train sped, the more impossible his escape. In trance, he saw the probabilities of the future - and in many of them, the locomotive went over the cliff, down into a gorge, straight into a wall.

He had to constantly accelerate his actions and remain unpredictable just to stay alive.

But if I were to stop now and disembark, surely someone far more dangerous will hijack this train.

Edward looked down from the mirror and breathed deeply. He was honest enough with himself to recognize the lie. There was no possibility that he would jump off that train, but not for any reason so humanitarian. He didn't want to keep the nirvana effect out of the wrong hands so much as keep it in his own.

The nirvana effect *completed* him, in a way so personal and so comprehensive that if he were to lose it, he would feel dead.

All his life, he'd dreamed of a golden path. He'd stood on its first brick, peering with squinting eyes through the fog that obscured it. He'd never gotten beyond that first brick, but he'd never stepped back, either.

Now that path lay in wait, welcoming before him.

He could reach his purpose, now. He was alive.

It was a total addiction, he knew. He'd known it innately since his first trance. It was not a physical addiction or a chemical dependency. Yet at no point for the rest of his life did he foresee walking away from this substance.

It was as though his entire life before the nirvana effect was simply background information for what lay in the *now* and in the future.

He had the fleeting thought that perhaps he was being too hard on himself. Of course he was thinking about the drug. In this span of his life, his decisions concerning it were matters of life or death. Maybe it would be different after he was safe. He did not see any future, however, in which he was ever safe.

It was ironic that the substance freed him into slavery. In one sense, his life was now his own for whatever short breadth he kept it; not his brothers', not his father's, not the Jesuits'. He had only himself and his God to answer to. And even his God seemed amenable to the suggestions Edward made about his life's course.

But there was the matter of the pressures he had to meet just to stay alive while he had those syringes in his pack. Possession of the substance brooked no weakness.

He knew he had many things to meditate on - his family, the Jesuits, Callista, his future. Much of this was surrounded in a black haze of pain that he resisted visiting while in trance. All that would come later, though. He knew it would be necessary to revisit all his past in order to set course for the future. But now all his concentration must be centered around the Onge "chosen one".

Mahanta may not be all bad, and surely not as bad as Nockwe makes him out to be. Mahanta may still be influenced. He is young, and I am the only man on Earth who can understand him.

Edward foresaw a future, tenuous and hazy as it might seem, where Mahanta assisted him on his golden path.

Edward grabbed his cloak, adjusting its hood so that as little of his face was exposed as possible without drawing undue attention. He shouldered his backpack.

"I'll be here another night," said Edward to the innkeeper on his way out.

The little man bent slightly and nodded, then belatedly called after him. "I hope you get to feeling better!"

"Me, too," muttered Edward Styles as he left.

26

The clinic had a brightness to it that distinguished it from the surrounding property. Its walls were clean and freshly painted. A red cross made of wood hung prominently over the door. The steps were swept and clear of loiterers.

Edward checked the street several times approaching. He did not really know what he was checking for, but he checked just the same.

A young Indian woman manned the clinic's desk. She was tall by Asian standards and wore a white hat with the same simple red cross insignia. Whoever ran this clinic had the best marketing and branding on the whole island. The innkeeper referred clients and her receptionist wore a uniform!

"Is the doctor in?" asked Edward in Tamil.

"She is not," answered the young woman in English. "She is making house call. But she will be back soon. Please have a seat."

Edward sat down. The receptionist walked around her desk and handed Edward a clipboard with a checklist of possible maladies from which he might be suffering. He left the contact information blank, checked nothing, and wrote at the bottom, "Need doctor's consultation."

She seemed puzzled when he returned the nearly empty form, but recovered quickly. "Thank you," she said. "Have a seat. The doctor will be in shortly."

"Shortly" was an hour, during which time the receptionist offered him a drink of water twice and a Coke once. The timing seemed scripted, as though to interrupt a caller from boredom at just the right moment.

"This clinic, how long has it been open?" he asked, after he'd long run out of things to mull over.

"Three years, happily serving the community of Lisbaad," she said. Edward smiled. He wondered how long it would take him to get her off-script.

Edward stood up and idled over to the window. He looked out into the narrow street. A car or two, some pedestrians. "The owner, the doctor, she's a white woman?" he asked, still looking out the window.

"What?" The receptionist looked up at him from her desk. Not long at all.

"The doctor?"

"Yes, she is a white woman."

"Where is she from?"

"From the United States of America. She is a fully licensed medical doctor, graduated from Oxford University." His American Cali had gone to Oxford, too, but not in medicine.

"That's odd."

"Odd? What is this, odd?"

"It's strange that an American would become an M.D. at Oxford, even stranger that she would open a clinic here."

"Why is this so strange, you say?"

"This isn't exactly the most profitable enterprise, is it?" he asked.

"No sir. It is not for profit. Those who can pay must, but most of the good doctor's clientele are locals whom she treats for absolutely free," she said.

Edward turned from the window. "Excellent use of whom," he said.

The receptionist smiled. "Thank you, sir." A door creaked from behind her. "That must be the doctor. Please wait a moment while I bring her your documentation." By that she meant the one empty sheet of paper where he'd scribbled on the bottom. *Certainly less red tape than America. Beats our health system any day…unless you're actually sick.*

The receptionist re-entered. "The doctor will see you now," she said with exquisite pronunciation, as though she were performing a Shakespearean drama. He could tell it was her most-used line. As she said it she swung her arm grandiosely, leading him to the doorway behind reception. "This way, please," she said. There wasn't a hint of accent in her voice as she said that line. She must have drilled and drilled it.

Edward followed her. She seated him in a small room and closed the door as she left.

The room was simply furnished: a chair, the doctor's roller stool, the examination pallet. A couple of cabinets and a receptacle for waste were on the far side.

The door clicked open and the doctor glided in. She was very young for a doctor, in her late twenties. Her blonde hair hung loosely in a bun. She was well, though moderately dressed, and had on no makeup. Her complexion didn't require any.

She didn't get past the door. She stopped in mid-glide and examined him with an odd look on her face. Her lips were perched sideways, frozen. Her eyebrows arched as high as they could go, and then they furrowed down. She disappeared. The door closed behind her.

Edward rubbed his face with his hands. He did not know whether to laugh or to cry. Apparently, Callista Knowles had stayed for med school after he'd left. Apparently, Dr. Callista Knowles had stationed herself on this island for the past few years.

For a moment, something occupied his thoughts other than the nirvana effect.

A moment later, she walked back in.

"Edward," she said, businesslike. He could not read her face.

"Cali," said Edward. "I mean, Callista." He could never read her face.

"You need a doctor's consultation?" she asked.

Now more than ever. She looked older now. She didn't look any worse, only different. He hadn't seen her in nearly a decade. He knew he looked different, too.

All the words he'd thought but never said in those lonely years rushed to his tongue to fill the air. Not a sound could come out.

He'd figured a one in a billion chance of their meeting again, but he'd played it over in his mind at least that many times. It had never gone like this. He sighed.

She watched him, waiting for an answer to her question. He watched her eyes. She had plain brown eyes. They were one of her more alluring qualities.

She broke eye contact by turning to the disposables closet and searching for a disposable. She had no need for a disposable, though Edward surmised from the tears that had welled up in her eyes that she needed something to do. She hadn't really changed at all.

He wanted to stand up and put his hands on her shoulders but she walked out again before he could do anything.

He had proposed to her seven years ago in his senior year of college. He remembered the goofy tux he'd worn to the restaurant ("Why did you rent a tux for a dinner?") and that frightful moment on one knee all alone at the park where the Earth had seemed to stop, and then roll right over him.

He'd written her dozens of letters. He'd never heard back. He'd figured she'd made a cold, clean break. And yet here were very warm tears in her eyes.

One thing that had changed about her: he'd never seen her this discombobulated.

He looked at the white wall and tried to not think too much. She'd be back again any minute.

He'd had no plan after their wedding. It was more an end in itself. They'd dated for years. She'd been his best friend. They had been two Americans in a sea of Brits. They'd become one another's home. It was them against the world.

The night she declined his proposal, where she'd ended their relationship, he'd sat on the edge of his bed with a handful of Tylenols trying to catch his breath. In the end, he couldn't come up with a reason to live, but he couldn't come up with a reason to end it, either.

In retrospect, he knew that joining the order, giving in to his father's and brothers' urgings, was his suicide, far more effective than over-the-counter medicine. *A cold, clean break.*

He thought he heard her call his name. His senses jarred to the present. Had she called his name or had his mind just drifted? "Callista?" he called weakly. No answer.

Finally he saw her peering out around the door. "Edward?" she asked quietly. "Come here."

He followed her to a small lounge area. Two chairs were positioned squarely facing each other across a table. A cup of coffee steamed at either end.

"We're out of tea," she apologized. "And I've come to like coffee better."

"That's because you're American." She wasn't looking him and didn't even acknowledge the attempted renewal of their longest running joke.

She had come to London with her parents when she was seven. Her father worked in the American consulate. It was her "flaw" - she wasn't a nice British girl like his father would have wanted. He used to pick at her endlessly on the point.

It was completely ridiculous. He was American, too, and the last thing his father would have wanted for him was any sort of girl at all.

Of course, she didn't have any real flaws. Not in his eyes.

Maybe she had flaws now. He had a feeling seven years had given him better vision when it came to things like that.

"Sit," she said, motioning toward his chair. She took the seat across from him and sipped her coffee.

"So..." she said, looking down into black cup. Her black blouse was distractingly form fitting. He just looked at her. She looked up, caught his eyes, and then looked down again. He couldn't stop looking at her. His eyes felt sore. "So, I got my medical degree. Peace Corps, couple other aid programs wouldn't accept my application, so I just..."

"Lisbaad?" he asked.

"I wanted to go to China, but it was too hard for me to get to the mainland."

"Lisbaad?" Edward repeated again, incredulous. She shrugged. "I like your clinic," he said.

She grinned ever-so-slightly. "Thank you," she said with a tired sigh.

"I got my Doctor of Divinity, just like pops and brothers wanted. I'm a full-fledged missionary now."

"How long have you been here?" she asked.

"Four months. You?" he asked.

"A few years. Not long after I finished my residency." He nodded. "What kind of work are you doing here?" she asked.

"The Onge. I'm working with them. The native tribe south of here."

Her eyes widened. "They are crazy. They won't trade. They won't even let me see their sick. Well, except once. One exception proves the rule."

"The rule that they're crazy?" he asked.

She nodded, then laughed. She was cheering up. Her laugh was the same, too. Edward felt familiar with her though they'd been so long separated. "I suppose you'll defend them?" she asked. "You've gone native?"

"Well, I've worked with a few tribes. All my work with the Jesuits has been with native peoples, missionary work. These Onge are definitely the most odd. They lack culture, and yet they are very organized. They are fixated on survival. And very violent. They only let one white man interact with the tribe at a time. I'm the white man right now…"

"That doesn't sound like a defense."

"They're crazy." They both laughed, then stopped suddenly. He'd forgotten for a moment that they hadn't spoken in years.

They sipped their coffee deliberately.

This is surreal. I finally meet her again and I'm talking anthropology.

Now she was looking at him. He felt a fleeting rush through his stomach. "I thought you -" he started to say.

"What, go back to the States? Marry an ambassador's son and never work a day in my life?" There was a bitter edge to her voice that she could not fully disguise from him; she was forcing playfulness.

"I don't know," he said. "You never mentioned becoming a doctor and saving the Sri Lankan coast from plague and pestilence."

"Well, you always mentioned being a Jesuit. One of us had to change things up." His father, his brothers, they always mentioned him becoming a Jesuit. He only mentioned his fights with his brothers and father.

She was digging at him. He didn't really know why, but he didn't feel up for an argument. Why did she want an argument? *He* could barely muster what it took to look at her and keep a goofy grin off his face. She apparently wasn't quite so happy to see him. *What's her deal?*

"Would you like anything to eat?" she asked.

"No, thank you," he said. She sipped her coffee. He watched. "I looked for you a few times, when I was back in London," he said. She continued sipping. "I looked for you in every city I traveled. I always thought that somehow we'd catch up."

She set the cup down carefully. Still, it made too much noise, and the drink almost lapped over the side. She smiled deliberately. "Well, it is certainly wonderful to see you, Edward." She sounded like a ghost in a creepy movie.

He remembered the day he'd asked her to marry him. Her "No, I can't, Edward, not now, it's a bad time," had carried the same hollow, deliberate sound and pacing to it. It gave him chills.

The receptionist poked her head in. "I am most sorry to disturb, madam, but the inspector from St. Mary's is here. He needs a moment of your time."

Callista rose. "If you'll excuse me, Edward, it will only be a moment. This clinic is funded, actually, by your Jesuits, and every few months they do an inspection."

"I don't want to be seen," said Edward.

"He's a Jesuit. Maybe you know him," she answered and started to walk out.

He grabbed her wrist gently. Her skin felt electric. "I can't be seen, Callista. Is there a place I can hide?"

Her eyebrows arched, then furrowed. "There's a closet. Maybe he won't look there. He's doing an inspection, though. He usually looks at everything. Follow me. Sorry, I can't put him off. "

She led Edward into a supply closet down the hall. The location gave him reservations. If the inspector were to open the door, Edward had a lot of explaining to do. "Is there a back door?" Edward asked.

A baritone drone rolled down the hallway. "Please tell Dr. Knowles that if she isn't available, I could return at another time." Edward recognized the voice. He'd met the older man at St. Mary's when he'd first arrived at the Isle of Lisbaad.

Callista turned abruptly and walked toward the entrance. She pointed to the back of the building.

"Hello, Brother Fields," she said. "I'd be more than happy to help you today." She turned the corner.

Edward darted down the hall in the direction she'd pointed. He passed the exam rooms. He saw no exit. He was trapped.

He skidded back to the closet and closed its door behind him.

As his eyes adjusted to the darkness he could make out white shelves filled with medical supplies - syringes, gloves, basic first aid materials, nothing fancy. It didn't seem like she had what he needed.

Maybe she can help me find it, though.

He could hear Callista's conversation with Fields through the door. It was obvious by the inspector's tone that the man was only going through the motions.

"How many patients have you had since I was last here?" asked Fields.

"At least a couple hundred, most of them locals," she answered.

"There was a plague..."

"In the southern stretches of the island. I got a few of the cases. Just influenza."

"Their outcomes?"

"All favorable. After isolation, of course. When my clients pay nothing, there is little benefit to me in having plagues sweep through the city. Unlike Western practices..."

Fields chuckled and asked, "Any change in your facilities?"

"None. Well, the paint, of course. Would you like a tour?" she asked.

"Naturally." Edward heard their footsteps draw near. He tensed. He simply had nothing prepared for the eventuality of Fields discovering him in a closet.

I should have just confronted Fields. I could have come up with answers to all the questions...why didn't you check in at St. Mary's? Why have you left your post? On and on. Easy fibs.

Why are you hiding in a closet? Edward didn't have a fib for that one.

Their footsteps passed his closet, down the hallway to the little rooms.

"How are your supplies?" Fields asked. *He's going to want to see this closet.* Edward wasn't home free yet. He had such an urge to *get out* that he felt like he was crawling out of his skin.

"Too low. Always too low. Here's exam room number one, if you remember from before, freshly painted like everything else," she said.

Edward drew his breath. He really had no right answer here. It was a roll of the dice.

He wished he were in the trance, but instead he'd have to rely on blind luck. He opened the closet door and made a beeline to the reception area.

Diane started to say something, but he urgently motioned for silence. Edward slipped out of the front door and didn't dare look back.

27

Podo's job was driver. He hadn't gotten the hang of it, yet. He'd told the Messenger this, but Tomy wouldn't hear it. Tomy the Messenger simply said that success was foreseen, so Podo could drive well enough.

Podo had mastered the accelerator, though. And he could hit the brakes. It was the steering and doing it all at the same time that had him worried.

Cars were such odd things. It didn't make sense to him why one would want one car instead of horses or mules. The car only did what it was told. A horse or any sort of animal was much smarter. There was no training a car, only its rider. And animals were much cheaper.

He and his crew were parked on the side of the road in a beat-up white Toyota truck. They'd stolen it from the other side of town. The Messenger had told them to drive to the most eastern road on the outskirts of the city proper.

It was wartime, so no one spoke unless it had to do with the battle. It was quiet. It gave Todo time to practice spinning the steering wheel left and right. Cars passed occasionally. The odd pedestrian walked by, staring into the truck before turning his or her head when met with the Onge's unified stares.

Finally, one of Podo's crew tapped him on the shoulder. "He comes." Podo jerked his head back. A strangely flat red car had pulled around a bend and was now approaching them rapidly. Podo slammed the gearstick into drive. The truck lurched forward. He heard a couple of his crew fall backwards into the trailer bed as he pulled onto the road.

The red car was coming quickly. It would take a god horse to keep up with it. Podo turned his truck sideways and hit the brakes, effectively blocking the road.

The car jerked to a halt just meters away. A white man was in the car. He wasted no time yelling gibberish and shaking his fist.

Podo nodded to Lew'tec, the Onge seated next to him. Lew'tec had a battle stick in his hand. On one end it was blunt like a baton, but on the other end it was sharp, with metal jutting out from the edge of the wood.

Lew'tec stepped out of the truck and approached the man in the car. The white man stopped shaking his fist and instead held out a hand. He suddenly became peaceful, even obsequious. He politely sounded out the same gibberish over and over again. It sounded like some sort of a question.

Once Lew'tec reached the driver's side door, he knocked the white man over the head with the blunt end of the stick. The white man didn't go out, even though the collision had made quite a thudding sound.

The man scampered to the passenger side of his car and tried to climb over the door. He was clawing to get away. He hadn't panicked.

Lew'tec simply walked over to the other side of the car in a business-like manner and hit him over the head again. This time the white man dropped limp into the leather seats of his vehicle.

28

"Dr. Knowles, there is another matter that I would like to discuss with you."

"Here is the second examination room." Callista Knowles showed it to him. "And what is that?"

"What was *that?*" asked Fields suddenly. His plump red face jerked to the side. He stared wide-eyed down the hall.

Callista followed his gaze. The closet had swung open.

"Someone just came out of the closet. I just saw it in a flash as I looked up. Was someone in the closet?" He was puzzled more than alarmed.

Callista chuckled nervously, filling in the time while her mind caught up to the situation. *Edward. The closet.*

"Probably Diane getting a pen or something," she said quickly. "Or perhaps a ghost." She laughed. "I may be needing *your* services, Father." He laughed but still kept looking at the closet. "Still, unlike her to leave the closet open," she said. "There are very important medications inside, and it's vital that they don't get stolen or spoiled. Excuse me for a minute."

She walked up to the reception area, playing the part of indignant doctor. In a suitable tone, using a dialect she knew Fields would be unable to decipher, she asked, "Did my patient leave?"

"Yes, just a minute ago," answered Duiyon. "He told me to stay quiet. I'm sorry if you didn't want him to go."

"It's fine he went. He might come back, though. Expect him. But speak to no one about him. He's a secret."

Duiyon nodded. There had been other visitors to the clinic who desired discretion on the part of the staff. This was nothing new.

Edward. Edward. Edward. She wanted to end this inspection as soon as possible. She needed time to digest this sudden shift in her life. At least he was gone for a moment. That was some respite.

Eventually he would be back, though, for whatever he had wanted to begin with. *At least, I hope.*

There was another part of her that hoped he went elsewhere. *Please.* Maybe he could go to the same place she'd buried all those memories from a decade ago.

When Callista returned, Fields was already poking around in the closet. "Dr. Knowles, you barely have anything in here that you need."

"I've been making do. I haven't been able to stock disposables since the last time St. Mary's gave us a grant." There were more basics in the basement, but who was counting? There was no other clinic on the island and no better use for the funds.

"Hmmm…" mumbled the old priest. He then turned to her suddenly. "Oh yes, the other thing I need to discuss with you. It's not in your province, actually, but maybe you've heard something from one of your patients."

"Yes?" she asked, trying to keep the nerves out of her voice as best she could.

"Do you know anything about the Onge village that lies some miles south of here?"

What sort of trouble has Edward gotten himself into? "I don't usually treat Onge. They don't trust Westerners."

"Treat any traders that deal with them?"

"A couple years ago I treated someone like that. From what I understand, they don't have much to trade - live off the land, basically."

"Basically," echoed Fields, walking back toward the reception area. "Well, there have been some alarming rumors from a couple of the natives that have dealings with them."

"What sort of rumors?" she asked.

"That they have a living god in their midst, a sort of Onge messiah that is leading them to liberation. There is a new structure in their camp, and all of their motions have changed. It is all quite peculiar," he said.

"Are these sources reliable?" she asked.

"Hardly. There are only two, they give conflicting stories, and they were both taken through a splotchy translator. But those fundamentals I just stated were in common."

"Tribal superstition. Maybe a new war chief amongst them. I hear it is commonplace for them to duel and kill each other off."

"Yes," acknowledged Fields. They had stopped walking. His eyes were on the clean floor of the clinic, but his mind was obviously elsewhere. "Dr. Knowles," he finally said. "I tell you this in strictest confidence, but it may help you to help me in case you run across any information that could be of assistance. One of our very own priests is on mission in that Onge camp. He's the only Westerner there. I haven't heard from him in over a month, which is not uncommon, but not common either. I fear for his safety."

"Of course, you'll be the first person to know if I hear anything," said Callista. *In other words, I guess I won't tell anyone*

Odd looking at Edward as a priest now, she thought as she saw Fields out. It was bizarre having Edward in the same category as Fields. *Edward certainly didn't act priestly when he was dating me back in our teenage years. And he certainly didn't act priestly hiding in my closet…*

After the priest left, she couldn't help but check the streets for Edward. She saw no signs of him. *He'll be back.* She hoped so, and she didn't.

What has Edward gotten himself into?

She didn't know. She was not one prone to worry. She knew she didn't have any way to determine an answer, so that was that. She wasn't going to think about it again until she had more data.

She would probably need to do a lot of thinking in the coming months; no use wasting all that brainpower.

She walked back to the exam room where she'd first seen Edward after a decade, only half an hour ago. She could almost see him again, sitting in that chair. It had been so long since she'd seen him. She hadn't expected to react like that.

She'd done everything she could think of to leave the door open for something like this. In one way it was a triumph for her. It was a painful triumph.

The seven years had been kind to him. He was more handsome now than before. He'd shed his boyish features for a more chiseled look.

Stop thinking. Think about it later. Stop thinking. There's nothing to think about now. So think of nothing.

Edward. Edward.

She closed the door so Duiyon couldn't hear her cry. She could blot out everything from her mind but his name. The name was all it took to make her bonkers.

29

Sala grew weary. She looked up from her work to her mother, who scowled and pushed Sala's hands back to the plants. There were hundreds of them.

Funny plants, the girl thought. They were thin, like brush, with hard trunks like pine. The trunks were covered in sap. She couldn't touch the sap. It was poisonous. One of the workers had gotten ill from touching the sap and still wasn't able to work. She lay under a tree vomiting all day and night. Sala wanted to sit under a tree all day and night, but didn't want to vomit. She just wanted to rest.

First, they'd transplanted all the plants to the secret garden. Now, they had to put them in special pots of clay. She'd never seen such pots before. They'd come from machines with wheels that sounded like monsters. They said the machines came from the city. She didn't understand any of it.

Well, she did understand something. She understood that her hands hurt from digging. The work was slow and tedious. Ten women were working, and they would be working late into the night, every night for many moons.

Once they put the plants into the pots, they took them to another secret garden. Every day they would move them, until the last day, when they carried them to their final destination, by the sea.

"Mother, why must we work into the night?" asked the young Onge girl.

"Because we are faithful," answered her mother.

"But why must we not see the village for so long? Why must we stay from the village?"

"These are sacred plants, Sala, these that we care for and nurture. We are part of Manassa's vision. We are part of something greater than ourselves." The mother glanced down at her daughter. Sala's eyes had glossed over. She hadn't heard a word of it. "It is as your father wishes," said mother.

Sala grabbed her mother's hands. "Even though I'm tired," said Sala, "I am happy to be with you." She loved her mother's hands. Her father's hands were often cruel. She did not miss him or his beatings. "It would be fine for us to always tend the secret garden," she said.

"And so we may. Your father will send word when it's time to come back. Now work, child. You must set a good example for the other children. We must get these plants into the pots. And don't touch the sap!"

Sala got back to work. She didn't feel tired anymore.

30

Edward took the opportunity to tend to the other errands he had in town - the I.V. apparatus, the electrodes. All was finished in an hour. If his tablet idea worked, he didn't need any of it, but he held true to the first recorded maxim of the nirvana effect: *never lie to a seer.*

To which he might add as a corollary: *never tell all the truth to a seer.*

If he said he was getting the materiel for these other ideas to reduce the after-pain, he had better make sure he did so. Mahanta could all too quickly find him out.

As Edward left a pawn shop in the center of town, he caught a motion out of place in his periphery.

He would never have noticed such a thing before, but not only did it catch his attention, but he had such presence of mind that he correctly refused to react to it.

He didn't turn his head, instead walking haphazardly in the opposite direction. Someone had reacted strongly to his coming out of the shop, ducking from sight.

Edward gripped his backpack, casually readjusting it and checking for the reassuring weight of the first aid kit within it. He was relieved to feel its hard metal edges sticking through the canvas.

The noon sun left no shadows on the dirt streets, and Edward walked a couple blocks down the road. He had no way to see who was following him without being obvious. There were very few reflective surfaces in Lisbaad.

Edward walked into a fabric store with a large window. He liked it because the glass was dirty, and with the noonday glare he couldn't see into the store.

The shopkeeper stood from his stool. He looked surprised to have a customer. "Just browsing," said Edward hurriedly in Tamil, then stepped down into the small display area. He went directly to the window; he could see out well enough through the grime. A few islanders walked the streets with totes on their shoulders with the day's produce.

"Is there a particular fabric you are looking for, sir?" asked the shopkeeper, who had joined him in the display area.

"Red," said Edward distractedly. *No men. Nothing that fit what he'd seen out the corner of his eye.*

"We have many excellent red products here, sir," said the shopkeeper. *Tamil obviously was not this man's native dialect. Half the fabric here is red.* "Is there any particular design you wanted?"

Edward craned his neck to try to identify his tracker. *Maybe there isn't one. Maybe I'm just getting paranoid — maybe a side effect of the drug.*

"No, thank you, just looking out your window," said Edward. Far down the road, a little boy begged at the curbside. He had no luck; the woman passing him was probably just as destitute as he was. The boy followed the woman for a little while with hand extended, then went back to his spot.

My imagination. I'm just jittery after the clinic.

The shopkeeper walked back to his counter and seated himself loudly. Edward felt the Indian's eyes burning holes in the back of his head.

Edward turned around. "Thank you, sir," he said, most respectfully. "I will be sure to return here if I need something red."

"You are welcome," said the scowling shopkeeper.

"Your window is excellent."

Edward walked out. He gave the street another long glance in each direction. An old woman walked toward him. Edward craned his neck to see the beggar boy behind her, but the young man seemed to have gone elsewhere to try his luck.

The missionary carefully made his way back to Callista's clinic. He turned a fifteen minute walk into several hours as he wound his trail through long alleys and shadowy corners trying to scare up a tail he wasn't even sure existed.

It would kill him if Callista came to any harm because he wasn't careful.

31

"Hello, Diane. I have returned," Edward told the receptionist. She was watering a plant in the waiting area.

"My name is actually Duiyon," she replied, setting down the watering pitcher.

"Well, hello Duiyon." He pronounced it correctly, much to her delight. "Is the doctor in?"

Duiyon covered her mouth, troubled. "Oh, she just left."

"When?"

"Less than a minute ago. I haven't even had time to lock up."

"Is there a back door she leaves out of?" he asked hurriedly.

"In the second exam room." *Of course. That's where Callista was pointing.* "If you hurry you might catch her."

Edward started to leave but Duiyon kept talking. "She seemed to be wondering why it took you so long to come back. She was troubled."

We have a lot of catching up to do. "Thank you," he said as he rushed past her to the back door. She grabbed his wrist and jerked him back.

"Priest," she said, shoving her face in front of his. She was surprisingly strong. "...or whatever you are...do not break her heart. She's already had her heart broken. There is nothing left to break." Edward's mouth opened but there was nothing to say.

"Hurry!" she said. She pushed him onward.

32

Nockwe stormed into Manassa's temple. The two guards posted at the door tensed at their weapons. They would never raise a finger against their chieftain, and yet in that instant he'd seemed more an enemy than an ally. Nockwe's eyes gaped wide, his every muscle taut. He was stifling a roar that caught in his throat and manifested as a persisting grumble.

"Manassa!" he shouted. Manassa was not in the main temple area. Nockwe ran to his quarters behind the throne. "Manassa!"

Where is he? "Here, Nockwe." Nockwe found him, sitting at the edge of his bed in his quarters. He actually had a real mattress, elevated from the floor.

"You had him killed!" shouted Nockwe. He was furious.

Quietly, Manassa said, "Remember the protocol, Nockwe."

"To hell with the protocol!" The guards were sure to hear him.

Manassa stood up and walked past him to the entrance of his quarters. He waved someone off - presumably a guard who was coming to check on the commotion.

Manassa pulled aside a rug to reveal the trap door he'd installed. It was an underground tunnel into the woods. He opened the trap and beckoned Nockwe to follow him.

They hunched to make it through the short tunnel. It took them to the jungle. Manassa walked briskly in silence, but Nockwe had no trouble keeping up.

"You have started a bloodbath, Manassa. Have you no respect for the tribe?"

Manassa was quiet. "I don't know what you mean."

"Your priests, your inner circle, they're killing dissenters."

"They're your inner circle, Nockwe," said Manassa.

"They do not act on my orders," said Nockwe.

"Nor mine." Though Nockwe spoke modern Onge, Manassa kept to the more ancient dialect. It made the whole conversation feel surreal to the chieftain. The adrenaline was already starting to flush out of his body, to be replaced by an empty dread.

Anger had caused him to play the fool. His reaction could have far-reaching repercussions. Moreover, he knew now he might never learn the truth.

"It cannot be coincidence that your three greatest critics are now dead by challenge."

The flow of the walking was draining Nockwe's outrage. Manassa did not stop. He climbed down into a ravine and changed directions. Nockwe followed. "Coincidence?" said Manassa. "I don't believe in coincidence. It was obviously planned."

"Inge was wise and cautious. Wisdom and caution make him no enemy of ours. He did nothing to malign you or Glis, and yet Glis killed him."

"Glis?" asked Manassa dispassionately.

"You didn't know?"

"I did foresee Inge's death, but not this way. All your sentiments aside, Inge was a stumbling block to our vision. But I didn't think he'd be killed by Onge."

Nockwe decided not to take up that point. It was moot. "He was challenged for sleeping with Glis's wife," said Nockwe.

"Did he?" asked Manassa.

"Glis and two others caught him in the act," said Nockwe.

Manassa finally stopped and turned. His voice was hollow, empty. "Then why do you come to me in this manner, my chieftain?"

"Glis's wife seduced him," said Nockwe.

"How do you know?"

"It is a fact. Inge has three times the years of Glis's woman. She is only sixteen. It is fact."

Manassa nodded. "You see conspiracy. I see it, too."

"The blood of the tribe must be preserved, as must its wisdom be. Glis committed murder, Manassa." *At your request.*

"Kill Glis." Again, Manassa was emotionless. He spoke in the traditional tongue. "I trust your judgment, my chieftain. His zealotry may be commendable, but his methods cannot be permitted. We are the greatest nation on Earth, Nockwe, but we are the smallest of nations. Our blood must be preserved. No murder shall be permitted."

"No more murder is necessary. The inner circle has slain your opposition," said Nockwe. He searched Manassa's eyes for insight. They gave no clue, no betrayal. The foot of space between the chieftain and the god felt like a great void.

Manassa spoke quieter still. "If you do not control the inner circle, then soon the inner circle shall be our enemy. Look not to me to displace the fault, Nockwe, for the murder of Glis and the deaths of the others. Look into the truth-water back to your own reflection. The inner circle is your dog, whether or not you desire it so. We agreed it was so. I trust you, Nockwe, but I fear that if you in turn trust too much, you will lose your faith in me and even in yourself. Don't trust the inner circle. Don't trust my priests. Get them into line, else they will be the dog that will eat us all up."

Nockwe was silent. He didn't know what to do. His mind was telling him to drop it, but his hunter's instinct still told him something was wrong.

"Nockwe," sighed Manassa. "I understand your frustration. I have foreseen it, in fact, for if I were you I would have done the same thing. But the fact of the matter is that even if I had ordered these peoples' deaths, you could have stopped it. You must own and control our priests. And we must trust one another. Do you see that with you over my priests, I leave myself defenseless to you?"

The sun was setting behind Manassa. The early calls of the beasts of the night disrupted the silence between the two men. *This inner circle, these priests, they are the jungle beasts.* Nockwe foresaw that one day he might become their target. He did not fear it. He would do what he must for the tribe.

"You have done me no wrong with your anger, Nockwe. You have done me no wrong. You are the sort who only trusts another man if you hold a knife to his neck. It is why you are so valuable to our people. I will permit you to hold it as close to my neck as you like. I know you will only threaten me if I threaten the tribe."

Manassa's voice remained quiet and firm. He edged even closer to Nockwe.

"Do not ever put the tribe at risk like this, again, Nockwe. I love the Onge as much as you do. My vision is the future of our race. Do not endanger it with stupidity. You may blame whoever you wish, but deep down you know the truth." Manassa walked past him.

Nockwe did not turn.

"Nockwe," said Manassa. "Do not waste any time in getting your dogs in line. Our world turns ever more quickly. I fear that we will need to move much sooner than planned."

Manassa left.

Nockwe knelt and mourned.

Inge had been Nockwe's father's best friend. He was as an uncle to Nockwe. The chieftain could see the corpse of Inge on the backs of his eyelids. The body had eight bleeding holes. Glis had stabbed him eight times. Inge's face was frozen in an awful contortion of pain. His body had reeked of feces and urine; his eyes stared out into the sky. Nockwe knew Inge's eyes were looking for his chieftain, for help and for justice. But Nockwe had been outside of the village on errand for Manassa when the challenge had occurred. Inge was dead before Nockwe ever set foot back into the village.

I must be smarter, and stronger, in many more ways than before. Else I may lose everything. He thought of his wife, children, and village. He thought of them all with bloody holes in their bodies.

He knew Manassa was right. He shouldn't have to trust Manassa. He should know. In such a situation as his, it was weak to trust anyone. It was better simply to know and control everything.

I will do this, starting with the inner circle. Starting with Glis.

Manassa may be a snake, but he is an enlightened snake…Onge through and through… fitting a god as any…

33

Edward rushed through the back door in exam room two. He tripped down the back steps to the dirt service road behind the clinic.

A car was pulling away, kicking up dust. Callista. Edward ran after her, yelling her name. Edward had an awful feeling that she wouldn't hear him.

The car stopped. The passenger door kicked out. He caught up and jumped in. His heart was racing faster than when Nockwe threatened him with his spear.

Callista was sitting in the driver seat. She smiled unnervingly. He looked away, reminded of the deliberate "It's good to see you," that she'd given him earlier. In his college days, that mannerism had meant the perfect storm was brewing.

She drove out of town. He stopped studying the road and instead turned his gaze to her. His eyes caught the curve of her lips. It was a real smile. She was genuinely happy. He could tell even though they hadn't spoken, yet.

He noticed he was smiling, too. He had a distinct falling sensation, the nervous jitters of temptation. Again he turned his eyes away. *We are on different courses, now. This is a nice twist, seeing her again, but that's all it is.*

Edward's future was too short in too many directions, now. No path he foresaw, however brief, included someone else. *Too risky for me and too risky for her.*

It didn't take long to get to the outskirts of Lisbaad. Once they reached the limits of the town, it was as though someone had turned off the car's mute switch.

"I'm going to help you, Edward, if I can," she said. Her voice sounded chipper, much younger than it had been just hours before. "And you're going to help me."

He was afraid of where the conversation was leading, so he pre-empted her. "Thank you, Callista. Maybe you can help me. And I'd be more than happy to help you if I can." He didn't want to know what that was, so he didn't give her time to say it. He just went right on. "I need help distilling an active ingredient and making it into a tablet."

"A tablet?" she asked.

"Right. I need some excipients, something to tabletize an active ingredient, to take under the tongue."

"A medicine?" she asked, curiously.

"Of sorts," he replied.

He knew her mind. There were many questions she would want answered. She'd keep asking questions until it made sense to her. And the prime question had nothing to do with the "medicine", but rather why he had avoided a member of his own priesthood. He hadn't thought up an answer for that one yet.

The car jostled over a few bumps in the road. Callista didn't ask any more questions. Instead, she said, "Okay. I can help with that." The simple statement surprised him.

That was easy. "Thank you." Edward had expected to have difficulty finding the necessary equipment. He'd feared that even after overcoming the hurdle, he wouldn't have the technical skill to make it happen.

He was sure that if anyone could tabletize the substance, though, it would be Callista, and with the greatest of professional ease. If anything, she was competent. If she said she could do something, she could.

"You know, Edward, I was very distraught when I saw you today," she said, not missing a beat. "I didn't expect that. Well, I didn't expect to ever see you, even though maybe I hoped I would. I don't know whether what you said about wanting to see me, looking for me, and all that was true." It was. "I don't know about that. But I think that maybe what it is…well…I'm just going to tell you everything. And you can take it or leave it."

"All right," Edward said. He had no idea where she was going with this.

"Edward Styles, when I first met you, I paid you no mind. I didn't. I'll admit that. I'll tell you why: I'd never heard of you. My friends, my parents had never talked about you. I'd never seen you at one of the parties that my father was always dragging me to. It was as though I couldn't see you. You were invisible, one of *those* handsome boys. Out of the question. I would marry someone with family."

Edward couldn't help but comment. "You sound very British right now."

Her smile broadened. He'd almost forgotten what it was like to create that kind of reaction in her. "Well, 'roight' you 'ah', then," she said, feigning a horrendous English accent. "And I know you know this. We've talked about it countless times, when we were younger. But I think it's important to mention again so that you can understand…with it all in perspective."

She drove for a little while longer. He had nothing to say. He couldn't say anything. It wasn't any sort of conversation he felt he could encourage. It wasn't that he was a priest; he wasn't a priest anymore, not in his mind. It was that to make her a part of his life would mean to pull her aboard the runaway train.

And yet he couldn't make himself stop her, either. The idea of getting some answers to all those questions he'd walked away from nearly a decade ago was irresistible.

"You told me you loved me from the first moment you saw me. You meant that?" she asked.

He was quiet, looking out at the road ahead. He hesitated too long.

"I know you're a priest, now, Edward, believe me, I know it. But I knew you before you were a priest…" Her voice threatened to lose the jocularity she had so enjoyed just moments earlier.

He laughed and turned to face her. She was still looking out at the rode as she drove. The sun was starting to set. They were making their way to a fenced residential area. "Of course I meant that. You'd always ask that and I'd always answer I meant it."

"Well, it wasn't that way for me. I might have told you it was the same for me, but it wasn't. It wasn't the same. And I think because of that it was far worse."

"What do you mean?" he asked.

"When I first met you, I didn't see you. But you made me see you. Your soul made me finally see you. It was nothing you tried to do. You just...you just shone."

Edward could not voice a single one of the replies that whizzed through his mind. He couldn't reminisce with her. He couldn't tell her, *you shone, too. You were the sun to me. You had me in orbit. You made me happy.*

She glanced his way before continuing her monologue to the windshield.

"It was my own choice, to be with you. It was probably the first choice I made of my own - my choice. Not what my parents wanted, not even colored by what they wanted. I knew from my own observation, from a total certainty deep within me, that you were my one - and that you would achieve great things - that together, we could be happy."

She'd never been so frank with him. In fact, she'd never been the one to tell him such things. He'd known them, he'd thought them, he'd felt them, but she'd never said them. Perhaps it had never occurred to her it needed to be said. But as she finally said it he felt an unexpected relief - that big question mark in his life was finally getting erased. Had it been real?

The relief disappeared as the next realization hit him like a truck. A painful exclamation point had taken the place of the question mark.

It had been real!

Because of that one question mark, he had buried his dreams. He had joined the Jesuits on that question mark. He had given up science on that question mark.

That question mark was disintegrating as he rode in the car next to the woman he had once loved to the exclusion of all else. A decade ago, his dream had consumed him. He'd studied her much more than school, he'd worked hard so that he might buy her things. His friends were only a way to pass the time when he didn't have her company.

It had been an immature love. In their senior year it had blossomed...He had to stop thinking about it. He was glad she started talking again.

"I know I never told you that. I'm sorry I didn't, I really am," she said. "I never thought you had a doubt. Looking back on it, I see you could. Looking back on it, I see a lot. As part of my schooling, we studied psychology…I had to counsel some people during my residency…seeing their troubles objectively - I saw my own. I didn't…"

"It's all right. It's fine." *You were wonderful.* He couldn't say that. Without saying it he came off conceited, but he restrained himself from saying it.

"It's not fine," she insisted. "I've looked back on it a lot. Maybe that's why…well…anyway, I didn't tell you. It was just a stupid thing. You were my one decision. I saw it all the way through. But I was trapped, Edward. I realized this now. I was trapped - so trapped that I didn't even see I had six cage walls all around me."

Edward felt raw, naked, his body locked in the seat. His mind rushed, but it all flowed to nothing. He was forgetting to breathe. He'd lost all context to their conversation. He felt ripped into another world.

For a moment, he'd never taken the substance. He'd never been a missionary. He'd never left her side. He was there, at his knee, opening up his ring box in the empty park in his stupid tux, looking for a "yes" in her eyes.

"You see, you were my one decision, Edward," she said. "But there were so many others. You were one drop of dew caught in a web. What school I went to, what career I took on - and then discarded for married life - where I traveled, who I knew, all these had been determined for me. They were determined for me in such a way and so thoroughly that I thought I'd determined them myself. That day…" Her voice trailed off. She looked over at him. Two tears ran out of his eyes, one creeping down each cheek. He turned his eyes down to the floorboard. It was too much to take in. The relief left him too open to the pain, and it was all he could do to still track with her voice.

She stopped the car at her house. He didn't see it - his line of vision stopped at the dashboard. Not that he even saw the dashboard.

She continued. "That day, I knew that day would come." He heard her voice beginning to crack. She still had her cheerful intonation, but under that rode an edge that made every syllable waver. "That day came, and you asked me, and I thought the word, 'yes'. And with that one word, the whole web of my life shook, it crumbled, it disintegrated. And I was left holding one single drop of dew. And I panicked. And I dropped it." She sobbed. He heard her sobbing. Nothing else was real. He was back at Oxford sitting in his car with her. He groped for her hand and gripped it tightly. He was sobbing, heaving for breath. He couldn't look at her. He sensed she was crying, too, that she was looking at him, but he couldn't think about it. There was too much to think about. Her hand dug into his.

They both finally stopped crying. He didn't let go of her hand. The sky reddened into darkness. It was much later when she said, "If I had known that dropping you once was dropping you forever, I'd have never let go. I'd have never said no. I was afraid, but that was worse. Far worse. That was torture."

She didn't cry anymore. She just told him that and rubbed his hand. She sounded exhausted.

Each syllable of what she said echoed a hundred times inside Edward's skull. He played them over and over in his mind. Over and over again he replayed the whole car ride.

In half an hour, she had vaporized his life's big question mark. The nirvana effect had started it and she thoroughly finished the job.

He reflected ironically that every constant in his life had become a variable now that his variable, his question mark, had become a constant.

He answered her silently with his thoughts - words he would not utter. They were words that would bind her path to his. It was his own monologue, one he could not voice to the windshield.

Callista, Callista. When I decided to become a priest, I felt free. After having gone through the darkest hour of a storm at sea, it was like I had seen the first glimmer of light on the horizon. I closed that chapter of my life, shut out the chapter of you. Every meditation, every exercise I went through in my training as a priest, I oriented to forgetting you and my dreams, to expunging every emotion I carried for you, to disciplining my mind from wandering to you. The sharp discipline of the Jesuit order was far easier than dwelling on you, than being stuck on maybe.

His mind wandered. *If only you hadn't rebuked me so sharply, so quickly. I'd have still held hope…*

But it was a false freedom. It was freedom in a prison cell. It was freedom from the outside world, and freedom from my dreams.

Now he had a choking, claustrophobic feeling, as though the walls of the car might threaten to close in and smother him. He'd never felt more trapped. She turned to look at him, wiping her own eyes as she did so. She reached to wipe his. He let her.

"I'm sorry," she said with her hand still on his cheek, making sure he was looking directly into her eyes.

"I'm sorry, too," said Edward. Everything he'd thought, he poured into those words. He wanted to say all of it.

It's too dangerous. There are no passenger cars on this runaway train.

She can't come with me.

Slowly, the skills that had let him survive this long without her came back to him. He closed his mind and took control of his breathing. It was far easier now than it would have been even a month ago. He pulled himself together. He looked at her. She looked brighter. She was watching him, as though waiting for him to say something.

"Thank you for telling me that," said Edward. "There is a lot I need to say, too. I just, well..." *I just can't say any of it. Except...* "Thank you, Callista, for giving me the happiest years of my life."

She smiled. "Thank you." She turned her head away, breathed deeply, and then turned to face him. "Thank you for listening. I needed to get it all out. I feel a lot better. All right," she said. She didn't sound a lot better. "So, a tablet, you say?"

"Yes, right. I need to make a tablet." *Or maybe just run away with you to Italy.*

"What is it all for?" she asked.

"Nothing I can really tell you about. I would love to, actually. I can't tell you how much I'd love to tell you about it. It's just..."

"Secret?" she asked.

"It's nothing illegal or a vice or anything. It's just something that needs to stay utterly confidential. As in, only I know of it."

179

She peered at him strangely. He held some semblance of a poker face. She shrugged. "Well, all right. Let's make a pill." She led him into her house.

34

The twelve chosen priests of the inner circle stood around the fire Nock-we had built for their meeting. He had chosen the clearing where Manassa had given his speech to the tribe, where the very trees had reverberated with the name of the Onge living god.

It was as fitting a place as any. It was a place of victory for the dozen. He hoped they were taking the time to revel in it. He needed them on their heels.

Nockwe watched from the edge of the clearing, unseen. He respected many of these "priests". They were among the strongest and the wisest of the tribe. Tonight, eleven of the twelve would learn to respect him. One would receive a deeper revelation.

The chieftain walked briskly to the fire. There were several nervous glances in his direction. He seemed to have appeared out of nowhere, much as their god did.

Nockwe acknowledged them with a nod. The priests began their opening ritual. They had met like this many nights since Manassa had risen to power. Manassa had stopped attending them. Still, the chant to their god was protocol.

The twelve formed a close ring around the fire. One by one they chanted.

"We are the chosen." The phrase echoed around the circle, each priest giving it voice in turn.

"Our god is the chosen." Around it went again.

"We are the vision."

"We stand for divine truth."

"LONG LIVE Manassa!" they shouted in unison.

Nockwe walked inside the ring of men, circling the fire in the opposite direction of their spiraling chant. He examined the face of every priest. He cast his shadow on every member of Manassa's inner circle. Many watched him with the deference they'd always carried for him. A couple cast the same jealous glances they'd always cast. Three amongst them were different, however. These watched him as adversaries, as equals. One was Glis. The others were Jurdan and Raol.

Nockwe weighed his options. Jurdan and Raol were on the opposite side of the fire as Glis. It would be dangerous to make assumptions. Of Glis he was certain.

"By all our traditions, Manassa is our living god," said Nockwe in their traditional tongue. All attending spoke the dialect or at least understood it. "By all our traditions, I am your chieftain." He twisted his head around to gauge their reactions. The priests were all around him. The fire gave no cover. The coolness of his knife hilt against his skin was reassuring. "And by the holy word of our living god, I am your head priest. Your purpose, as a priest of this order, of this inner circle of followers, is to further the tribe by furthering the vision of Manassa. For those who do this, there is abundant hope and eternal life. For those who do not, there is death and fire. And none in this ring are exempt. Those of this circle shall be first to receive both reward and punishment."

Nockwe continued his circling. He neared Glis. He felt butterflies in his stomach, and he had to force himself to continue speaking. Something was wrong. He never got butterflies. It was not the warrior's way.

He was not sure of what came next; he did not know if his traitors outnumbered those loyal to him. He would soon see. "No vision of Manassa includes the destruction of the tribe or its laws," said Nockwe. "The laws of the tribe are supreme."

He stopped circling and looked directly at Glis. "One of our laws is that no enemy shall be given quarter." Glis tensed. Nockwe heard some rustling noise from Jurdan's direction. It was inconsequential at this point. No matter what Jurdan did, Nockwe was too close to Glis. Loudly, Nockwe cried,

"Glis, I wish to commend you, for slaying one of our movement's enemies!"

Glis relaxed. Then his face took on a gray, slackened recognition. It was too late for him to even react.

A flash of metal by the firelight. A gurgling shriek. Glis dropped, clutching his throat.

"Glis! Nockwe!" The priests shouted to one another. No one moved toward Nockwe, though.

Nockwe shouted, "It is a higher law not to murder Onge!" He gained their silence with his volume. He met their every eye. "And it is an even higher law not to betray our god! This priest acted without authorization and without direction. A vigilante is more dangerous than a traitor. There were other killings, perhaps prompted by Glis, perhaps by others. They will not any longer be tolerated. You may meet with me in secret at any time and gain my advice. You will not act on your own!"

The priests around the circle looked frightened, every one of them. They were looking at Glis's dead body and taking in Nockwe's words. None of them could put up a fight against a healthy Nockwe. The limp form of Glis bleeding at his feet reinforced that.

"Manassa is god. I am his high priest. His revelations come to you only through me. Is that clear?" Nockwe asked the silent members of the Circle. They nodded.

"Lee'tep, Jurdan, Raol, and you two - you are to go now to Lisbaad with your warriors and fortify Tomy's position immediately - tonight. The last phase of our planning is about to come to fruition. Manassa foresees events taking a quicker pace than even he predicted." Nockwe had planned on Jurdan and Raol staying at the village, but that was no longer tenable. Lee'tep, Nockwe's cousin, would keep an eye on them. "The rest of you are to stay here and report to me at the throne of Manassa in the morning." Nockwe looked at Glis's body, a bloody hole in his neck. It saddened Nockwe to see Onge blood spilt. "Give this man a proper burial. He was a servant to the tribe, and a great man. Let it be known he was investigated by the chieftain and found guilty of murder. Good night."

Nockwe walked away. He did not check his back. He did not even wait for them to acknowledge him. He was certain of their compliance.

He was uncertain of something else. He still had the butterflies. *And something with Glis's gray face…Something wrong…*

35

With Callista's assistance, it was only a matter of a few hours for Edward to isolate the active ingredient in the substance. The agent was an extremely soluble compound bound up with a liquid that was at least half the culprit for the after-pain. This unnecessary liquid was similar in structure to caffeine, but obviously had a lot more kick.

Edward picked over his memory for the sensation of the "upper". It was there, definitely, but had nothing to do with the positive effects of the substance. It just taxed the nerves heavily. Just the fact of purifying the substance would reduce the after-effects.

The simpler matter of tabletizing the drug took far less time.

Edward and Callista skillfully limited their conversation to the task at hand. Edward, for one, was glad to be on a much more manageable subject.

"What do you want to call it?" she asked.

"Hmm?"

"Well, we can call it T or Z. I don't have 2 flat ends of the pill presser, just one. And two ends with letters."

"Why T and Z?"

"It was supposed to come with every letter, but the person I got it from - let's just say they don't take returns."

"Well, if I've got to have a letter on it, give it a T," said Edward. *For trance. Trance pill.*

She pressed the first pill.

"You have to press every single one individually?" asked Edward.

"I'm not Pfizer. This is what you call home cookin'. Here you go," she said as she dropped the pill into his hand.

I hope this works.

The pill felt heavy. He knew it weighed only a few milligrams but its significance seemed to add to its mass. It was his next step ahead of Mahanta, ahead of being predicted. It might very well be his only lifeline. It was certainly his only assurance of guiding his own destiny. If it worked, it was a game changer; he would get to be the maker of the game.

Right now, he didn't even really know what game Mahanta had him playing.

This pill had better work.

"What's wrong?" asked Callista.

"What do you mean?" asked Edward, looking up his hand. Callista had pressed a pile of "t- pills". She was finishing up with the last powder in the bowl.

"Forty-five pills," she said, pressing the last one. "What do I mean?" She laughed. "You've been standing there staring at that pill forever."

He rubbed his face.

"You know, you've been rubbing your face a lot today," she said.

"I'm tired." He set the tablet down and stretched his arms and legs. He'd been standing for hours.

"Me, too," she said. "I'll go get you a medicine bottle for the pills. You know, I don't understand why you can't tell me about this. I'm a doctor, you know."

When she left the kitchen, he popped the t-pill into his mouth.

He had to find out if it worked.

Edward looked out the window while he waited for her to return. It was dark, now. Lisbaad nights were darker than London nights. Of course, Onge nights were darker still. His tired mind drifted momentarily to the panther chase, to the air so dark that he couldn't see his hands in front of his face.

The window gave him a view of her back "yard". It was more a jungle clearing than anything else, with a few potted plants here and there. Edward idly flipped the light switch off to let his eyes adjust to the scene. It was beautiful, really, with the moon and the stars the only light in the sky. Everything in her yard seemed to glow.

It seemed like that moment where she poured her heart out to him had been eons ago. It seemed a detached moment on the track of an alternate reality. *I'll have to tell her something before I go.*

He saw motion in the yard, and for a second he felt the adrenaline start pumping. His spine snapped straight, his eyes widened, and he leaned against the glass.

It was only a cat. He relaxed, resisting the urge to chuckle at himself. *Well, it pays to be alert.*

A moment later, his body tensed again. A hand gripped his neck.

Callista. He recognized her before he jumped. She was massaging him. Still, knowing it was only her didn't relieve his tension. He continued to look straight ahead, out the window, becoming slowly intoxicated by the caress of her soft fingers on his neck.

Edward experienced the slow sensation of the room shrinking (or was he getting closer to it?) then expanding (was it going away?). The back yard lightened. It looked like it was a blue noon, with the moon as bright as the sun. He felt like he didn't have a body at all.

He felt momentarily queasy, and then it all passed. All was back to normal with his perceptions, but only because he willed it so.

The trance. It's working…much more gradual than the injection. It's definitely working.

Her hands worked a rhythm into his neck that resonated through his whole body and irresistibly into his mind.

In the park. On my knee. I pop the question. He looked at her face in that freeze-frame. Her eyes do say "yes". And a lot more. She told the truth.

He played through it again and again, a hundred times in less than a second. A dim realization that the trance was on in full was overshadowed by the clarity of the hundreds of recalls that defined his relationship with the woman whose skin was touching his.

He'd never meditated on Callista in trance. He hadn't let himself. Now he could not help himself. The lid was off Pandora's box.

Four years of college. 1,461 days. Only 97 of them spent without her.

He knew because he saw them all, re-experienced them all, so quickly it was almost instantaneous.

He drove her from the campus up to the Uni Parks, walked her to their sequoia. *The grass, the blanket sometimes, the pressure of her head resting on my stomach. She tells me not to laugh so much. I laugh more.*

The times she saw the look on his face that told her he'd just talked to his family. *She just holds me.* She delighted in the person that was actually Edward Styles - a person who happened to be totally unacceptable to Edward Styles. She understood him because she'd gone through the same.

He sighed. *All those conversations. The conversations and conversations.*

He had a million snapshots of her beautiful face and body. He'd spent much of his college life staring at her. He stared at her now, in trance, through his mind's eye.

I'm indulging. He willed himself to stop. He only needed to learn one thing from this meditation. He needed to know only one thing and then he'd shut the book one way or the other.

Edward took a moment to visualize all of the factors involved. Himself. Her. Mahanta. Nockwe. The tribe. The Jesuits. The drug.

All these things created a future. In one equation, he took her with him. In another equation, he left her behind.

Probabilities did not pop up at the end of the equation. Rather, he saw a vision.

The first one, with her in his arms, was dim to the point blackness. *It's not real.*

The second, the same bright future, the future he didn't even dare say out loud for fear of it disappearing, was still shining and brilliant. *It's real. It's without her.*

It didn't seem quite as appealing as it had yesterday. But there it was. He had to leave her. That was final.

He decided.

The massage had stopped. He opened his eyes. He was looking straight into hers.

He kissed her.

She pulled away. "Edward," she said.

"Shh," he said.

"I don't…"

"Shh." He held her and watched her. He could read her in the trance. It was the first time he'd ever been able to read her. She was afraid. She had been afraid he was going to hurt her by walking back out of her life. Now she was afraid that he was going to hurt her far worse.

"Callista," he said. He searched for the words. He smiled and stroked her hair. She leaned into his hand slightly. She was hoping.

"Callista, there's something I need to tell you. It's quicker than your story. It's simple, actually, quite simple." He breathed deeply and looked at that first vision, the vision he desired. It was a little brighter. It was possible.

"I love you," he said. He kissed her again. This time she didn't resist. He tasted her tears as they ran down into their mouths. For long after they kissed, they held each other. She sobbed into his shoulder. *Relief.*

Edward saw a flash of metal in his peripheral vision. He jerked his head. It was a boy peering through the window across the room. Edward's eye only caught him moments before he pulled out of sight, but in the trance it was enough to identify the intruder.

It was Tomy. *The eyes and ears of Manassa.*

Edward pulled her away firmly. He held her cheek. "Something's in the yard. I'll be right back. Stay here." Edward checked the window outside. The kitchen opened directly to the yard. "No, scratch that. Go to the furthest room from this door and lock the door. And don't open it until I come get you."

"Edward?" Her voice quivered. "What's happening?"

"If I don't come get you in an hour, call the police." *Not that they'll do any good.*

"Edward," she said.

He had to move. "Just do it," he yelled with an urgency that she could no longer resist. As she started to follow his instructions, he bolted out of the door. He got into the yard in just enough time to see Tomy disappear into the thick jungle.

36

Edward ran. He concentrated on getting every iota of momentum possible out of his leg muscles. He pushed with all his might. He had to catch up with that boy. Tomy had a head start, but Edward was closing on him. Though the Onge boy had been raised running the jungles, Edward had the trance and longer legs.

The boy darted behind bushes and plunged through underbrush. If he got out of eyesight long enough, he could hide. Then Edward would be one step behind Mahanta again. *Dangerous. Gotta get him.*

Edward felt the sharp thorns of plants ripping at his skin. He stumbled, but managed to launch himself back up without slowing his pace.

For a moment Edward lost him. Tomy was out of sight, and all Edward had to track was the swaying of vines and limbs in the boy's wake.

Their chase had taken them deep into the jungle, where the moon had a harder time piercing the treetops. Even with his trance vision, Edward had a hard time seeing what was ahead of him.

He forced his eyes to dilate further as he ran, so that he could pick up motion more easily but caught less detail. Edward didn't feel the fear he'd felt during his first nighttime race into the jungle. Rather, he felt calm, detached, as though he were playing a game of cat and mouse.

He heard moving water, some sort of stream. He kept following the branches whipping back, the leaves waving under the moonlight. It was harder to hear the footsteps and the boy's path because of the water, but he could still make it out.

He started being able to hear the boy's breathing. Edward was getting closer, still, but the jungle was growing thicker. He strained his eyes to catch a glimpse of that boy's dirty shirt and dark skin.

The finer calculations of his predicament were starting to enter rapidly into Edward's mind.

The spear. That flash of metal had been a spear. He had to keep the boy on the run, or else Edward might have Tomy's weapon run through his gut.

Edward heard Tomy shout. He was close. Edward lunged through a wall of brush, pushing hard into the jungle floor for more leverage.

There was no leverage. His foot pumped through the empty air.

He gasped. His right leg plunged downward. His left knee smashed into the ground and then he was flipping in the air. Directly below was water shimmering by the moon. It was a thirty foot drop to a rocky bed. The jungle stream had carved a gorge into the bedrock.

Edward stopped time. At least, that was how his sense channels perceived it. He could think so much more rapidly than the events unfolding that he may as well have been suspended in the air for an hour. His mind took in everything. *The rocks below. Tomy on the ground near the water, hurt, dragging himself up. The spear on the other side of the water.*

The stream was shallow and only a few yards wide. There was no sense in landing in it.

The roots. They projected out from the other side of the gorge. They were insubstantial, but his only shot at avoiding injury. He could reach them. He spotted a long, fat root hanging out from the other side about ten feet down. He extended his body out of his aerial roll to catch it.

The root creaked, but he stopped his fall.

Below, the boy started moving away in a gimpy sprint, cradling his arm. The way he moved reminded Edward of the beggar boy. *He'd been the beggar boy.* Edward hadn't recognized him in the shirt, with his dirty skin and his hair so much in his face. Tomy was picking up speed. Edward kept his eyes locked on him, adjusting his grip on the root.

It started to give. Edward's hands slipped as the root bent down towards the stream. The root was too moist to really grip well. He saw another root ten feet below, but it was too far downstream to reach.

The root gashed his hands, but he willed himself to hold on long enough to swing slightly downstream. He fell.

Edward caught the next root, but only for a moment before he dropped down to the creek bed. He landed hard. The whole bed of the gorge was rock.

Had he not been trancing, the impact even from twenty feet up would have knocked him out. Instead, he willed himself through, rolling toward where he'd last seen Tomy and launching forward.

Tomy had slipped out of sight. Edward raced along the bank, moving much more rapidly with firm ground underfoot and every muscle working in perfect harmony under the trance.

He didn't feel any of the exertion he'd just gone through. He could tap into the pain of it if he so desired; he didn't so desire. *I could probably will myself to sprint until I drop dead. Gotta make sure I don't overdo it.*

The gorge stretched long and straight. He could see far ahead, but no saw no sign of Tomy. He must have gotten out somehow.

There. Edward almost passed it - a steep yet navigable slope out of the gorge. Edward climbed up, back into the jungle.

He tuned his ears to every sound of the night, but the one noise he was looking for he couldn't find. He heard no footsteps, no rustling, just the howls of the animals, the croaks of the reptiles, the calls of the insects. Nothing human.

Breathing. He heard human breathing. It was only one sound of thousands, but in the trance, he heard it. It came from above.

Edward craned his neck. He knew Tomy hid in the tree branches, but couldn't see him.

A thousand calculations whirred through Edward's mind. Edward was no Onge; he wasn't physically able to scale a tree. Even if he tried, Tomy would just jump down and escape. It had been a wise move for the boy to take the high ground.

Edward edged forward slowly, alert for an ambush. None came. He knew Tomy was watching his every move from high in the branches. For fifteen minutes, Edward continued on, expecting at any moment to hear the dull thud of Onge feet on soft jungle ground and the boy running again. Once Tomy was on the ground, Edward would have him.

But Tomy didn't drop. Finally, Edward decided to head back. He didn't know how much longer the trance would last, and didn't particularly want it to end before he got out of the jungle. As Edward turned to go back to the gorge, he heard the rustling of tree branches, but no thud.

The Onge boy was wisely sticking to the treetops.

Edward thought about his next move as he ran back. He knew he had a little time to think. It would take Tomy over a day to get back to the village on foot, even at a breakneck speed. Edward could make it in a car in just three hours.

I've got time. Think it out.

He had to cut off Tomy at the pass. He didn't know what Tomy would report to Mahanta. Edward had to assume Tomy had seen the pills and that he'd seen Callista. That put her in danger and him in danger.

Edward found another exit to the gorge on the other side and ran back to Callista's home through the jungle.

As he ran, he wondered if he hadn't made a mistake.

I did. He had known he was making it when he kissed her, but he would have never have done it if he'd known Tomy followed him.

He mentally cringed at the idea of what he must do. He had to end it with her now. Now that he didn't get Tomy, his vision with her was not just dim; it was dead. It would only be selfish of him to cling to her. If he didn't stop it now, she might end up dead as his vision. He could not predict Tomy or Mahanta. Both would have no compunctions against harming her if they saw fit.

He hated it, though. He was about to hurt her worse than he'd ever hurt anyone.

He was glad that the trance allowed him to will his thoughts away from it.

He would do what must be done when he got back to the house. For now, he would just run through the jungle.

He willed away the sick feeling to his stomach, as well. It was the same sick feeling he'd gotten when he signed his life to the Jesuits. It was the feeling that she was gone.

37

Tomy dropped out of the trees and ran as fast as he could to his car. "Back to the base," he ordered his driver.

He tried to stop the racing of his mind. Edward was betraying the tribe. Of that, he was certain. He had no orders for this eventuality. He was only to watch Edward and report. He would need a nod from Mahanta to take care of Edward.

The woman needs to be taken care of, too. Edward must have shown her the secret.

Tomy's thoughts diverted. *Before I do anything, I must bring word to Manassa. The others can tend to business.*

Once he arrived at their Lisbaad base, an abandoned three-story tenement at the outskirts of town, it only took a few seconds to issue his orders. There would be no questions, only compliance. Such was the way of the Onge.

He got into the car with Da'lin and left for the village.

38

"Cali," he called into the house. "It's Edward. I'm back. It's safe, now."
She was hiding. "Come out, now."

She appeared at the end of the hallway. She had a marble doorstop in
her hand, and when she saw that it was indeed Edward she dropped it to the
floor. "How'd you know where I was?" she asked quietly.

Edward shrugged. "Are you okay?" he asked. "Did anyone come in the
house?"

"No. No. I'm fine. I'm fine."

You're beautiful. Edward examined her. The moonlight cast into the house
in slanted rays through the shutters. They caught her and drew lines across
her skin as she walked toward him. He could feel her fear, saw her shaking
and trying to cover it. He understood. She had no idea what was going on.

He purposely slowed down his own breathing and calmed his counte-
nance. She responded and relaxed a bit as well. Her eyes were searching his
for answers. Her gaze froze on his cheek.

"What?" he asked. Edward put his hand to his face. He followed the line
of a deep scratch and found blood. "Just some scrapes. Nothing serious,"
he dismissed. Her shaking hadn't stopped. He pulled her to him. "Don't be
afraid," said Edward. "I'm sorry to frighten you. It's just…"

She embraced him back. He felt her drawing strength from him. It was
the sort of thing that gave him strength, too.

"Just what?" she murmured. "What's happening, Edward?"

"I'll explain everything to you, I promise." He stroked her hair.

"Are you in some sort of trouble? You're in hiding? What happened?"

He pulled from her slightly to look her in the eyes. "Nothing that makes any sense. I promise you I'll tell you everything. It's just, there's no time right now..."

"What was that out there?" she asked.

"Just a boy. He was following me."

"Just a boy? Why'd you react like that?" She flipped the light switch behind him. The harsh light illuminated her face and the two trails of tears must have run down her cheeks.

"I thought it might have been something else."

"Just tell me what's happening, Edward. I need to know what's happening." *She needs to know if this is going to work out. And I've got to tell her it's over.*

"Listen, Callista, I want to answer all of your questions. I really do. But I can't. Right now. And I need to talk to you before I go right now."

"Before you go right now?" she asked, incredulous. "Before you go *right now?*"

"Sit down. We need to talk." He tried to lead her to a seat. She sprang back up and paced to the other side of the room.

"Listen to me, Edward," she said. She twisted her hair up frantically, then let it go again. She turned to face the wall and then spun back around. "Something happened out there, Edward. And now you're trying to break up with me before we've even gotten together. And you hid from a Jesuit. And you've just been acting *weird.* If you honestly think that you're going to get out of here without telling me the truth, you've got rocks in your head."

"It's only to protect you," said Edward.

She gave him a withering glare. "There's one person who will definitely need protection if he leaves here without telling me what the hell's going on."

She stood with her hand on her hip. She was resolute.

For the second time in an hour, Edward denied his vision. He would have to make this future work. He had demonstrated conclusively to himself that he could not trust himself to be rational around Cali, even in the trance.

"It's called the nirvana effect," he said. "And Mahanta."

39

An hour later, Callista sat straight-backed at the edge of her seat, still quizzing him. She had the kind of posture that never necessitated a chair back. In contrast to Callista, Edward slumped into the couch.

He'd told all, but all wasn't ever enough for Callista. The drug had worn off, and its effects were replaced by a dreary exhaustion and a dull body ache. *So much for the after-pain. I guess we could call it an after-ache now.*

"So what do you make of it?" she asked. "Who's telling the truth? Nockwe or Mahanta?"

Edward rubbed his forehead and sat up. He sighed. "I can't tell you how much of a relief it is to communicate this all to another human being instead of just bouncing it all around my head."

"No problem," she said, smiling. "So what do you think?"

"Well, Nockwe told me Mahanta wants to rule the Earth - that he has to, basically..."

"What do you mean?"

"I mean that because of the way the prophecy works in his tribe, the same tradition that *made* him a god to his people could also kill him if he doesn't follow what that tradition predicts. And part of that prediction is that he'll guide his people to rule the Earth."

"Literally or figuratively?"

"Quite literally."

"That's crazy. Can you imagine the President or the Prime Minister bowing down to a boy in a loincloth?" she asked. She laughed at the idea. He didn't.

"Well, he probably wouldn't be in a loincloth at that point," he said.

"Wait. You're seriously considering that possibility?" she asked.

"I'm not debating what he's capable of. I'm just trying to figure out what he's capable of trying. But anyway, I asked him point-blank while I was in the trance if he intended that. He said no. I would have been able to tell if he were lying."

"Wouldn't have you been able to tell if Nockwe was lying, too?"

"Well, I wasn't in the trance then…but it seemed like he was telling the truth."

"Why would Nockwe lie to you?"

"Power. There's always a power struggle in the Onge. He would want to undermine Mahanta."

"But from what you said about Nockwe's actions before this situation occurred, that sort of thing doesn't sound characteristic," she said.

"Maybe not. But Nockwe might be under new stresses, new pressures that force his hand. I don't know the new Nockwe, and barely know the old."

She nodded.

"One thing about what he said, though…what he said made sense. As a matter of fact, I don't see how it could possibly be a lie…"

"What did you ask Mahanta?" she asked.

"Hmmm?"

"What did you ask him exactly?"

Edward rubbed his forehead again. He felt the need for coffee or, better, another trance. He sent his dull mind back to that moment. "I asked…well, it wasn't a question, actually. I said, 'I do not fault your desire to have the Onge rule the Earth.' And he said, 'I have no such desire.' Of course, we said it all in Onge."

"Hmmm…"

"Any ideas?" he asked.

"No, not yet. I don't know what to tell you about that one," she said.

"Yeah, seems like he's being honest. You know, it's totally possible that Mahanta's being honest and so is Nockwe. Nockwe might just be being cautious, and not really know what Mahanta intends."

"So what do you do now?" she asked.

He was looking at his hands. He studied them, looking for an answer written along one of the lines on his palms. "Well, I..."

He stopped because he'd looked up at her. She looked hopeful, a bit like a school girl sitting there waiting on the bench for her boyfriend to get to recess. When he stopped the expression evaporated.

"You're not going back there, are you?" she asked.

He started to nod.

"Edward, you said it yourself. You're playing their game, and you don't even know what it is. Nockwe said Mahanta could kill you."

"I know," he said.

"And I'm here. Look at me. I'm here, Edward, flesh and blood. You're here..." Her voice trailed off.

"It's the nirvana effect..." he started.

"You've got the pills. We can just go. We can get off this island."

"It's not that..."

"Edward," she said quietly. She looked down at the ground. He waited for her to speak. She seemed uncomfortable. "I set up a clinic here, on this island," she said, "because I'd heard from your father...that you specialized in anthropology...and in tribes resistive to adopting the basics of Christianity. I mean, I wanted to set up a clinic, but I chose here because the Onge are one of the classic examples of such a tribe. I..."

He didn't believe his ears. She wouldn't look at him. Her face reddened. Her eyes watered.

"I couldn't forget you," she whispered. "I know that sounds stupid, childish, ridiculous. I..."

He held her. She still wasn't looking at him. "I turned down travel," he said, "to half a dozen cities I would have otherwise killed to see, just to get back to London. I've probably 'thought I've seen you' a hundred times. I couldn't forget you, either." She looked back up at him, her lips quivering into a smile.

"I just thought," she said, "that maybe if I set up here, I might somehow see you again…"

"Good plan," he said, squeezing her shoulders.

She laughed. "Stupid plan. Took long enough." She laughed again. "Just stay," she pleaded. "Or let's leave."

"I'd love to," said Edward. "I can't. I have to find out what Mahanta is up to. I've got to confront him and ask all the right questions this time. I've got to go spy on him while he doesn't suspect I'm there. I can't leave the drug with him if he's up to no good."

"Why not?"

"There could be a lot of people dead on account of him," said Edward.

"You didn't ask to get into this," she pointed out.

"I'm trying to fix this. I just can't drop it, Cali. I've got to make sure I do it right."

"Why?" she asked. But she already knew the answer. He could see that she'd resigned herself to it.

Instead of responding, Edward just sighed and kissed her forehead.

"Don't we already know he's up to no good? He sent a spy after you."

"It's the Onge way," he explained. "Trust but verify."

"I don't think that's an Onge quote," she said.

He shrugged and kissed her hard.

"You're going now?" she called as he walked to the kitchen. She sounded disappointed.

"I've got to. I don't have much time." He started pouring the pills into the small bottle she'd pulled out for the purpose. He felt her slender fingers slide around his waist. She'd quietly slipped up behind him. "You don't have to do anything," she whispered, kissing the nape of his neck.

Even if Edward left in the morning, he could probably still out-pace the boy. But there was too much at stake and too much that could be decided by minutes.

Edward twisted his neck to kiss her. He felt her fingers slip under his shirt to touch his stomach. He turned around and kissed her more. Her smooth hands rubbed his back.

"Callista Knowles, I love you," he said.

"I thought you were going to say, Callista Knowles, will you marry me?"

"That, too," he said.

She poked him. He kissed her again and then he pulled away slightly.

"I have to go," he said.

She laid her hands on his chest. He was still holding her to him. "You have to go now," she said. The pleading left her voice.

"I do," he said. "Can I borrow your car?"

"Will I get it back?" she asked.

He just looked at her. *Good question.* She tossed him the keys off the table.

"It's good we go way back," she said. He smiled.

He held up the keys. "This is my insurance you don't run around on me while I'm gone."

"There's a doctor with a Corvette in the neighborhood. He could come pick me up."

"I'll take my chances," said Edward. He kissed her once more and let her go. He had to get moving. He pocketed the bottle of "t-pills." "Can you do me a favor?" he asked.

"Sure."

"I'm going to ask you a few questions and give you a few directions before I go. You are in no way in danger personally, but I don't want you to take any chances. You don't need to worry, but you need to be careful. Does that make sense?"

She nodded. "Do you think that boy saw me?" she asked.

"Yes, I think it's possible. Like I said, I don't want to take any chances. I'd like for you to lay low until I get back."

"That makes sense," she said.

"Is there anyone you feel you can trust here?" he asked.

"James." She cleared her throat. "Dr. Seacrest."

"Corvette?" he asked. She laughed. "I see." She laughed again. "Is he in town?" he asked.

"Yes."

"Could you shut the clinic down and stay with him for a few days until I get back?"

"Is that really necessary?" she asked.

"Please?" he asked.

"Will you not go if I don't do it?" she asked. He narrowed her eyes at her playfully. "All right. I'm sure that will be fine."

"Start this morning first thing. And if you see any Onge or suspicious-looking natives in the neighborhood, promise me you'll go into town and hole up at Seacrest's office? He has an office?"

"Yes and yes."

"It's just precaution," he said, more for his own benefit than for hers.

"I know," she said.

"I love you, Callista."

"I love you, Edward." She kissed him again.

He stepped out the back door. "Goodbye."

"Goodbye," she said.

He turned around to look at her once more. She was beautiful, leaning on the countertop. She still wore her black outfit. Her blonde hair casually framed her face. Her blouse hung loose with a couple of the top buttons undone. He knew that under any other circumstance, he wouldn't be leaving until the morning.

Under any other circumstance, I wouldn't be leaving at all.

40

Callista's town car drove much faster than any other mode of transportation Edward had used in the past months. It was an older model; he was taxing it to its limits on the roughshod road.

Rain began to splatter and then pour onto the windshield. The only lights he had on the road were the moon and the headlights. Still, he took his chances and kept up the pace.

The highway would only take him to the edge of Onge territory. From there he'd have to hike through the jungle. The most direct route to the village was straight through the thick of the wild. Otherwise he'd be forced to make a long trek on the winding cart path of the traders.

Edward slowed as the rain intensified. He couldn't keep track of everything - watching the road, the potholes, the curves, riding the hydroplaning, focusing through the beating of the water against the car top, and all between the wipe of a windshield. 160 kilometers per hour had been quite easy to manage twenty minutes ago before the rain. Now 60 kph was quite taxing.

The dull ache in his body had lessened even further. *It worked. It worked it worked it worked!* He smiled, thrilled, and pounded the steering wheel with his hand. He hadn't had time to celebrate. The revelation had been smothered in the other, equally momentous revelation: *She loved me. It had been real. She loves me...*

His mind turned to the trance substance once more. There was no sense in getting giddy. If he did not solve his problems with the nirvana effect and Mahanta, there was nothing to celebrate.

Part of the problem was solved. He had in his pocket the t-pill, the answer to the after-pain and the key to keeping a step ahead of the Onge. Edward's trance was longer and barely hurt. He wondered how many times he could take it in a day.

Three times in less than two days had been unbearable. It was quite likely that he could trance four or more times each day with the t-pill and still not get the same after-pain as one injection.

He quelled his excitement. He needed to concentrate on the road. The rain eased, and he accelerated. The road dipped downward.

Edward saw a pair of lights ahead. He squinted past his windshield wipers. At the bottom of the hill, he spotted an old purple car parked on the side of the road. Its headlights were still on, illuminating the rain, and it was parked cock-eyed on the shoulder. Edward could not slow down. He couldn't waste any time. As he zoomed by, he could make out two figures. They seemed to be natives. The adult figure was changing a tire. The other was a boy, pacing in the rain, as though supervising. The boy jerked his head up to Edward's passing car as soon as he heard it. Edward could see the face distinctly. *Tomy.*

Onge in a car? It was one of the most bizarre things he'd ever seen.

His spine chilled. If he had stayed the night, it could have been much more complicated. Cars turned the "sun and moon" trek to Lisbaad into just a few hours. *How did they get cars? Why?*

The *why* was obvious. Mahanta had more secrets.

Edward watched them in his rear view mirror. He saw just the headlights for a moment, then the silhouette of Tomy jumping up and down in excitement. As Edward reached the top of the next hill, he saw Tomy's car swerve back onto the road. The boy must have somehow recognized him.

Edward accelerated further. Still, the headlights in his rear view mirror were getting closer. It wasn't until he hit close to 150 kph that he began to gain some distance. He hoped that the road didn't swerve. He was relying on blind chance. The windshield was smothered with water mere moments after the wiper passed. He could only see a good twenty meters in front of him, and at that speed on that road, he may as well have been blindfolded.

Edward resisted the temptation to pop another t-pill. For every danger he faced now, there were ten more waiting for him once he got to the jungle. He would definitely need a trance to get through that trek; and then there was his encounter with Mahanta, if he ever reached the boy-turned-god. He would have to take his chances, here.

Edward hit the top of another hill. The car caught air, and Edward wrestled it into staying on the road. Tomy and his tribesman were almost out of sight. Edward needed to get several minutes ahead of them to be able to hide his car without their detection.

Will I get it back? He remembered Cali's humor.

That depends on if I die. He smiled. He wondered what she would have said to that. Probably, *well, then you can't have the car.* He'd be in her bed right now.

I should probably start slowing down. I'm getting close.

The car hydroplaned, then skidded through a muddy spot on the dirt road. He shot past a windblown sign: "Hard Right Turn Ahead". Edward slammed the brakes. The car slid further.

Ahead Edward saw a massive clump of trees. He had reached the edge of the jungle. The road twisted at an odd angle to shoot into the woods. It was meant to be taken at 40 kph. Edward was still zooming at 120. He pumped the brakes, then yanked up the hand brake as he took the turn.

It wasn't enough. The car responded to him, but the rain and the terrible road were merciless. In his slide, the back tire slammed into the dirt incline at the edge of the curve. The car spun left. It started rolling. Edward braced himself, getting as low as possible in the vehicle, thankful he'd buckled his safety belt.

The car only made a quarter roll before its hood slammed into a tree with a deafening crack. The back swung around and made its own impact against another. The collision jerked Edward sideways towards the roof of the car, the seat belts digging hard into his shoulders and torso and knocking the wind out of him. His head got dangerously close to the roof of the car, but stopped with a jerk before he hit it.

The engine had stopped running. The car had no power. The only sound Edward heard was the rain. Except for the bruising pain from the seat belt, and the soreness in his neck, he was uninjured. The collision had thankfully left the cabin more or less intact. He sat there just listening to his own breathing. Any minute now Tomy's car would be coming by.

Edward took a moment to pray before he did anything else. *God, thank you for sparing my life. It's a sign to me that I'm not working against you.*

Lord, please forgive me for the breaking of my oath. Please do not forsake me. Every sin I have committed against you I will make up tenfold.

I know you have a purpose for me, Lord. Please give me the strength to fulfill it. Give me the strength for what I must do.

He didn't say, "Amen." He felt it wiser for his whole night in the jungle to be a prayer. He felt he somehow had a better chance mid a direct communication to his maker.

And God, I know it's stupid, but please let me have Cali. Please don't take her from me.

His scientist side told him that there was no evidence of a God that actually meddled in the affairs of men. At that moment, he hoped there was. After all, he'd just seen his life flash before his eyes.

Edward tried the door facing up. It wouldn't open.

Edward pulled himself out through the smashed windshield. One of the remaining glass shards scratched him. He ignored it and strained his eyes to the north. Down the road a couple kilometers away, he saw the pair of headlights he was looking for peek out over the hill. He still had a minute before they reached him. They were driving much more slowly, now. *They must know about the turn. They've done this trip a few times.*

Edward's mind started down the path of, how long have the Onge been doing this?

The pressing necessity of dealing with that pair of headlights, however, forced his thoughts to the task at hand.

41

Next to Da'lin sat the boy Tomy, the Messenger of the living god. Using Manassa's magic nectar, it had not taken Da'lin long to learn to drive the car.

Da'lin had never been a courier to a boy before. It was Manassa's law that one must speak to the messenger as one might speak to the god, and one must listen to the commands of his messenger with the same deference. It seemed odd to Da'lin, listening to a fourteen year old as he might respect one of the tribal elders.

But Tomy only said what Manassa told him. And Da'lin was never one to question the holy. Manassa was a god; it stood to reason he was always right. That was fine for Da'lin.

Tomy was irritated. His feet were covered in mud and were everywhere in the car - on the dashboard, on the door paneling, on the seat. Tomy could not sit still.

Da'lin was not a clean man or a neat freak, even by Onge standards, but it was his car. At least, he drove it. No Onge in living memory had even rode in a car, let alone driven one. He preferred to keep it like the white man had it when Da'lin stole it from him.

If Tomy were just a child Da'lin would just knock him over the head or throw him out of the vehicle. But he was not a child. In many palpable respects, he was Manassa.

The boy kept talking. He wouldn't stop talking.

"That was the white man, the white man I was following. He hunted me. He tried to get me. He saw me. Manassa will be *angry*. Manassa will not be pleased. He'll be *angry* with *you*, Da'lin. And he'll even be angry with me. Edward is ahead of us, Da'lin. You must go faster. It is as Manassa wishes."

"How do you know what he wishes?" asked Da'lin even as he pressed his foot on the accelerator. The rain was subsiding, but he was already going far faster in the storm than he felt he should risk.

"He speaks to me, even as we sit here now. His word to me is as the air I breathe. His whispers are the wind." He was quoting some of their oral history, now. Da'lin didn't believe him but did not want a bad report from the boy to get to Manassa. "We must catch him. We must bind him and bring him to our god."

"Didn't you just want to watch him?"

"I'm afraid that he's already betrayed us. We must take every precaution." They drove over another hill. "Why are you slowing down? We can't even see him anymore."

"There is a curve here, just before we enter the wood." As they reached the bend their headlights illuminated the undercarriage of Edward's car. It was bent forward in the middle, wedged between two massive trees at the jungle's edge.

"The white man!" screamed Tomy. "Stop the car! Stop the car!" Da'lin slowly braked. He was not about to flip his car and join the white man. *The Messenger of Manassa needs to learn the patience of his master.*

Before the car even stopped, Tomy was outside of it, sprinting to the wreckage, climbing around it, looking for the missionary. Da'lin cautiously stepped out of his car, leaving it running in case they needed to make a quick getaway. "His body's not in here," said Tomy.

"Maybe he survived and is now making his way on foot," said Da'lin, taking a few more steps towards Tomy so he could see him better. The rain was still coming down hard enough to obscure his vision.

"Maybe so," said Tomy. "It would be a long way for a white man to travel in the jungle."

"I saw him duel Dook. He is no normal white man," responded Da'lin. He looked around for signs of the missionary. Tomy saw them first.

"Tracks," he shouted, pointing at the muddy road. Da'lin walked over to examine them. They were pointed away from the village.

"The white man goes the wrong way!" shouted Da'lin over the rain. Tomy was still at the wreckage. Da'lin's eyes followed the path of the footsteps into the darkness of the jungle.

"There is no sign of him here," shouted Tomy.

"There!" yelled Da'lin. He spotted Edward first. Da'lin had never seen a white man move in such a manner. As a matter of fact, he'd never seen a human being come close. It was as though the white man were held up by strings, as though the unseen god of gods were pulling and tugging his body as a toy. Da'lin was reminded of Mahanta's supernatural duel with the panther.

The white man *leapt* onto the car, *slid* all the way across the top, and *flipped* down through the door in one fluid, graceful motion. Da'lin ran towards him.

"Get him!" yelled Tomy. "Get him!"

Da'lin did not want to lose his car. Moreover, he did not want to lose his life at the hands of this boy. The adrenaline let him overcome his fear of the white demon. There was some awful, dark medicine, some white magic in him that was making him dance like a god.

The white man started the car moving, but its wheels spun out in the mud. The rear tire in a rut in the dirt road. The white man tried again. Da'lin drew closer. He would reach him.

The white man did something funny with the brakes, tried again. The car lurched forwards out of the rut. Da'lin grabbed him and hurled him out of the car. Cat-like, Edward landed a meter away and in the same motion launched at Da'lin.

Edward's blows lacked power, but they came with such speed and fury that Da'lin could only stagger back. The white man used not only his hands and feet but his knees, his elbows, his head, his every body part to strike Da'lin, and Tomy could only get halfway to the fight before the Onge driver had fallen.

Da'lin watched the white man leap over him back into the car. He saw

Tomy charging, but this time it was too late for the Onge. In a blur of mud, Da'lin's car lurched off. Tomy was shrieking.

"Get up! Get up you weakling! Get up! We must hurry! The white man crushed you! Just wait until Manassa hears this! You have failed our god!" Da'lin was in a fog. Tomy slapped his face to wake him up. *My car*, Da'lin was thinking. *My car...* "Why would you leave the car running!" yelled Tomy. "He stole the car! He'll make it to the village before us, now! Get up!"

Da'lin pulled himself up from the mud. His nose bled. He wished that the white man had hit him hard enough to have his ears stop functioning, but no such luck.

"We must run," said Tomy.

Da'lin obligingly started trotting down the road. He had no problem with hoofing it. If he hurried, maybe he could get his car back.

"Wait," said Tomy. He pulled out two vials from his pocket. "We must *run.*"

42

Lila, newly widowed adulteress and girl of sixteen, walked past the guards of Manassa's temple. They were expecting her, at Manassa's instructions, and let her pass without so much of a glance. As was customary with the Onge, she wore little clothing, but she made it a point to lose her skirt on the long walk to Manassa's bedchamber so that only a loincloth remained.

She walked into his quarters with impunity. He was working with a microscope at his corner desk. He had turned before she even entered the room.

"My husband is dead, my lord," said Lila. "Glis is dead."

She stood in the doorway. She resisted the urge to walk closer still. She wanted him to look at her. She wanted the eyes of the living god upon her, much as she'd had his eyes for years before he'd risen to power. She hoped she still had his eyes.

He looked at her and half stood up in his seat. She smiled. She had his eyes, though she knew she didn't hold the same power as before. He had the power in all things but a few. He could have any woman he wanted. For now, he desired her. This fact didn't repel her, but rather drew her closer. She had to hang onto the doorway to keep from falling in.

"I am sorry for your loss," said Manassa.

"It was as you had foreseen!" shouted Lila, ecstatic. "It was exactly as you had foreseen!"

"You have kept our promise? You have told no one?" he asked.

"Not a soul," she said. "I won't tell a soul. It's our secret."

"As a god, Lila, I hear all things. I love you a great deal, more than any other, but I will cut out your tongue if you break our agreement." He spoke with sincerity. There was no menace in his voice. He was making a statement of fact.

She gulped. She had known their relationship was different now, but in that moment she realized how different.

"I have much better intentions for your tongue than that, though," said Manassa. He smiled. For a moment he was Mahanta again. She sighed and felt warmer. "Well done, Lila. You were very brave and loyal. You may enter," he said.

He watched her walk into the room. She stopped in the center so that the candlelight could dance all over her dark body. She saw she was overcoming his discipline. He moved forward from the chair, but then sat back down.

"Lay down on the bed," he told her. "I've just got to finish this." He turned back to his microscope.

She eased herself across the sheets. *Yes, he has the power in all things but a few.* Despite his godly discipline, she'd seen that look in his eyes.

43

Edward had amazed himself at his own motions. As he flew down the road in the Onge's old purple Lincoln, he played the scene over and over in his mind.

Before, when he'd fought Dook, he had tried to tap into whatever martial arts he had seen in movies and boxing matches. That data hadn't served him well at all. As a matter of fact, the only thing that kept him alive with Dook was the moment by moment evaluation of what Dook planned next, and Edward's own response accordingly.

This time, Edward applied that to his attack. Instead of using some pre-determined fighting style, Edward simply evaluated and fought moment by moment in trance. This made his assault unstoppable, even with his relatively weak muscles compared to the Onge. He had simply evaluated every perception as it came through his mind, one quantum at a time.

Every step occasioned a counter-step. Every change in his momentum was calculated so as to leave the Onge defenseless. Every motion of his opponent, every countermotion, all led him to action with each muscle in harmony.

Edward had no training in martial arts, but it was as though his mind had manufactured a special martial art for that exact scene. The muddy terrain made him rely on rapid blows. He couldn't get a grip with his feet to land any heavy hits. If he had fought in different terrain, he would have moved in a completely different yet appropriate manner.

He needed more strength, he learned. He didn't need to learn how to fight.

Now his mind left contemplation of the present and looked to the future. It seemed to be more and more likely that Nockwe was right. Maybe Edward just couldn't tell a liar, even in the trance. He hoped that wasn't true. It would render this confrontation he was manufacturing worthless.

Of one thing Edward was certain: he was glad to have 43 t-pills in his pocket. Mahanta obviously had something very different than science in mind.

He stopped thinking. To think further was pointless. He knew what he must do no matter if Mahanta spoke the truth or was deceiving him. He had calculated all the possibilities while in trance.

Edward reached the point in the jungle he needed to. He drove another quarter mile, however, before finally parking behind some trees out of view from the road. He checked out the car, finding a knife in the glove box. It fit at his belt. He turned off the car and locked it. *Like that will do any good…*

Edward sprinted into the thick of the jungle, plunging in at a dead run. He would have put Nockwe to shame. He ran through the woods as another might run a track race, bending or turning the slightest amount necessary to avoid the foliage, his feet always finding the exact right spot, and all in the budding dawn, with only the slightest red of the sky to guide him.

The rain made it difficult to find footing, but only because he was sprinting faster than he'd ever run in his life. It was five miles to the village. After the first mile, Edward kept running but let up slightly, quite aware of the fact that his body might give out on him even if he could will himself through it.

As long as I keep trancing, I'll be fine. After the trance – well, that's a different story.

He eased his speed even more. Again, for all the dangers of the jungle, the dangers that lay before him held ten times the force. He slowed to a jog. He did not want to be winded when he got to the village. Still, he had to make it before daybreak to keep his advantage over his trackers and Mahanta.

The whole trek, which would have consumed most of a day even for an Onge, took him less than an hour. His navigation was dead-on, taking him to the "back" of the Onge village.

44

From the edge of the jungle, Edward could see the spark of a few of the cooking fires lit up in the village. The relatively colossal temple of Manassa dominated the landscape over the little huts.

Edward spotted Nockwe's hut in the foreground. His black family flag still flew over the roof. *Nockwe rules another day.* The chieftain must have recovered some of his health. Though the tribe knew he was weak, no one else must have challenged him.

Edward felt an odd sort of relief. He had hoped that Nockwe would still be living when he returned. There was a definite kinship between them that Edward could not explain.

Edward felt the trance starting to slip. He wasted no time in popping another t-pill. He was in the belly of the beast, now.

Almost instantly he felt a resurgence of his consciousness. *This could become a very painful parallel to chain smoking.*

Only a few Onge women maundered around their fires in the early morning. Dawn's pale tones were leaking into the sky. In another half hour, the night would evaporate.

Edward evaluated the scene. He knew the village like the back of his hand. He skirted around the edge of it until he could get a good view of the temple. Two warriors guarded the front entrance, weapons at the ready. He hadn't expected that. That was quite a change since a few days ago, and another clue that Mahanta had hidden plans.

Edward needed a diversion.

A cooking shack was situated only a few meters from the temple. It had been converted from a house to prepare Manassa's "holy food". Edward saw smoke already billowing out of its side.

He scampered into the village, careful to avoid the eyes of Onge women making their morning rounds. He wriggled through a hole in one of the walls in the shack.

Edward took only an instant to survey the primitive kitchen. A hog roasted on a spit, and a pot of cooking grease lay nearby. Edward grabbed the pot and pitched the grease all over the walls. He used a pair of tongs to hold a burning log up against the corner of the wall and straw roof. The grease and the roof lit quickly.

Edward turned from his handiwork to find himself face to face with a large Onge woman holding a bowl of water in her arms. Edward knocked the bowl out of her hands and waved the blazing log inches from her face. "TAUN!" he shouted, the ancient curse of the witch doctor that Edward had heard during Mahanta's coming-of-age. He had no clue what he said.

The woman's eyes jolted wide. She fled screaming, "White devil! White devil! White devil! The fire!" *That worked too well.* Edward wriggled out of the shack as the guards ran to investigate.

Edward edged out of their line of sight, their vision burned out by the building fire. He made it to the temple entrance undetected. He knew he didn't have much time, maybe a few minutes before the guards checked the temple after putting out the fire.

Edward saw Manassa poised serenely on his throne, his eyes closed in meditation. Long purple banners hung from the ceiling on either side of the god's throne. *That's new.* New guards, new ornaments. As soon as Edward set foot into the hut, Manassa said, "Hello, Edward." He still hadn't opened his eyes. His voice boomed out across the open space.

45

Callista Knowles left the house shortly before dawn, unable to sleep. She'd been living alone in the house for three years. For the first time in all those days and nights, the place felt *empty*. It gave her a creepy worry and led her mind to dark thoughts that she did not wish to contemplate.

Dr. Knowles did not scare easily, but Cali did not want to see Edward go. It had been too long.

I have him back. She contemplated that. Her doubts ate at the thought, but she refused to release it. She sat on her couch and smiled at the ceiling. *I have him back*.

She had actually gotten interested in her work, here. She had almost forgotten Edward. She really had. She enjoyed her work. She was actually making an impact. She had developed a couple vaccines that had put quite a dint in local illnesses. She was really happy with that part. And it was nothing like England. Her parents could send her a letter once every couple months and that was about the extent of their influence: the postal service did their bidding if they affixed the correct number of stamps. No one else cared in the least who her parents were or what they did.

Her work, her accomplishments, the entire life she had built in Lisbaad all disappeared into the backdrop the moment she saw Edward in her exam room. Looking back on it, she saw that was why she had reacted so strongly when she first saw him again. She had nothing to meet him with. She had felt naked. She was just a little girl with a crush on a boy for those moments. It was a giddy sorrow that she hadn't felt in a long time.

Focus. She had to focus. She needed to follow Edward's instructions. And

Edward needed to come back in one piece.

She wished those pills would just disappear.

That look in his eyes had told her though that she wouldn't be able to argue him out of it.

She hoped he wasn't addicted to them. That would be unlike Edward.

The dark sky just beginning to catch the sun's reflection. It wasn't yet morning but it was close enough. Callista grabbed her purse and walked across the street to Doctor James Seacrest's front door. She gave it three sharp raps. She hadn't seen the Corvette, but perhaps he'd parked on the street behind. She hoped he was home. She didn't want to have to wait for Edward any more without company.

Callista heard footsteps inside the house. It sounded as though there might be several people inside, but no one responded to her knocking. She tried again, but still no answer. Curious, she walked along the porch so that she could check out the driveway. As she passed a window, the curtains inside abruptly parted, revealing a face of a nationality she had only seen once in all her time in Lisbaad.

Dark, dark skin, half Indian, half Chinese in feature. He was almost invisible in the shadow, his face only lit by the porch light. His wide, surprised eyes peered out at her. She restrained herself from sprinting back to her house. He regained his composure as well.

She waved, friendly, as though just calling on a friend.

"Not home," said the Onge in Tamil. *Odd, maybe I'm wrong. The Onge only speak Onge...*He waved his hand in a side to side motion. *Maybe he's not Onge.*

She nodded. "Thank you," she said, also in Tamil. She turned and walked away down the porch. She had to measure every step, carefully planting one foot after the other to resist the urge to flee. She gave one quick glance back to the house. The dark eyes were still watching her.

She walked around her house to her back yard. As soon as she was out of sight, she leaned against the wall and breathed deeply.

Focus. She had to collect her thoughts. She couldn't just run. She had to somehow leave Edward a trail.

Callista bolted inside and grabbed a pen. She had to force her hand to stop shaking as she wrote him the note and hid it in her bedroom. She kept checking out the window for the door to Seacrest's house to open and half a dozen Onge to come after her.

Had they been there the whole time, staking us out? she asked herself. It didn't seem so. There would have been much more of a reaction to her knocking on the door. *Are they on Edward's side? Probably not.*

She didn't know. Only what she didn't know could hurt her.

She started running through the jungle behind her house. There was a neighbor, seven houses down, who was always home. Her husband owned the only ship supply company on the island. She stayed with her two children. She would let Dr. Knowles borrow her car.

Callista knocked on the lady's back door. She quickly answered with a four-year-old on her hip. She looked slightly bewildered to be greeting Callista at her back door, but still friendly. "Hello, Dr. Knowles," she said. "Can I help you?"

"Hello, Lindsay...Ms. Webb. Maybe you can. I'm sorry I'm knocking on your back door like this. Just...in a hurry, you know. I got a call from the clinic, it's an emergency, and my car's on the fritz again. You know, I'm a doctor, not a mechanic. Not in my job description." Callista forced the joke, forced the chuckle. All she could think about was that dark face in Seacrest's window. She hoped Seacrest hadn't come to harm.

Lindsay laughed overmuch. She seemed starved for adult conversation.

"I know what you mean. I'm not a mechanic, either, Dr. Knowles!" she said, laughing again. It wasn't funny at all but Callista laughed with her. "Whenever my car breaks, I have to nag Mr. Webb 'til it gets fixed or I get a new one...so I guess you could call me a mechanic."

"I'm only a body mechanic," said Callista. She was hoping Lindsay would offer. If not, she would ask. If Lindsay said no, and if Callista's pulse kept rising, she would probably take it anyway.

Lindsay's face suddenly took a look of concern. She frowned. "Is it a bad emergency?" she asked.

"Just an average, run-of-the-mill emergency..." Callista looked at the four-year-old. He was playing with his mother's hair. She could see a staircase behind Lindsay to the second floor of the house. "Just a child, couldn't be more than five years old, one of the merchant's kids, had an awful spill down a flight of stairs. They think he broke his neck. They got him to my clinic, but I wasn't in. I don't want to have to move him to another clinic and risk disabling him permanently just because I need a new mechanic."

"Oh, God!" shouted Lindsay. She covered her face. There were tears welling up in her eyes. She looked at her own, impressive staircase. "I just keep telling Donald how we need to get an elevator. It's just not safe for the kids, and so wearisome for me, doing the laundry, up and down, up and down. Oh, God!"

Jesus Christ, lady. I need this car. At this rate, I may as well have just hunkered down on Seacrest's porch.

"Yes, would be a terrible shame…" Knowles said.

Lindsay's eyes darted around. "Listen, promise me you won't tell Donald, he has no compassion for children, but I could lend you my car. It's a mess inside. I hope you don't mind."

Callista smiled warmly. "I won't mind. You're sure it won't be any trouble?"

"Just don't tell Donald. He'll have a cow. He's out of town on business, but he'll be back next week. You won't need it for that long, will you?"

Callista shook her head. "No, just for today. I just need to get to the clinic."

"Yes, that's fine. Oh, I'm sorry, I'm such a terrible host. Would you like to come in, have some tea?" She motioned warmly. The kid just stared at Dr. Knowles from her hip.

"No, no, I need to get to the clinic to help the child." Geez, this woman is off her rocker.

"Oh, right. Let me go get my keys."

"I'll get them, mom," said the little boy. He jumped off her hip and ran down the hall.

Callista checked behind her. She wondered how much time she had. She wanted to grab the keys herself and leap into the car, but she had to restrain herself. She made wise use of the time.

"Have you seen Doctor Seacrest?" she asked.

"No, no," said Lindsay. "I haven't seen him in several days. As a matter of fact, I always see his Corvette pull in, he always comes in at three and I'm just waking up from my afternoon nap, but I haven't even seen him pull by in the next couple days. Is he on vacation?"

"I guess so," said Callista. "I guess so."

"He's got such a fine car, don't you think? I've been trying to get Donald to get one. It's so fine. Doctor Seacrest is a fine man, too, don't you think? And single. If I weren't married to Donald 'the fish' Webb--"

"Here you go, mom!" The kid ran up and handed her the keys. Lindsay passed them to Callista. Callista grabbed them. Lindsay kept them gripped in her hand.

"You'll come by some time, and have tea?" she asked, eyes like lasers into Callista's skull as though searching out some deep, embedded truth.

"Yes, of course. What are neighbors for?" chuckled Callista. Lindsay let go of the keys. "Thank you. You just saved a child's life today. I'll see you tonight."

"Wonderful. I'll see what they're making in the kitchen and have them add a plate!"

Callista had already started walking to the car. It was a black 2007 Lincoln Towncar. It was immaculate except for a couple children's toys on the seats. *Very messy.* "Actually, I might be late with this surgery."

"Oh, we'll wait. You're a guest of the house."

"I wish you wouldn't. I might be all night with this case."

"Another time, then."

Callista got into the car. "Absolutely!" she called out before closing the door and starting the engine. She pulled out of the driveway, waving. When she got to the road, she saw three men sprint from Seacrest's house across the lawn to her own. Two were dressed casually, one in a business suit, all natives with the same build and skin tone as the man in the window. She pulled away, watching them in the rear view mirror as she left the neighborhood. Two went around back. The man in the suit peered into the front windows. She accelerated. Seacrest's clinic would be no refuge for her. She had to think and stay safe.

46

Edward was not impressed with Mahanta's stage presence. "Hello, Manassa," he quietly answered as he sidestepped away from the temple's entrance. He preferred not to move any closer to Manassa. He didn't know what sort of weapons the Onge had behind his chair.

"You'll call me Mahanta before we are done today," Manassa said pleasantly.

"I'll call you as I see you." Edward kept walking until he had an optimum distance between himself and the door - closer than Manassa, but far enough away to give him wiggle room should the guards come bursting through.

"We'll give me one of your Western names, yet." Manassa smiled. He held his eyes closed.

"How about Judas?" suggested Edward.

Unperturbed, Manassa said, "And I will call you Simon."

"I think the man who doubts is the one who sent a stalker," said Edward. As long as Manassa was talking, he would play along. He needed the whole truth from the Onge god, and he wouldn't get that just from reading his eyes.

"I foresaw your coming today," said Manassa.

Edward didn't know whether this was true or not, but fenced. "Or else, you're in trance, and heard my footsteps in the entrance."

"You were keeping something from me, Edward," said Manassa.

Edward laughed. "I think you kept something from me, too." Manassa did not find anything funny, but just kept sitting on his throne.

"You had an idea about the substance. Something for the after-pain."

Never lie to a seer. "Yes," said Edward. "And you have a plan you've been hiding meticulously. The guards, the cars." He focused all his attention on Manassa's face, eyelids, hands, muscles. He now knew why Manassa stayed in the meditation position. It would be difficult to read him.

Edward recognized the need for an overt strike.

"Yes," said Manassa.

"Out with it, Manassa." Edward pitched his voice into the beginnings of fear. It was an honest emotion. It was all honest, what he would say, but from a far corner of his mind which he never let out. He hoped it was a sufficient deception. Just by the careful tone of Manassa's "yes," Edward could tell that the Onge god planned to deceive him once again. He wondered how deeply Manassa could read *him*. "In Lisbaad," Edward started, "I did something that has committed me on this course. I will no longer be able to remain in my Order. Please tell me you have not betrayed me."

Success! Manassa opened his eyes to look at him. Edward had taken the encounter down an unpredicted course. Manassa doubted him, needed to read him, hadn't seen through him yet. Now Edward had the god's eyes. They told him everything he needed to know.

Manassa watched him, modulating his voice to a deadpan. "I did not betray you, Edward." He saw that Edward did not believe him for an instant. "I may have hidden things from you, but I never lied to you, nor have I betrayed you." Edward willed himself to believe it in part. It was key that Manassa thought he had the upper hand, and just acting wouldn't do. He made himself believe it. *He is acting in my best interests. He is working in a logical fashion.* And the one other assumption that he now sensed Manassa was looking for: *I am willing to follow his lead.*

"But why did you hide things from me?" asked Edward. He knew the questioning sold it, as though he'd already accepted Manassa's premise.

"You were not ready," said Manassa.

"For what?"

Manassa stood from his throne. He walked forward idly. Edward matched his step towards the door, maintaining his advantage. Manassa raised an eyebrow.

"I do not trust you, yet, Manassa. Explain yourself. I deserve an explanation. I am not your subject or your villager." He threw some real anger into the mix. It was an acting job of life and death. "For what, Manassa?" he repeated.

Manassa returned to sit at his throne. "This road we are on has many forks, but there are three of consequence that we must face."

"Yes?" Edward prompted.

"The first is darkness. The second is chaos. The third is order."

"Go on." Edward had to force himself to be receptive. He remembered how forceful Manassa had gotten with him after the fight with Dook, how easily the young man had assumed the role of teacher. Edward hoped Manassa's trance certainty and desire for subservience would mask Edward's deception.

Manassa seemed to be taking the bait. Of course, Edward also had to weigh the possibility that Manassa was a step ahead of him, that Manassa wanted him to make those exact conclusions. The young man might have been planning this all day and foreseen the whole encounter. It was a deadly dance of wits. In the trance, every flicker of face muscle, every beat of an eyelash, every modulation of the voice betrayed vital clues.

Edward had to trust that he had the advantage, that he'd taken Manassa by surprise, that he could take what was being said at something close to face value.

Manassa continued. "One course is that we could destroy this substance in its entirety, destroy every plant, every ounce of sap, abolish it from the earth. That is the path of darkness, the snuffing out of a candle that could light the world."

Edward nodded. "I had considered that," he said. *I hate it, but that might be what needs to happen.*

Manassa continued his teaching. "In that way, we could step away from it in peace."

"Go on," prompted Edward.

"The second path is that of chaos. At first that seems the only path beyond darkness. We could take this substance and plunge the world into death. If we keep it much longer, someone else will get their hands on it, someone else will use it stupidly."

Edward again nodded. "I had considered that, too."

"At first, when looking into the future, this chaos seems to be a cloud that consumes all paths that lead beyond. For weeks it was all I could see. But I would not have started to use this substance, to risk unleashing it upon the world, if that was all the future held."

"What is the path of order?" asked Edward.

"The path of order is the path of control. It is the path of enlightenment, of a Golden Age. You could say it is the path of an Order. If we control the substance, we could…"

"Lead the world," Edward finished for him.

"Yes. And we would have in our Order the first people who were ever truly fit to lead."

Edward let the idealistic part in him speak, the part that had foreseen this path, before throwing it by the wayside. He had studied far too much history to really allow himself to fall into such a trap. "But how could it be done? I saw that, too, but my vision kept going back to the chaos."

Manassa smiled. "It can be done." Edward gave him a cautious look. Manassa waved his arms. "We will use the Onge. It is why I ascended to godhead. They will be our Order."

"That's why the cars."

Manassa nodded. "And more. I have developed a half-drug." Edward hadn't suspected that. It was nowhere in his calculations. "I have my Onge take the substance orally. It produces a trance of a sort. It heightens the senses, but it's not enough to awaken them, so to speak. My Onge call it the Lightness. It is enough to give us what we need to start. We shall be the Seers. And we shall have an Order. It is all as I have foreseen."

Edward, in the merciless logic of the trance, saw why Manassa had chosen him for his plot. "You knew when you read my journal that I would follow you," said Edward.

Manassa didn't answer.

"You knew I wouldn't be able to resist the drug. It brings my dreams back to life. It brings me back to life," said Edward.

The Onge shrugged. "So it is with me," Manassa said simply.

"And now you expect I'll follow you, for the same reasons."

"Or perhaps better ones," said Manassa.

He's got me wrong.

"Do you think you are some sort of Messiah?" Edward asked. He knew Manassa would be suspicious if he didn't challenge him there.

"I think I've been given a gift. And so have you. And with this gift comes more responsibility than anyone has ever had laid on his shoulders in millennia."

"You feel fit to rule the world?" asked Edward.

"I feel fit as any to guide it...with you..." Their eyes were locked on one another.

"Tell me this. What is your plan after we train our Order?" He said it like he wanted to be convinced, like he wanted to be reasoned with, but that he didn't see any future. He could see Manassa biting. It was his last necessary deception.

"We will build up a power base. We will increase our resources. We will not, as the fools of history have done in the past, give up our discovery to the bigger fools who govern. We will control our weapon and lead the people of Earth..." Manassa trailed off. Edward had stopped his acting. The tension released out of him. The Onge detected it in an instant and knew what it was. "You've already made up your mind."

"It's a weapon to you, isn't it?" Edward asked. There was anger in his voice.

The Onge surged toward him. "It is what we say it is, Edward. It is what it is. It is higher than anything on this world. It is higher than the atom bombs, than your Vatican City, than all the sciences of Earth. To name it is a pretense!"

"You'll rule this world to what end?" Edward asked.

"I'll lead it."

"Why?"

"Because I can!" Manassa got in his face and shouted furiously. Edward didn't react. He did not fear this boy. In his peripheral vision, he saw the guards rush in, responding now to the shouting as they had to the fire. Manassa waved them to hold back at the door without so much as a glance. He would not take his eyes off Edward.

Edward was quiet. "Manassa," he said. "You have decided to rule a world you have never seen. You wish to lead it to a goal you cannot even foretell. You seek power for the sake of power."

Edward could tell the boy was listening to what he said, that every part of his mind was dedicated to understanding what Edward was saying, and yet he knew in that instant that Mahanta would never hear. Mahanta was gone and only Manassa remained.

"I will see it. I will have it," said Manassa, defiant.

Edward knew that he would, or die trying. The Onge survival pattern was part and parcel to Manassa, enlightened or no. Just as the Onge who feels most powerful seeks to take the tribe by force, so did Manassa think he could take the world by a subtle force. There would be no convincing him otherwise.

Life amongst the Onge was a much more black and white proposition than Western culture, and the business of living was handled with the utmost precision. It was an Onge law, for instance, that if a hunting party were more than two miles from the village at dusk, and a member of the party is injured, that the injured must be left to fend for himself. If this were violated, the leader of the party would be put to death for his weakness.

No leader was ever put to death. Very few Onge allowed themselves to be injured, but if one did get injured, he would insist on being left behind.

The Onge are the last people in the world who should have the trance substance. With their discipline and lack of "civility", they could wreak untold destruction to civilization without even realizing it. To them, it would be the natural order of survival.

Edward arrived at a conclusion. He knew there was no talking, now, no turning back. He would try anyway, but he already knew the answer. And yet he still had to try.

"Mahanta, this substance, used properly, could give mankind freedom. Or it could create freedom just for one. Or it could plunge everything into chaos." Edward face was only inches from the young man's. "You told me when we started this that there were certain people who could not be trusted with the trance drug. Mahanta, you're one of them." Manassa didn't say anything, only stared at him. It seemed to actually be sinking in. "Mahanta, we must destroy this substance. I need your help. We must destroy it, so that no man can ever reach it again. What seems to be a great blessing is in fact only a curse."

He could tell that Manassa was actually torn. The young man's eyes glazed over.

At long last, Manassa looked at him again. It seemed his trance had worn off. Edward could see the pain and tension suddenly consuming the god's body. Lackluster, Manassa asked, "You discovered something for the after pain?" He asked as though reminiscing, as though it didn't matter. He said it as though he'd decided to help Edward end it all. Edward almost subconsciously nodded. He stopped himself, but it was too late. Manassa was glaring eagle-like into his eyes. *He saw it in my eyes.*

"I must think on all this, Edward," said Manassa tiredly, and walked away from him to his bedchambers behind his throne. "I must think on this. *He't'cari'nya.* I must think on this." It was an odd Onge phrase he'd said. It meant, literally, "the world turns." As he disappeared by the curtains, Manassa chuckled. "I told you you'd call me Mahanta."

Edward was stunned. He could not believe that he actually had Manassa deliberating. He thought there was no chance of changing his mind. Now he was thinking.

Edward heard the call of one of the guards outside. *"Tanyan."* More.

More…Edward heard footsteps far in the distance.

"Tanyan. Tanyan! Tanyan! Tanyan-to-to!" All.

Edward sensed it before it was too late. Mahanta had given an instruction with his odd phrase.

Edward sprinted to the doorway. His muscles ached from his journey in the jungle, but that was a trifling matter compared to the footsteps. In his state of elevated consciousness, the pounding of the earth was growing deafening. Even outside the trance, he could have heard them. The whole tribe was being risen.

Edward heard war cries.

The god lost his trance and so sent his dogs.

47

Callista reached her clinic in less time than she thought possible. She must have had her foot to the floorboard the whole trip.

She had debated risking a stop there. She'd left all her money, though, at her house. She was defenseless without a bit of cash.

Callista's hands were shaking when she tried to open the door. It took her five times with the keys to get the door unlocked.

She stopped in the lobby. All the lights were out. She always left them on. She flipped the switch.

Chairs were out of place. The door to the supply closet was open. All these things would have been tended to by Duiyon.

She thought she heard the clinking of instruments down the hall. Her hair stood on end. She tip-toed further into the clinic, but didn't see anybody.

She checked the exam rooms, but found nothing else out of the ordinary. *Footsteps.* She whirled around.

Must be my imagination.

She was nerve-wracked, this much she knew about her state of mind.

Calm down.

Callista marched to the back of the building with all the aplomb she could muster. A car was parked on the back road that she hadn't noticed before. She scanned the whole area, up and down the empty streets. Maybe she *had* seen the car before.

Calm down.

She tried to unlock the basement door. It took her even longer than the front door. She put her hand on the door and breathed slowly. She tried the lock again. Still, her hands shook too much to get the key in. She cried out, then hit the door with her fist. Finally, with a steady, frustrated hand, she slid the key onto the lock and jerked it open.

The lab was situated just as she had left it. She went to the back corner of the basement, behind a particularly long work counter, and knelt down to unlock her safe. She was so *angry*. It seemed as though she finally had gotten what she wanted, only to have it all taken from her. She just kept thinking over and over about seeing Edward as a corpse. She gripped the safe. *Edward*.

She grabbed the cash and her passport.

Footsteps.

They were clear and unmistakable. Not her imagination.

She slowly rose, until she could see him over the countertop.

48

Edward ran. He had to escape that thunder of feet.

He reached the doorway of the temple and cracked the nose of one of the guards with the butt of his palm. He moved too fast for either opponent to react.

The guard jerked back. Edward wrenched the guard's staff from his hand. It was a hunting staff, a heavy, bludgeoning weapon. It was weighted carefully, fast and strong.

Edward lashed out twice with the stick. Both guards dropped. Edward had simply chosen a path for his weapon that neither Onge had a chance to block.

He turned around. Forty armed Onge were charging the temple. They saw him drop the guards.

Edward tossed the stick down and started running again. He could outpace them.

At the jungle's edge, near the trading route, Edward spotted a trail. It would serve his purposes, helping him to transform the mob into a more manageable line.

The path snaked him through the jungle. The pounding feet of the Onge drew closer. As the path curved more and more intricately, he began to doubt his choice. He heard some tribesmen up ahead taking the more direct route through the brush.

One leaped out from the foliage ahead of him, spear in hand. Without breaking stride, Edward sidestepped the Onge's weapon and buried his elbow into the native's face. The Onge just dropped, and Edward swiped his spear with a spin move.

Edward saw two more Onge through the foliage on his right, closing in on him through the woods. He kept running. One stopped to throw a spear. Edward ducked it and rolled, relentless forcing his body ahead. The second tried to tackle him. He spun around him, whacking him on the back of the head with the spear handle without giving up his pace. Edward sensed he was losing those Onge that were on the path. He didn't see any more in the woods.

After several minutes of all-out sprinting, Edward reached a clearing. Fifteen cars were parked in a semicircle, all facing a newly cut path which could fit a car one way. *Probably leads to the road.* Several muddy divets in the clearing marked where cars had once taken up the semicircle. It seemed a few vehicles had peeled out in a hurry.

One thin Onge stood stunned and unarmed amidst the cars, gaping at the white man.

Edward stopped and let his eyes rest on each vehicle for a moment. He chose the Jeep far to the right. It was bright orange, but he wasn't picking it for its looks. The key was already in the ignition, as he suspected. He cranked it up. He glanced over at the Onge. He had backed even further from Edward.

The rest of the tribe, however, was starting to reach the clearing. Edward threw the Jeep into gear and kicked it out to the path. He heard the Onge rev up cars behind him.

The four-wheel drive let Edward really tear up the muddy path and hang the curves without sliding. The Jeep bounced over huge holes in the road and kept right on rolling. Finally, Edward reached a flat part of the jungle, and it seemed that about a kilometer down the path he could see the road, or at least a clearing. He stood and looked over his muddy windshield. *Definitely the road.*

A red car pulled onto the path from the road. It was directly in his way, moving slowly toward him.

Edward stood up again. He saw the car was low to the ground, some sort of sports car, and it definitely didn't seem to be made for the rough jungle terrain.

Edward glanced behind him. He could hear a few of the vehicles pursuing him, but none were in sight. He was definitely outpacing them. Of course, a road race in his Jeep would be a different story. The rain had stopped, and he knew it would only be the matter of an hour or so before the road dried up. His Jeep would be a disadvantage, then. They'd catch him in a race to Lisbaad.

He focused on this vehicle ahead. *First things first.* Unless the path unexpectedly widened, there was no way around the red car. He'd either have to try to go over it or seize it. Edward started being able to see its occupants.

The driver was definitely Onge. A white man with slick black hair sat in the passenger seat.

The car was a Corvette.

49

Dr. James Seacrest's head hurt. His wrists ached and itched. The sunlight burned his eyes, and he had to make quite an effort to open them. He felt ill, and the bull-like jostling helped little.

When his eyes adjusted, he screamed. He also tried to throw his arms up, but he couldn't manage it past the ropes which bound his wrists.

A huge bright orange Jeep hurtled directly at him and his car. He wasn't driving his car. Rather, it was being steered by a dark-skinned man in a loin-cloth. He looked dirty. He shouldn't be sitting in the Corvette dirty like that.

James did a double-take on the dark-skinned man before he remembered what had happened. His head started hurting worse. That Jeep didn't look like it was stopping. The dark man threw himself out of the Corvette. James felt neglected as a hostage.

The Jeep skidded to a stop on all four tires, fishtailing out. It stopped just before impact.

A crazy white man in priest robes leaped out of the Jeep and jumped the native.

James tried to rub his head. It was all so much to take in. He couldn't rub his head because of the damn rope.

The white man hit the driver in the face and the stomach, but the native recovered quickly by rolling with the punches. He counter-attacked with fists and elbows. The white man twisted to the side in response, bracing himself on James's precious Corvette to land a kick. The native swept back to dodge it, and the white man, still spinning, planted a high kick onto the native's chest.

Amazingly, the native was pushed back, but did not fall. He didn't even seem shaken.

James heard the roaring of engines. Far down the path, he saw cars and trucks approaching single file.

The native charged the priest. The priest sidestepped him again, but this time the native came at him with a fist he couldn't dodge. The white man took it straight to the gut. James was shocked to see it didn't even seem to wind the man.

The native hesitated and muttered something in a foreign tongue. He must have been shocked, too. He lunged again at the white man.

The priest's back was to James. He was only a meter away from the Corvette. The priest dodged the native's fist, then grappled him by the hair and arm and sent his head crashing into the side of the Corvette. James felt the sickening thud reverberate through the precious car. He hoped it didn't mess up the paint job. A dent was easier than a paint chip.

The native's head didn't jerk back like it was supposed to when he hit the car. Instead, he just dropped.

The lead pursuit cars skidded to a stop behind the parked Jeep. More dark men poured out of their vehicles before they had even stopped moving. The priest jumped into James's Corvette and shifted into reverse. He was using mirrors to keep to the path, launching back up the trail. James eyed the speedometer. It only read zero.

The natives were tilting the Jeep. They were rolling it off the path so they could get through.

"Hello," said the strange white man.

"Uhm, hello." James debated which driver he liked better.

"Dr. Seacrest, I presume?" asked the priest.

James wanted to scratch his head. He made up for it by squinting. "Yes, I'm Dr. Seacrest. And you are?"

"Edward Styles." Styles extended his hand to shake and then put it back onto the seat when he saw James wouldn't be able to reciprocate.

"Father Edward Styles?" asked James.

Styles scowled. "Just Edward Styles will do fine."

"All right, Edward Styles. Mind untying me?" asked James.

"In a minute. Got my hands full right now." The cars in pursuit loomed larger in their vision. Styles revved the engine.

"If you push it too much it'll…" James started to say. The car suddenly shook and jerked sideways. "…bottom out," he finished.

Styles kept the car zooming. Five cars chased after them, at least twenty men, all less than a hundred meters away.

"Oh, God," said James. One of the natives leaned out of the lead SUV with a shotgun and trained it on the Corvette.

"About fifty meters away," shouted Edward over the high whine of the engine in reverse. "We're okay," said Styles. "You don't have a gun, do you?"

James braced through another jolt from the road. "Under the seat," answered James.

"What seat?"

"My seat," said James. Edward sighed.

"Can't reach it."

"Me either."

"Duck," said Edward matter-of-factly.

"Beg pardon?" asked James. He wished he'd heard more clearly, because the next moment his head was between his legs, forcefully shoved there by Edward's hand.

The shotgun sounded like a thunderclap. The tinkling of shattered glass rode the echo of the shot.

James felt hot glass on his neck and cried out. Edward did not react. James jerked his head up and saw that his windshield was shattered.

"Stay down!" shouted Edward. He shoved James down again. This time the shot flew high.

James looked up again careful. James had been in some tough scrapes before, but never had this much harmful intent leveled at him in one sitting. *They're literally trying to kill my arse with a shotgun!*

The SUV was only twenty meters away. James glanced back and saw they were only a hundred meters from the road.

"DUCK! DUCK!" screamed Edward. This time James reacted quickly enough. He saw a puff of upholstery and interior where Edward's head had been situated only a moment before. "Stay down!" shouted Edward. "Just stay down."

Edward was staying down, too. "How are you driving the car?" asked James. Edward ignored him. "Styles? What's going on? Don't you need to see the road?"

Edward had closed his eyes.

The car revved faster.

"Oh God!" shouted James. He envisioned his Corvette wrapped around a tree. A huge bump jostled him down to the floorboard. He could only watch Edward, now, with his closed eyes.

Edward jerked the steering wheel. They bumped over a small tree. They were on the road. Edward rocketed up into his seat and jammed the accelerator all the way down to the floor. They rocketed down the paved highway.

James thanked God for a miracle and cursed the priest.

50

Tomy finally reached the temple. He collapsed at the feet of his master. He had run in the lightness faster and longer than any Onge had ever run in their oral history. His body was shaking. He had thought that if he had run fast enough, he could warn his master about the white man

It was obvious as he ran through the village that he had arrived too late. The whole place was in uproar. No warrior was to be found. The women and children were running here and there, collecting their possession. Everyone was talking, jabbering to one another, not making sense. "It is time… we are traveling…the white man…I hope they get him…Manassa…the temple…Manassa." He'd only heard them in passing. He had but one goal - to relay his information to his lord.

"The white man," wheezed Tomy, unable to even look up at his god.

"He has come and gone," said Manassa. Tomy could hear the anger riding under Manassa's tone. The god yanked Tomy up to his feet. "He came without you warning me, messenger! He came and surprised me and now knows of our plans. He is a traitor of the worst degree, that white man, and you let him beat you!" Manassa's face was beat red. He slapped Tomy, who collapsed on the ground.

Tomy groaned.

"You were weak, messenger! I know you had a moment of weakness, where you acted as a child, and he got the best of you." He was down in Tomy's ear.

Tomy's terrible sin flashed in his mind. "I got too close…" groaned Tomy.

"What?!" yelled Manassa.

"I…I got too close on the porch," he mumbled. "I was watching the house, and watching them, and they started kissing. I was thinking about a girl…I got too close…he saw me. I didn't think he'd see me." Tomy sobbed his confession to the ground.

Manassa kicked him. "Get up! Get up, fool!" He kicked him again. Tomy just rolled over.

The living god knelt down over him, menacing just inches from his face.

"Listen to me, Tomy. Tomy, you are dead. When you stand up, Tomy is dead. Tomy will never be any more. Tomy is just a child, an embarrassment to our race. You will kill him, now. And when you arise, only Tome will rise. As Mahanta died, and Manassa rose, so it will be with you, Tome. Tome, 'word,' the word of your living god. Now rise up, and leave Tomy dead in the dirt."

Tomy forced himself up on shaky legs. He dried his tears. He had failed his master utterly. He did what was asked. He let Tomy die inside of himself. It was a quick and easy thing in the half consciousness of exhaustion. He would be only what his living god would need of him now. *Tome.*

Manassa pulled out a vial from beneath his throne and emptied its contents into Tome's mouth. He was giving him the lightness again. He knew the boy had just used the lightness to get here. He did not care. There were penalties for failure.

"I will tell you this once. We are leaving now. There is no time. The white man could ruin everything. Go now to Lisbaad and raid Liang's mansion. Then come to the launch point. Bring everyone. Evacuate Lisbaad."

"There is a woman," said Tome. "A doctor. The white man worked with her in Lisbaad before he saw…Tomy." he said, hesitatingly.

"You have her?" asked Manassa. Tome nodded. "Then bring her along with you."

"What about the white man?"

"There's no need to find him. He'll find us. We must only be ready. Be sure everyone is on the highest alert. We must move NOW," said Manassa.

Tome felt the effects of the lightness surge over him. "Yes, master. Thank you for your forgiveness."

"There is no forgiveness, Tome. There is only living, and on the other side, death. Now, go."

51

"Callista," said the priest. "What happened to her?"

"Callista?" asked James vaguely. "Callista...who..."

"We're on the same side, Seacrest, so just tell me what's up."

"I'm not too sure of that. I'm still tied up."

Styles slammed the brakes. He did a rough job of untying James and then started driving again.

James rubbed his wrists. "I don't know what happened to Callista. How do you know Callista?"

"An old friend," said Styles cryptically.

"Wait a moment. You must be *him*." Seacrest laughed. "Am I right? You're *him*!"

"What do you mean?"

"Funny that you're American. I would have taken her to be one who fancies the foreigners and not the down home cooking. Though that was why she had started falling for me."

"Falling for you?" asked Styles.

"She must like the accent...Don't worry about it, old boy. Now she's got the real deal." James patted Styles on the back humorlessly.

"So when's the last time you've seen Callista?"

Old boy's got a one-track mind. Kind of like his girl. "Last week. I brought her flowers."

"She didn't make contact with you today?"

"No, no contact. She didn't even say hi."

Styles taxed the engine further. The Corvette started catching air over little bumps in the road. James didn't like it but wasn't going to say anything.

"Mind filling me in on what the hell's going on?" asked James.

"You first. How'd you end up here?"

James took a moment to collect his thoughts.

"Listen," said Styles, more softly. "I'm only interested in protecting Callista. I'm afraid she's been abducted just like you were. So the more you can tell me the better. I promise I'll fill you in, too. I just need to know what's happening. When were you abducted?"

"About three in the afternoon yesterday. I had just shut down my clinic and was on my way home when I was stopped in the middle of the road."

"What happened?"

"They were natives, with no shirt, just loincloths, guns and clubs."

"Onge."

"Is that what you call them?"

"Yes, Onge."

"Well, these Onge were parked in the middle of the road. When I stopped one of them clubbed me over the head a couple times. When I woke up they made me take them to my house. At first they didn't speak any English. One was reading a book, though, and somehow learned pretty quick. Amazing, actually, sort of fightening. Wanted to know if I knew anything about pharmacology."

"What did you say?"

"I just acted like I still didn't understand them. It was freaking me out, really, watching some guy in a loincloth learn English in half an hour."

The priest nodded understandingly. He seemed to know what James was talking about.

James continued. "Even though he was speaking some English, he kept saying this word."

"What was the word?"

"Lay-yek-tah?"

"*Lleychta?*" Styles asked, putting the emphasis on the first and last syllables.

"Yes, that's it. That's it exactly." James snapped his fingers. "That's just how they said it! What does it mean?"

"You've been in this sort of situation before, haven't you?" asked Styles.

"What do you mean?"

"I mean this whole life and death thing. You're a bit chipper for having just been kidnapped, rescued and now on the run from a band of vengeful Onge."

James shrugged. The priest was right but James really didn't want to get into it. "What's the word mean?"

"It means nectar," said Styles.

"Nectar…nectar…hmm…" reflected James. "Ahm…What do you suppose that means?"

Styles winced. The car skidded and Styles slowed it down.

"You okay?" asked James.

"Fine. We're well enough ahead now," said Styles. He didn't look fine, though. He looked a bit green and was rubbing his head.

The road took them into lower terrain. Mud covered portions of the road. The sun was rising, and James hoped it dried things out. James leaned over to check the gas dial. The car still had a quarter tank, more than enough to get them back to Lisbaad.

"Thanks for bailing me out, there," said James.

"No problem," said Styles. "Another question for you."

"Shoot."

"How far is your house from Callista's?"

"Directly across the street," said James.

"And you haven't seen her in a week?" asked Styles.

"I think she's been avoiding me. Like I said, starting to fall for me."

Styles didn't comment. "When did you leave your house?"

"I suppose around midnight," said James.

"Did you see any Onge at Callista's house?"

"No, I don't believe."

"Anything suspicious? Are you sure? Any cars in the driveway, anything out of place, any Onge coming from her house?"

James looked over that wild night through his mind's eye. "No, no, I don't think so. Ahm…no. Nothing like that. They were at my house. Only mine."

"All right," said Edward.

"Do you know why I was abducted?" asked James.

Edward nodded. "At least, I have some idea," said Edward.

"Well, all right, I answered your questions…"

"Right," said Edward. The priest hesitated for a moment before he started his explanation. Just that little pause told James's experienced ear that he wasn't going to get the whole truth. "The 'nectar' is what you could call a designer drug," said Edward. "A sort of an upper. The Onge have a new young leadership that's trying to export is to the mainland, but right now it's got a nasty kick that makes it unsalable. I'd assume that they were going to use you to try to fix it."

"Why me?" asked James.

"No idea. Ask yourself what might lead them to you in particular. There are a few other doctors on the island, no?" Edward asked.

Liang. I'll never get away from that bastard. Especially while I'm stuck on this damn island. James shrugged again noncommittally. "Maybe it was just bad luck," said James. "I seem to be running long on that."

"Maybe so," said Edward.

"So what's your gig?" asked James.

"Hmm?"

"How come you're kicking 'Onge' ass left and right?"

"Excuse me?"

"Well, you know…"

"Just bad luck, I guess." The priest smiled a bit too knowingly. He could tell that James was not satisfied with that answer. "Actually I was the missionary assigned to that tribe. They tried to get me to do what they were 'recruiting' you for."

"And what's Callista got to do with all this?" James smelled a rat, but he tried to keep his eyes from slanting in suspicion. *This priest is in the drug game. I don't care what he tells me.* James knew bishops, politicians and superstars all in the drug game. A priest was no surprise to him.

Edward hesitated. "I escaped a few nights ago. I ran into Callista by accident. Then I discovered that I'd been spotted, that the Onge had seen me with her. I told her to go hide somewhere she felt safe – which she said was with you. I came back to the Onge village to try to reason with the leader of the tribe. He had been my pupil for a time and I stupidly thought I could change his mind. I almost got captured again in the process."

James nodded. He wasn't convinced, but would act like he was.

"So now I don't know where Callista is because you're sitting in this car," said Edward.

"What's your plan?" James asked.

"Find Callista. Get off this island."

"Aren't you a member of some order of priests or something? Couldn't your church help you?"

Edward hesitated again. "Dr. Seacrest, this may or may not be a surprise to you, but that option is not open to me, if you know what I mean."

Paydirt. At least he's an honest crook. If it were me I wouldn't tell the truth. As a matter of fact, I won't.

"I do," said James.

The reached another hilltop. James could see Lisbaad through the hole that used to be his windshield.

"You don't mind if I bail when we get home?" asked James.

"I don't mind. Wouldn't advise it, though," said Edward.

"Do elaborate."

"Thing is, unless you're getting off this island, they'll get you again."

"What makes you so sure?" asked James.

Edward shrugged. "Educated guess."

"On your word as a priest?"

"For whatever that's worth," said Edward.

I'm starting to like this guy.

"I want to get off this island, anyway," said James. "But I think I'll need some help in that department."

"You help me find Cali, I'll do what I can to help you."

"Who?" asked James.

"Callista, sorry."

"What makes you think I'll be so helpful?"

"You're a crook," said Edward. "Crooks are always helpful."

James just stared at the priest for a moment. He couldn't help but laugh. "It takes one to know one, Edward. Takes one to know one." He laughed again.

Edward shrugged.

52

Edward and James reached the neighborhood. Edward had never seen it in the daylight.

The street was a jumble of houses. Obviously foreigners of many different backgrounds and nationalities occupied this small territory carved out of the edge of Lisbaad. It had no rhyme or reason. Edward was sure the words "building" and "code" had never been uttered together on the island. Still, this neighborhood comprised the "finest" residences of Lisbaad - meaning they weren't ancient piles of firewood.

Edward resisted the urge to barrel down the street, launch out of the car in yet another trance, kick down Cali's door, wipe out Onge by the cartload with his trance fighting, and carry her off into the sunset. Reality was a factor he could not ignore. Physically, he was exhausted. Trance or no trance, he could only direct his body to do what his body was already capable of. With no sleep and after having gone through what amounted to a combination marathon/boxing match, he felt he could at any minute blink his eyes and wake up two days later. The after pain only made it worse.

What was more, he had no exit strategy. There was no plan once he reached Callista. He hoped she had some ideas. Maybe this crook Seacrest could help. He'd managed to subtly convince Seacrest that he was criminal; hopefully that would increase the doctor's willingness to trust and help him.

Edward had no idea what the Onge's strength and position was inside Lisbaad, or even inside the neighborhood. He didn't even know if Cali was home. It was pointless to risk death fighting a troop of hunter-killers only to not even find Cali. Stealth was his best option at the present.

"Is there a back road?" asked Edward.

"There is behind my house. Not behind Callista's," said Seacrest.

Edward didn't like Seacrest using her first name.

"Show me," said Edward. The doctor pointed the way. Edward puttered the car up the road, idling as much as possible. The roar of a Corvette engine would have been too much of a tip for whatever Onge were stationed inside the houses. "Tell me when we're a few houses away."

"Stop, then," said Seacrest. "We already are."

"Are they home?" asked Edward, pointing to a nearby house.

"No, not 'til 5:00 or so," answered the doctor. Edward pulled up into the driveway. He parked and pulled out the key. "I wouldn't run," said the doctor. Edward smiled at him.

I know you wouldn't. I have the key.

"Not just because you have the key," said Seacrest. "As a matter of fact, a key wouldn't be much of a barrier for me. But I want off this island. I really do. And Callista is a friend of mine. I wouldn't play a part in her coming to any harm."

Edward's tired mind couldn't help but contemplate whether Seacrest had ever managed to pick up Callista in his red '95 Corvette. He was suddenly very happy to see it riddled with shotgun pellets.

Edward acknowledged Seacrest with a nod as he stepped out of the car. He kept the key in his pocket. "Stay here, then, will you? I'm just going to go see what's happening. I'll be back soon."

Edward's legs were killing him. He'd never moved so much in his life. His whole body was dragging. Somehow Earth's gravity had doubled overnight. Again he fought the temptation to pop another t-pill. He only had forty-two left. They might be the last forty-two he would see in a while.

Moreover, he felt he should be cautious. He played with something he still did not even vaguely understand. Its effects begged many questions. In a way, he felt like the child who after his tenth time watching the thrilling adventure movie began to wonder how the film was shot.

In the minute alone as he crept from house to house, he finally had time to think. *What's Mahanta's next move? Stop reacting and start ACTING.*

And stop calling him Mahanta. He's Manassa through and through. He's enemy.

Mannassa will protect the substance first and foremost. He'll guard the sap from me. That's foremost on his mind. Probably he has all the plants mobile by now, without my knowledge.

Edward picked over the situation – the cars, the "lightness", what Manassa told him about his plans.

He'll make the big move soon. Maybe tonight. He won't risk anything after our confrontation. He's got to assume I'm bringing in the Jesuits. He can't take any risks.

I'd never bring the Jesuits into this.

Edward looked at his chances. Trance or no, his gut betrayed him. *Manassa will win.* He would have to find some way to change that, but Mahanta had everything in his favor - the initiative, the resources, his own personal army.

He toyed again with getting help from the Jesuits. They *would* help him… but there goes his freedom…and who knew what General Pizo would do with the drug.

That was idiotic to ask Manassa to destroy the substance. There will be no tricking him, now. He knows what I intend. He can predict me. Edward had always had a talent for berating himself with the brilliant clarity of his own hindsight.

He watched Cali's house from the neighbor's, but saw nothing amiss. No lights were on.

Edward crept back around to the other side of the house to spy on Dr. Seacrest's domicile. It looked to be a combination between an Asian garden and a log cabin. No motion there, either. No lights.

Think. Think. Think. Something was bugging him. He wished he was in trance. *Something obvious. Damn it!* Edward closed his eyes and breathed. He forced the exhaustion out of his body. He forced his attention to the matter at hand. Now that he'd done it in trance, he at least knew what the state felt like. He could approximate it.

Clarity wavered in and out of his consciousness. As soon as he would turn his attention on the houses, the exhaustion would work back in on him. He pushed it out again. He decided most firmly that it was gone. *The houses. The houses. The lights.* The lights were a subtle point in the daylight, but they told him what he needed to know.

53

The Sri Lankan posted at the heavy iron gate of the Liang estate pulled his legs off the control board.

Four cars were barreling over the horizon, directly toward him. He pulled up his binoculars. They were a mangy hodge-podge of vehicles - an SUV, two sedans and a Bug all covered in mud and grime. He saw some dark tribesmen leaning out the windows of the vehicles. One native peered back at him with his own set of binoculars.

The guard pulled his gun out its holster and radioed for help.

"I've got four unidentified vehicles coming at high speed to the gate. Do you hear me? Do you hear me?" He was panicked. They were closing the gap quickly. In less than a minute they would be upon him.

The captain of security's voice crackled back over the radio. "Roger that. We're sounding the alert and manning up. Hold your position. Are they armed?"

The guard checked his binoculars again.

"Can't tell. Just see some guys leaning out of the windows."

"What are they?" asked the captain over the radio receiver. "Cartel, you think?"

"They look like natives, sir. Almost look like blacks." He felt exposed. It would take the security force a minute to get up there. Dozens of Liang's soldiers manned the estate, all armed to the teeth, but they didn't do him a bit of good while they were at the mansion.

He heard the telltale clicking noise of a gun behind his head. He started to jerk around.

"Don't move," said an insistent voice in Tamil. The cold metal against the back of his head reinforced the mysterious assailer's words. *How did he get in the gatehouse?*

The cars were only a few hundred meters away.

"Open the gate. Now." It was a young voice. The gatekeeper did not move. "Now!" He tripped forward as the metal was shoved violently into his head.

The gatekeeper fumbled with the controls. His vision was blurry from the blow. The cars kept flying towards the gate. Finally, he got the gate to start opening. "Thank you. Now step away."

The cars didn't even slow down for the gate to fully open. The first zipped through the gate, scraping both of its sides on the iron and knocking off its side mirrors. The other cars were following.

The gatekeeper didn't hear the shot that ended his life.

54

Tome got into the Bug. It had skidded to a stop at the gate, and one of his warriors had opened its passenger door for him. He slammed the door and shouted, "Go!" He could already hear gunfire in the distance, near the brick mansion.

The young man was on his third lightness in a day. He knew he might die from the after-pain. He did not care. That might have been a concern of Tomy but not of Tome. It was what must be done. No one else could be trusted to get the money and the guns.

The top of Liang's house was crenelated. Automatic weapons were manned at each corner and firing wildly at the Onge vehicles.

Tome watched as two of his Onge leaned out of the front car windows. Each fired a few shots with their rifles. The two machine gunners atop the turrets dropped and their guns fell silent. The Onge reached the house. A flatbed full of Liang's guards were pulling out from the back. The Onge fanning out of the vehicles shot it to pieces before the guards even had time to fire back. One bullet dropped each man, in just the way that Tome's men had been trained. *Efficiency.* Their assault had come too fast for even the hardened criminals and ex-military under Liang to make a stand.

The power of the nectar.

His Onge warriors ran one of the cars through the front door of the estate. It was an iron door, but it could not stop an SUV. They were in.

Tome followed behind with gun in hand. His job was the safe. It turned out being in the music room, and quite obvious. There was a guard he had to drop, which was his first tip-off.

The floor sounded different near the grand piano. Tome shoved it into the middle of the room and flipped away the throw rug. One of the floorboards beneath had a recessed handle. He pulled it, revealing a passage below. He checked his gun. He was sure there would be a few more surprises before he got the cash.

Liang wasn't home, but his hideout reserves would be down there. It would be quite a sum, all they needed to set up shop in Sri Lanka.

55

Cali's house had several lights on when Edward first saw it. She had left them on during the day while she was at work, probably as a security measure. And at Seacrest's, Edward remembered the same.

Edward tossed this around in his mind. Cali may have turned the lights off at her house before she left, but the only people that could have changed Seacrest's lights were the Onge.

The Onge are definitely still there. No tribesman would have bothered to switch a light off to save electricity. There were many tactical reasons for it to look like no one's home. Chief among them: *the fact that someone's home.*

Edward grasped for something else he could learn from what he'd already learned. He wished he could discern Cali's situation. It seemed that if only he were in the trance, some telltale clue would present itself.

He wanted God to tap him on the shoulder and whisper in his ear, "Cali's in Seacrest's house, in the third room to the right. You can get in through the side window and save her."

He doubted there would be any divine intervention today. He'd have to use his logic, despite his weariness. He backtracked several houses and then crossed the street to Cali's row.

Now that he knew the disposition of Seacrest's residence, he needed to know what was happening at Cali's. He found an empty driveway and followed it all the way back, hopping a fence into the same jungle area where he'd chased Tomy the night before.

He leaned out of the foliage see through the windows facing Cali's back yard. The glare kept him from seeing all the way inside. There didn't seem to be any motion, however. Outside, he saw no signs of activity: no cars, no footprints. The whole neighborhood felt abnormally still. Edward checked the sun. It would be many more hours before the workaday crowd started making its way back to this community.

Edward gripped the t-pill bottle in his pocket, then released it. *It would be a lot easier.* His eyes felt droopy despite the adrenaline flush in his veins. He maneuvered behind the tree closest to Cali's back door, then calmly walked up to the house. He kept his eyes peeled for motion in the window but saw nothing. He tried the door handle; it was unlocked.

He hadn't expected that. The door swung open easily and quietly. Edward froze. The doorknob slammed into the wall. He listened for a reaction, but heard nothing.

Edward stepped inside and closed the door behind him. He resisted the automatic impulse to rub his feet clean on the mat and walked light-footedly to the kitchen. He'd never been able to walk quietly, before, but he poured his attention into his feet, tweaking their position and the shifting of his weight until no sound came from his steps. Cat-like, he reached the opening of the living area and leaned his head around the corner. He positioned his body so that he could respond to an assault at any moment and quickly gain the initiative.

The living room was empty. Edward walked in. He was starting to relax. No one seemed to be here.

He looked out the window to the front yard of Seacrest's residence. The house's front door swung open. Edward dodged behind the curtains. He didn't want to take any chances of being spotted.

Edward peered out as four dark men, two in casual tourist clothing and two in suits, stepped out of Seacrest's front door. One of them had a paper in his hand. One toted a suitcase. The two in suits carried briefcases. They were obviously Onge. At least, that fact was obvious to Edward. *Probably not to anyone else, though.* He'd been right about some of Manassa's plot. That fact was reassuring, although it felt akin to being able to predict the path of a boulder but not being able to step away.

The group entered a black sedan parked on the roadside and pulled away.

Edward started in the direction of the back door but stopped himself.

Can't just leave. Got to see if Cali left me any clues.

Got to rest. *My mind just isn't functioning.*

He made a quick but thorough check of the house. He was glad he did. In the nightstand drawer, written in Cali's hand in French: "Corvette had company. I have patients to tend to under the clinic. -C."

The hope pushed an elation through Edward's body that drowned out the exhaustion. Edward stuffed the letter in his pocket and sprinted out of the house back to the Corvette.

Seacrest wasn't there.

56

"We will go soon to the sea," said Nockwe to his wife Bri'ley'na. "By the evening we'll be leaving. Are the children ready?"

"They are," she said. She called for them. "Children?"

They ran outside of the house to join their parents. They had their packs. Nockwe took time to inspect his first sons and daughters. There were four, the oldest of them only six years old. Bri'ley'na had given birth to him when she was only sixteen. He was the strongest, a born leader. Nockwe was very proud of him. The one he loved the most, however, was his younger son. He was almost five, and had been sickly most his life. He was the most loving of his children.

Nockwe had been blessed by the unseen god with four children from his wife's four pregnancies. Looking at them lined up before him, shortest to tallest, he could not help but smile. Even amongst the turmoil, there was some small joy to be found.

"How are my warriors?" asked Nockwe.

They shouted in unison, *"Tendo!"* *Ready.*

He knelt down in front of them. "My children, Manassa will soon muster the tribe and begin the march. It is a great day for our tribe. We will leave our homeland, but create a new home. I will be very busy with matters of the tribe, so you must be strong and stay close to your mother and do whatever she asks. No matter what happens, follow the directions of your mother."

"Yes, father," they said. "Okay. Okay. Yes, father."

"Good." He stood up and turned away from them for a moment. There were tears in his eyes. *Why?* He wiped them away and walked into the hut to gather his own pack. *It is a great day.*

Bri followed him. "Nockwe," he heard her say. "What is happening?"

"The move. It is unexpected." He looked up at her. His bluff didn't work. She just looked at him knowingly with her hand to her hip. "Glis. I killed him."

"We already discussed this, Nockwe. He was a murderer. You did justice." She held his hand and guided him to sit with her on their pallet.

"There is something I didn't tell you. It is why I can't let it go. There is something that plays in my mind again and again."

"Tell me."

I must. It won't stop unless I do so. "Just before I killed him, the shock on his face…" He paused to gather his words. He shifted her hands back and forth in his. He looked up. "It was the shock and the disappointment of an innocent man."

He looked into her eyes. There was no redemption there. He wouldn't find it there, he knew, but he had hoped somehow just by saying it the ghost would leave him. Her eyes were more like mirrors, no matter how much she might want to soothe him.

"I have tried to deny it to myself," he said, "but I know I brought justice to an innocent. I was wrong. Manassa was wrong. It must have been an honest challenge, and I slit his throat."

"You did what you thought best for the tribe."

"Perhaps I can't see that, anymore," said Nockwe.

She took his face in her hands and made him look at her. "Nockwe. All you see is the tribe. If you cannot see it anymore, there is someone blinding you. Look around you," she said. She touched his chest. "Look into your heart. You are the eyes, the ears, the heart, the head of this tribe. You are its chieftain. If you do not see, do not hear, do not feel, do not think, your tribe is dead."

He considered her words. She had a terrible habit of saying the right thing at exactly the right time. He restrained a smile and shot up out of his sitting position.

"Where are you going?" she asked.

"I am going to watch, to hear, to feel, to think. I love you," said Nockwe.

"I love you, too," said Bri'ley'na.

He walked back to kiss her, then ran to the temple.

57

"Seacrest!" muttered Edward under his breath. He pulled the car out of the driveway and idled it in the direction of the doctor's house. He would give the doctor sixty seconds before he pulled off.

He could see the back of Seacrest's house. It was all windows. Light flashed inside as a gun cracked. One of the windowpanes shattered.

Seacrest burst through the broken window. He held a briefcase in one hand and a gun in the other. He twisted his body backwards in a dead run so he could shoot as he fled.

"Seacrest!" shouted Edward.

An Onge crawled through the window after him, but ducked when Seacrest fired. The doctor was a lousy aim.

"Go! Go! " shouted Seacrest as he leapt into the back seat of the car. Edward kindly waited until most of Seacrest's body parts were in the vehicle before roaring away toward the city.

"What the hell is that?" Edward shouted above the over-revved engine.

"My briefcase," said Seacrest. The doctor gasped. "Oh, mother of God, Virgin Mary, Jesus Christ of Latter Day Saints…"

"I hope you're praying," said Edward sharply.

"I hope I am, too, *father*," said Seacrest. Edward took his eyes off the road long enough to look in the passenger area behind him. Seacrest sat sideways staring into an empty briefcase.

"What was in there?" asked Edward.

It took the doctor a long time to answer. Edward made it half the way into town before getting a reply. He trained the rear view mirror on his passenger.

Seacrest had no color to his cheeks. He just kept staring down at the briefcase, as though he could will its former contents back into existence if he focused hard enough.

"Some personal effects," was Seacrest's answer at long last.

Edward slammed the brakes on the car. It skidded to a halt. He twisted around to face Seacrest. His patience was worn thin by the exhaustion and the aching. He could hardly think anymore. He had no idea how he had managed to keep on driving despite his weariness. "Listen! I'm not a cop, I'm a priest. And I'm not even a priest. I've never known you until now. After today, I will again not even know you. You have no reason to lie to me. There is no harm I can do to you with the information. But there is a great deal of harm I can do to you for not telling me what I need to know. If that briefcase is empty, then that means the Onge have what was in it. If the Onge have it, then I need to know what it is. You can tell me on friendly terms or on any terms you wish, but you've got to tell me."

If that briefcase had money, Manassa could use it to make his move. The very idea panicked Edward. Edward had expected it to take more time for Manassa to gather his resources. A sudden infusion of cash could be disastrous. He could move immediately.

Seacrest climbed into the front passenger seat. "Your Onge are wearing off on you, old boy. Drive. I'll tell you everything. No need for threats."

Edward started the car. "What was in the suitcase?"

"My insurance," said Seacrest matter-of-factly.

"Your what?" Edward's asked curtly.

"My insurance. I'll explain," said Seacrest.

"Go on." *He'd better finish before I get to the clinic.* The clinic was all Edward could think about. He had to get to the clinic basement before something happened to her.

Something already has happened to her. They have her. He somehow knew this, and yet he still had to hope and try.

270

"I am an exile, my friend."

Tell me something I don't know. "Yes?"

"I'll explain," said Seacrest.

"You've got ten minutes." *Or less.* Edward managed to keep the kph slowly climbing. He was getting more comfortable with the Corvette at high speeds.

"I'm telling you this because you need to know it to help me get off this island. But if I tell you, you've got to tell me the real reason you're at war with the Onge."

"I can't tell you why. I can tell you how. That's all you need if you can help me."

"Very well. Well, since it doesn't matter anyway. I don't have any insurance...I was a doctor in Melbourne. My practice was failing - the economy and so forth. This was more than a decade ago. A punk with a gunshot wound knocked on the back door of my clinic and collapsed in the staff lounge. I took him under treatment, sewed him up, and accepted a couple thousand bucks cash for the job. I started getting backdoor guests every week. Turned out the first kid I treated was the nephew of a very dark name in the city. A man approached me about turning my practice into a night clinic, and eliminating expenses by firing all of my staff."

"An offer you couldn't refuse?" asked Edward.

"It was an offer, mind you. But I took it. Business slowed a couple years later as this man consolidated his territory in Victoria. No turf wars meant no doctoring. They could no longer justify my fat salary, and I was getting hounded for taxes, so I took a transfer to Sri Lanka and a raise. They had started an operation out here and there was big demand for doctoring. Not to mention that Sri Lanka is more cash-friendly."

"How did you end up on this island?"

"I took too many clients. Once I set up shop in Sri Lanka, I started accepting pay from a couple allied gangs, in addition to my own clan. The local cartel got hostile with us. The main man at the cartel, Liang – well, his son was wounded near my clinic and he knew he could get help there. He was a personal friend of mine. I took him even though relations were strained.

He died in my care within minutes. There was no way to stop the bleeding. Liang blamed me, said I let his son die on purpose, and put a price on my head."

"What about your…"

"Gang? My employers?" Seacrest laughed. "Don't kid. They sought peace with Liang, and came after me, too. I exiled myself to Lisbaad."

"Why Lisbaad?"

"It was a deal we made. Liang controls practically all ships going to and from Lisbaad. He may as well own this island."

"Then why aren't you dead?"

"The deal is, I live in Lisbaad and never leave. If I leave, Liang kills me. And in return for his consideration, for allowing me to live in this cell, I don't allow certain photos of him dealing with a known CIA operative to surface amongst his cartel underbosses. My insurance."

"And your ex-employer?"

"Let's just say that certain photos of white mobsters raping heretofore missing in action yellow women of the cartel would put an end to all the profitable operations they have going here."

"Your insurance." *This is far worse than cash in Manassa's hands. Instead of a bird in the hand, he gets five thousand in the bush.* Edward prayed the Onge didn't know what he had. "How'd you get these?"

"A lot of money paid to people who didn't know what they were worth."

"Was there any money in the briefcase?" asked Edward.

"No, just the photos," he answered.

"Well, why are they so important to you? If this truce you have is already negotiated, then why does it matter whether you have them there or not?"

Edward's question struck a nerve. Seacrest screamed spontaneously, "Because I want *off this island!* That's why! I want to renegotiate. I don't like the deal, for Christ's sake." Seacrest sighed. "Sorry."

Edward waved.

"Sorry," Seacrest repeated. "Anyway, I'm miserable on this island. I'd rather be dead. My ticket out was this briefcase. Now I'll need to do plan B."

"What's plan B?"

"Get a friendly ex-priest to smuggle me out on a boat to Sri Lanka and I will in return assist him, in ways that only I can, in his odd battle with the Onge." *His underground connections. Manassa just got a lightyear forward but so did I.* "If it's drugs you're dealing with, I can help."

"You could get off this island without me," said Edward.

Seacrest shrugged. "Maybe I can, maybe I can't. I think my chances are better with your help."

"It's Callista," said Edward.

Seacrest shrugged. "I get it, she's your gal."

Edward just watched him.

"Look," said Seacrest. "She's a friend. We can talk. I don't have many friends. I've spent my life running from good guys and running from bad guys and only helping where it pays. I don't know."

"How do I know you won't start running?"

Seacrest shrugged.

I need Seacrest if they've taken Cali to the mainland. I'd have no way to find her without him.

"You could just jet when you hit the mainland, is my point. How can I trust you?" asked Edward.

Seacrest leaned forward. "What is your first name again, Styles?"

Edward was taken aback by the abrupt change in tack. "Edward," he answered

"Well, Edward, although you are pushy, and have threatened my life on two occasions in less than four hours, I can understand that you are a man on a mission - and the fact still remains that you saved my life. So both you and Callista fall under the friend category. If you help me you will not regret it, Edward."

"What kind of help do you need, exactly?"

"We can burn that bridge when we get there. Nothing too difficult. We need to get back to burning this bridge we're on right here, though, don't you think?" asked Seacrest.

Edward studied the crook's eyes. *Well, if he deserts me on the mainland I won't be any worse off.* The greatest thing he'd learned in his experience with Manassa so far: never trust a human being completely.

Except Callista. There were some things that ranked over mere survival, Manassa's philosophical drivel to the contrary. But Edward had no plans of forming a lifelong love with Seacrest. Here was a man who'd survived in the underworld. Every one of his words had ten intentions behind it. The only thing Edward could be sure of was that Seacrest would help him as long as it benefited Seacrest, regardless of whatever words might spew from his mouth to the contrary.

"Fine. I'll help you, you help me," said Edward. Seacrest put out his hand. Edward shook it.

"Styles," said Seacrest, acknowledging him with a nod. *Yes, I'll have to watch this one,* thought Edward.

Edward looked behind him. There was a car pulling over the nearest hill. It was the first one he'd seen in a while. Edward started the Corvette down the road. He could feel Callista calling for him.

58

Edward felt an awful drop in his stomach when he reached the clinic. The first thing he noticed was its front door swung wide. He braked the Corvette at the curb. Seacrest followed him as he raced inside.

Edward raced to the back door. He still held out a glimmer of hope that they hadn't found her, that somehow she was safe. He imagined that he would simply swing open the basement door and take her into his arms.

When he got to the basement door, he didn't need to swing it. It was already open.

He saw that Callista had built up quite a lab beneath her clinic. It had a great deal of equipment and he could see stores of medicine on the walls. No sign of conflict, but he knew the Onge had definitely been here. He knew because there was no Callista, even though he called for her and checked the room three times. No note, either.

The Onge had her.

Edward forced himself to play out the scenario in his mind. As tired as he was, he could still make the connections if he willed himself to think.

Manassa would value Callista because Tomy would tell him he'd seen her with Edward. He would know she was a doctor and try to use her as he planned to use Seacrest. Manassa would suspect a relationship as a matter of course. If Manassa discovered her name, however…he had all of Edward's journals.

Edward put himself in Manassa's shoes. *What does Manassa want? Manassa wants me dead. He'll do anything to kill me, at this point. I'm the only threat to him, and a thin one at that.*

Edward shook his head clear. He was too tired, and his thoughts were running together. He really needed someone to talk to, to bounce his ideas off of. He only trusted Cali for that. He'd already had to tell Seacrest too much.

"I need a safe place to rest," said Edward.

"Sure," said Seacrest. "I know just the spot."

"Can you drive?" asked Edward

"Sure."

Edward slammed the door as he got in. "Dammit!"

"We'll get her, old boy."

"Right. Any idea where they might be keeping her?"

"You think she was abducted?" asked Seacrest.

"Yes."

"Sure she's just not out on a stroll or something?"

"No, they got her, Seacrest. Got it?"

"Got it…"

"Any idea where they'd be keeping her?"

"Not a clue. You're the Onge expert. The only thing I know about them is that one of them hit me over the head. Everything else I've heard from you. But a safe place to rest, we can start there."

Edward leaned back as Seacrest drove but refused to close his eyes. In a few minutes, Seacrest pulled up by the inn Edward had used the night before.

"That's a no-go. That's only place in this town I *know* isn't safe for me."

"Come on, I know it looks rough. But it's the perfect spot." joked Seacrest. "Nobody would look for you there."

"Right. Let's go to spot number two. I need to rest." He yawned. "Wait!" Edward said. Seacrest hit the brakes. "Go! Go!" The Corvette lurched forwards again.

"Christ, man, what's your problem!?"

"The Onge, they're in the inn. The same car that was at your house, it's in the parking lot." Edward looked back. The car was empty. "Park here." He pointed out an inconspicuous side street. "Let's go scout them out." Edward led.

"Aren't you tired?"

Edward scoffed. He was practically dead. Yet what was another half hour at this point?

"What is it about this inn?" asked Seacrest.

"They know I went there my first night in town."

"When was your first night in town?"

"Two nights ago."

"Why do they know? I thought they spotted you later."

"It's complicated. Do you see them?" asked Edward.

"What do they look like?" asked Seacrest.

Obviously, he hasn't seen them. I've got to sleep. "Two are in suits, two in casual wear. All four dark, Onge. Short. The two in suits had briefcases."

"Perhaps with photographs."

"Perhaps. I doubt it, but perhaps," said Edward.

"I don't see anyone, period," said Seacrest. He was right. The streets were pretty dead. There was no activity at the inn.

"Let's wait 'til they come out. They have no reason to sleep there. They've got your place and probably a few other bases around the city," said Edward.

Seacrest looked the street up and down. "We're pretty much in the open right here in broad daylight. If they saw you, they'd recognize you?"

"Yeah."

"Why don't I keep scouting it out and you go back to the car? You can catch a nap in the event it takes more than a few minutes, and I can wake you up as soon as I see any activity here. That way they won't know we saw them."

"I want to tail them," said Edward

"I know. So do I. I want those photographs. I'd much rather the photographs than having to hide in your luggage. I could go back to plan A," said Seacrest, his eyes occasionally darting to the inn's door far on the other side of the street.

I want you to have those photographs, too. Edward weighed the factors involved. He did not trust Seacrest, but he was increasingly unable to trust himself, either. He had to rest, even if for fifteen minutes. Moreover, the doctor was right. If the Onge came out, they had a better chance of recognizing him than the doctor.

He trusted Seacrest to serve his own ends and protect what was left of his car. For these two reasons, Edward felt safe leaving the watch to him.

He dragged himself to the passenger seat of the car, leaned back, and closed his eyes. The sun was hanging overhead, but it felt like glorious night.

59

Callista had little difficulty pretending she didn't know Tamil. Their pronunciation was so bad, it was difficult to understand their questions anyway:

"Why did white man meet with you?"

"Who Edward Styles to you?"

"What know about nectar?" Maybe she didn't hear that last word correctly.

They were Onge, she presumed. Dark faces, an apparent mix of Indian and Chinese. She was bound in a rough-hewn wooden chair. She just kept squinting at them, at whoever was speaking loudest, occasionally saying, "I only speak English. Does anyone speak English?" No one had hurt her. She hoped Edward was coming. She hoped he wasn't dead. She felt he wasn't. Maybe that was just hope.

She didn't know where she was - some sort of warehouse. They'd blindfolded her when they'd brought her in. They'd carried her up two flights of stairs to get her to this room. She knew because she counted.

There was a single window that faced toward the city. The way the sun was seeping into the room, she figured that she was on the east side of Lisbaad. Her mind was making needless calculations. There were only a few that were really relevant.

First of all was that she sat bound in a barren room with a concrete floor, a torn out ceiling, and at least twenty different Onge in and out all day.

Second, they were all armed and alert. She had no hope of escape. There was only one door in the room. Who knew where that might lead. Probably past more Onge.

Third, the Onge were buying her not understanding their language.

Fourth, they hadn't hurt her yet.

Still, she felt sick. She wanted to crawl out of her skin. She didn't let on. But at any moment one of those natives could get a funny idea in his head and shoot her with his rifle. It would be all too easy. She controlled her breathing. At least she could control that. Hysteria was not an option. *At least, not yet...*

One Onge seemed to be the leader. He had a khaki hat on which made him look like a safari guide. He wore clothes as one might wear a costume; he definitely didn't seem used to them.

The native walked back into the room. He had a book in his hand, and he was quite intent on it. His gaze perturbed her. It looked as though his eyes were devouring his book, one page at a time.

Finally he dropped the book on the floor and bent down to eye level with her.

His speech was broken, pronounced horribly, but understandable. It shocked Callista. Only an hour ago, he was only able to yell at her in Tamil and five other dialects she didn't recognize. This time he spoke English, biting out each word. "I...speak...English. You... answer...my questions. I... beat you...until...you answer."

She screamed. He slapped her, then put his face just inches from hers, holding her by the collar of her shirt.

"Why...did...Edward Styles...the...white man...why he...meet you?"

60

For the last time, the tribe assembled on the holy grounds. The priests had been playing their instruments for a while, long enough to have to light the torches to fight off the dusk. Manassa ran into the clearing through the more obvious entrance, this time, giving an opportunity for his followers to scream and bow and wave as he walked up to his tree.

Manassa had hung a small rope from the lower branches of the tree. It was dyed the exact color of the bark so no one could see it. Manassa used it to run up the side of the trunk before leaping up to the branch and walking out to be seen. It looked as though he'd defied gravity. The crowd went into uproar. Manassa acknowledged them with a wave. Finally, the gongs of his priests demanded silence.

"MY PEOPLE!" shouted Manassa.

"MANASSA!" shouted the crowd. They resounded more deafeningly than ever before. He was the savior of his people. He exalted in the electricity of their fervor. *And I had been worried they wouldn't want to move.* He had elevated himself above tradition.

"YOU ARE THE CHOSEN!" he screamed, filling up the heavens with his words

"As are you, our god!" Manassa had to wait a long time before the crowd was quiet enough for him to continue.

"Hear my words, my people! Today we end a chapter in our history books, and begin anew! We are the tribe over all tribes, the greatest of nations, and we begin today a challenge that will end with our taking our seats at the right hand of the unseen god as rulers over his earth! Today, we begin our march towards our eternity - immortality, prosperity, and peace! In years to come, you will look back at this day as the day we staked our claim to inherit the Earth! Follow me, my people, to the sea!"

61

Callista gets an Onge funeral. They burn her to ashes. Her messenger walks into the jungle with her ashes in a sieve and doesn't come back until the ashes have all fallen to the earth. An hour later the messenger comes back with her head in the sieve.

Her head says, "I love you."

Edward lurched awake drenched in sweat. "Oh, God," he said. His head was wrapped under something. He was having a hard time breathing. He struggled up for air. He realized it was just a blanket over his head. He calmed down and slowly pulled it off.

He was surprised to see that it was dark outside. It wasn't just the blanket. He must have been out for hours. His body had needed the rest.

Edward noticed that the after-pain had strengthened further. It was still nowhere near when he'd been forced to stand before the tribe and proclaim himself healed, but it was far worse than any hangover he'd ever experienced.

It'll be gone once I trance again. It was a weak thought, but it was true. He would be trancing until he found Callista. He was certain of that. Even if he dropped dead from the after-pain, he did not care. He would do everything within his power to find her.

Consider it an experiment, he told himself.

Where the hell is Seacrest? Edward's faculties returned to him fully. Yes, he had needed to rest, but he had needed every moment to find her.

The dark sky sent him into a panic. Callista might be on a boat by now.

Manassa will learn who she is once he sees her. He'll use her to get to me.

283

I should have told her no. I should have left her out of this.

Edward clambered out of the car after Seacrest. He almost collided into the doctor.

"Boy, were you *out*," said Seacrest.

"Are they still in the inn?" asked Edward.

"Yeah, been in there since noon. It's eight, now. Figured they're staking you out, hoping you go there. We need them to lead us to their little hideaway, so I just took care of some business."

"What did you do?" Edward rubbed his head.

"I went in there and paid the little Chinese man a hundred bucks to go upstairs and tell those guys he saw the white man they were looking for. The white man poked his head in, I told him to say, then spooked and left in a hurry before China boy could go tell them. I think he'll do it."

"He already took the money?" asked Edward.

"Yeah, but I think he'll do it."

"Why?"

Seacrest kept his eyes on the inn. "He asked me if you were feeling better and wished you good health." Edward smiled. "There they are!" shouted Seacrest. "They're running! Hurry!" Seacrest ran to the driver's seat. He glanced at Edward before taking his seat.

The Edward waved his hand and hopped into the passenger seat. *By all means, take the wheel.* Seacrest marked time, waiting for the black sedan to drive past the alley. "Oh, God," he said after a good minute.

"What?"

"They must be heading south..." said Seacrest. Edward's head slammed back into the headrest as Seacrest floored the accelerator. The car whipped around the corner. Edward almost collided with the doctor. He had to brace himself with the dash and the seat. A horn sounded. A car swerved passed them as they picked up speed. Seacrest used the handbrake to power slide around the corner across from the inn. Far down the road, Edward saw the sedan turning right.

"There!" he shouted, pointing.

Seacrest *flew* his Corvette. Edward wished he'd had Seacrest driving the whole time. The doctor wove the car full speed through traffic and the fickle curves of the narrow road that was designed for speeds six times less than what he was pushing.

Seacrest yanked the handbrake again to whip around the next bend. Closer, now, they saw the Onge's vehicle turn left. Seacrest reduced his speed as he neared them. The Onge were driving pretty slowly. If he'd ripped around the corner he would have surely been spotted.

The doctor found a slow moving truck to lurk behind. Edward kept his eyes on the red tail lights of the sedan.

They followed for fifteen minutes to the eastern edge of town. Finally the sedan pulled up next to an empty warehouse. It seemed to have been some sort of industrial facility at one time. The Onge got out and ran under a gate that had opened for them. The gate closed. *They have radio communication, now. Moving up in the world.*

Seacrest slowly pulled his vehicle up to the hideaway. They both scanned their eyes over the building. Windows stretched across the top of the third story. A couple lights were on. Edward thought he saw movement.

"Do you see anybody? Anything?" asked Seacrest.

While the doctor was looking away at the building, Edward popped a t-pill. The trance came almost instantly. "Callista," he said, his eyes closed.

He saw her not in the present, but in memory. He broke down that flash of motion he'd seen as they pulled up, frame by frame for inspection. It was her dark brown hair, and the tip of her forehead, almost in silhouette. The features, to him, however dark, were unmistakable. *They're moving her.* There was something dark on her forehead. *Maybe blood.*

A moment ago, his mind had been a maelstrom of speculation and emotion.

Now, there was no thought at all.

"Stay in the car," said Edward. It was not a request.

62

The tribe had never moved like this. A pack of twenty might go out for the first hunt in the spring, as ritual, but nothing like this. Not in living history. The ground reverberated with their footsteps. They had heard of the militaries of old in their oral histories. This, Tinti supposed, was what this was like.

Tinti held his mother's hand as they walked. They were moving faster than he could comfortably pace. His mother kept pulling him along.

"Will we see Sala?" asked the boy. He hadn't seen his friend in several weeks.

"We will see everyone that we're supposed to see," said his mother. "It is all in Manassa's vision. We are destined for greatness."

"Where are we going?"

"To our new home." She tugged him again. "Across the sea."

"We have a home, there?"

"Our god has made everything ready for us."

"Sala!" the boy cried. He saw her at the other end of the clearing. There were a couple priests ordering men to pick up potted plants by harnesses. There were other men grabbing carts full of the plants. He'd never seen anything like them before. A couple hundred plants were lined up to be moved, much more than he could count. The priests were organizing getting them carried. The majority of the tribe just continued marching forward.

Sala was watching her mother load a cart. She ran toward Tinti. He wrenched his hand from his mother's and ran to her. "Tinti!" she shrieked, overjoyed. She was laughing and jumping up and down. "That was forever!"

"Yes, it was!" he said back. He hugged her. "You're okay?" he asked.

"Yeah," she said, running her hand through her hair. He saw her hands were roughened. Her clothes were covered with dirt and mud. She looked worn out.

"Do you want to walk with us?" asked Tinti.

Sala looked over at her mother. "I need to stay with my mother," she said. She looked disappointed.

"It's okay. I'll see you at the water. There is a big thing we're supposed to get on…a boat?"

"What's that?" asked Tinti.

"I don't know," said Sala. "But it has benches. It is a cart on the ocean. Maybe you'll sit near me?" he asked.

"Yes, if my mother approves." She smiled at him. He smiled back at her.

"Okay," he said. He ran back to his mother, who hadn't stopped her walking but kept her eyes on the ten-year-olds.

As Tinti ran he looked at the tribe. He'd never seen such strange looks on their faces. His mother had called it "hope" and "determination."

Some people looked downright scared.

The old looked very tired.

But the young did seem hopeful. All of the priests were young. Perhaps he would be a priest someday. He was young. He'd ask his mother about it.

63

Nockwe had his men begin torching the place. The village had been home for his entire living memory. The tribe never moved. An Onge never settled other lands. Home was always a thousand paces in any direction from the village center, marked by an ancient rock. The food moved, but that was why they had hunting parties. The tribe never moved.

Change. Change. Change. His mind chanted in time with his steps. He toured his village. He would have others burn it. He would not light a single straw himself. He could not bring himself to do so. And he could not get Glis's face out of his mind.

He walked to where the white man had been staying so many moons ago. Nockwe remembered his threats to the missionary, to try to keep him from witnessing Mahanta's coming of age. He wondered if things would have been different if Edward had never left that tent.

He walked to the open area of the village, where Dook had almost slain him. He remembered the white man's courage. The duel would have been the end of Nockwe's life. Nockwe knew now the white man had fought with the lightness, but he had risked his life for Nockwe still the same. The magic didn't diminish what he did.

Or perhaps he'd fought with more than the lightness...there are whispers that he moves and fights as our god. Maybe it's the same for him as it is for Mahant--. He corrected himself mentally. *Manassa. Maybe the lightness does something different to him.*

There were fires starting at the northern edge. It would only take his boys half an hour before the whole village was up in flames. They were quite efficient. They had been trained in efficiency.

Nockwe found himself at the temple. He walked inside. The throne was bare, its ornaments stripped for the erection of the secret temple on the mainland. He reflected on all his meetings with Tomy, now just Tome, and Manassa.

He walked behind the raised area with the throne. He'd only seen Manassa's quarters a few times. He wondered what the Onge god had left to burn.

His priests had taken his mattress. They'd taken his books. The furniture, Manassa's servants had left. Footprints were everywhere - there had been quite a few people in here emptying the room to prepare for the move.

A glint of metal caught Nockwe's eye. It was situated in the dirt under where the mattress had been, near the wall. Curious, he picked it up. He had nothing to do until the village became ashes.

Then there will be a lot to do.

Nockwe dusted off the metal. It was a ring of sorts. It was octagonal, fashioned of polished brass. A memory flashed to his mind. It came easily; everything about Glis was too easily remembered.

Glis stands at the front of the tribe. Nockwe and the medicine man bless his marriage with whomever he so chooses, so long as she be willing. He chooses Lila. She walks to the front of the tribe. She says she is willing. The medicine man says other words. She walks away with him.

The tribe sings the marriage song. Nockwe, watching them, sees him hand her a shiny octagon. She holds it up to the light, admiring it. It is quite a fortune, quite a find. He slips it onto her finger, in the Western way. He says something to her in her ear. She smiles and kisses his cheek.

She gives a long glance to Mahanta, who stands next to Nockwe. The newlyweds leave for their hut. The tribe sings on.

Nockwe stared at the ring.

Nockwe felt as though the trinket were wrapped tight around his neck. He didn't know how long he was stood there.

He felt heat. The temple was burning. He was tempted to throw the ring down, but instead pocketed it.

Nockwe burned far hotter than the temple. *I am a fool.*

64

James weighed his options as he watched Edward jog to the entrance of the abandoned establishment. *Is he just going to go to the front door and knock? Ask for his girl back?*

The most sane impulse James felt was to run. There was an idiotic, honorable side to him that was winning out, however. He tapped the steering wheel of the car nervously and checked the windows above for guns. *None yet.* He checked the other side of the street for guns. *None yet.*

He'd abandoned plenty of chumps in his lifetime. It would actually be quite intelligent to abandon chump #74, who apparently had a death wish.

He considered his position. It would be nothing for one of those men to pop out of the shadows and pump him and his car full of holes. On second thought, they would probably just shoot him and save the car. He'd heard of it happen enough times. He'd cleaned up the messes from plenty car chases and drive-bys. He'd tended to the wounded of both sides.

This priest is no priest. And these natives are no natives. Drugs? Guns? I don't know.

He knew what he was seeing. It was the same sort of pattern he'd played out in Melbourne. It was the same game he'd tried to play in Sri Lanka.

Was this white man one of them? Certainly things weren't as they seemed if he was just going to walk into the warehouse unarmed.

The more Edward explained to James, the more questions he was left with.

James thought about Callista. Edward had said Callista was in there. *I do care about Callista.* Maybe Edward was just playing him. How could he even know that she was in there?

The door to the building was unlocked. Edward opened it, about thirty meters away from Seacrest.

"Actually, I just need something to care about," James said aloud. It was the first genuine sentence he'd uttered in a while.

He promised himself that if anything came out of the warehouse besides Edward or Callista, he'd jet, all handshakes to the contrary.

James could no longer see Edward, but he heard gunfire. The ricochet of bullets echoed through the street. James tensed and gripped the gearshift.

More gunfire. He saw flashes of light and heard odd screams, shouts in the Onge tongue.

The struggle moved deeper into the building, muffled now but far more intense. It sounded like a full-blown war in there. The noise moved up to the second floor. More shots. *What the hell is going on?*

Surely, the priest was dead. *What the hell was he thinking?*

James eased up to the open door. The interior lighting cast a soft glow into the dark street. He kept his feet just centimeters from the pedals, ready to jam the accelerator at the slightest motion.

Let's have a see. James craned his neck to get a glance inside without having to leave the car. Two dead Onge lay just inside the door. *Jesus Christ.* He saw no sign of Edward.

James put the car in park. He fumbled in his glove box for his gun. The Onge had stolen that one. He groped under his seat. His backup was still taped there. He yanked it out and checked the street again. It was empty.

The gunshots grew sporadic and seemed to emanate from a higher point in the building. James got out of the car and scrambled to the side of the door. He poked his head around the side and got no reaction. He lowered his body and swung out into the doorway for a full view, gun at the ready.

The room was large, originally a shipment receiving area. Huge, decaying pallets full of boxes made up the pathway he had to navigate. James counted eight bodies in the room, but no Edward. All the bodies were Onge, all were armed, all but two had shots to the head.

Jesus Christ. Styles never was a priest. James had no idea what he was.

The spatter of guns ceased. The screaming stopped. James heard a car start in the distance. It seemed to be on the other side of the building.

"Here we go," muttered James. Other cars revved.

James ran back to the Corvette. He sent it roaring around the corner of the warehouse. Several cars were ripping down the road ahead. He had a feeling Callista was with them.

Edward ran out to the sidewalk with an assault rifle looped around his back. James braked as hard as he could. The car fishtailed. He almost hit Edward, but the man did not even react or move. The car stopped just inches from him. He got in. "Go," he said. "They have Callista."

James started driving. He suppressed his thousand questions. A man such as this was not asked questions. Rather, he divulged information when he wished. That was just the way it was. James had run into a few of such men in his lifetime, and had survived because he understood the nature of such relationships. He found it odd that he did not feel threatened in any way by Edward.

"Get behind them. Get closer," said Edward.

There were two sedans, then three Jeeps.

"They'll be going off-road," said Edward. "There are no highways in that direction. They're going away from port. We'll need one of those Jeeps. Get closer."

They drew near the first sedan. Edward stood up in the Corvette despite the bumps and swerves. James checked him. Somehow, Edward kept his body steady. He reacted to every motion of the car at the moment it happened, almost as though he could anticipate what bump or swerve was next. His legs and hips were like shock absorbers. James had never seen anything like it.

Edward lined up his shot and fired twice.

The two back tires of the sedan popped. The car spun out of control. The corvette zipped past. James was able to stay cool, not unused to gunfire, but this was a bit up close and personal for even him. He took care of business *after* all the shots were fired.

They travelled a long, ill-used road that ran alongside the eastern side of the city, northwest to southeast. It led to nowhere before looping back into town.

"Get behind that second one," said Edward, concentrating on the car ahead.

A man stood from inside the sedan with his head out the sunroof. He brought a rifle to bear on the Corvette and started firing. The man only got out two errant shots before Edward took him out with another bullet.

James stopped trying to figure it out. Maybe he would wake up in a minute, hopefully still alive.

Two more shots from Edward. The second sedan spun out, too.

"Duck," said Edward. This time, James heeded with no argument. He was glad he did. He heard bullets whiz directly over his head. "Clear."

James looked back. There had been several Onge in the sedan who had fired at them from the window as they passed, even as their car still spun.

James realized these Onge were strange like Edward. Their shots were fired so well they would have killed them both, even though they'd been aimed from a vehicle doing a 360 spin on two wheels. James swallowed his panic. Panic would do him no good. For now, at least, he was joined to this crazy American's hip.

"The Jeep," said Edward. James accelerated. The Onge had already started firing at them. Potshots whizzed by. "Just a little closer." They were still a hundred meters away. James closed the distance cautiously. He had no desire to have three Onge with semi-automatic rifles filling his Corvette with holes.

A bullet nicked the hood. "Dammit!" yelled James.

"I think you're entirely too emotionally attached to this vehicle," Edward deadpanned. He stood up from his seat and leveled his gun at the jeep. He emptied the clip into its gas tank. The Jeep exploded. They sped past. James watched in the rear view mirror as the surviving Onge pulled their dead and injured from the wreckage.

"My God," said Seacrest, eyes back on the road.

"Watch it," said Edward.

"I think you're entirely too emotionally attached to this God of yours," deadpanned James.

Edward glared at him, slamming the remaining clip in noisily. "I meant watch the road. This is a used clip. It only has four bullets in it."

"How do you know?" James asked. Edward didn't answer. James looked over to see why the American didn't reply.

"They're firing," said Edward matter-of-factly, pointing to the road. They'd gotten in range of the second jeep. "We'll need to go closer. I can't miss a single one of them. We're about a kilometer away from the end of the road and we'll need the jeep by then. The last jeep we'll need to track down off-road. Cali must be in it."

James swerved around a truck parked out in the lane. Edward stayed down. The shots were getting more accurate. James yelled, "How do you know how many bullets are in the clip?"

"It's simple. Each clip has thirty bullets," said Edward. James just shook his head. This priest didn't make any bloody sense.

"How much closer do you need to get?" asked James.

"Now is fine." They were still sixty meters away, quite a shot. Edward stood up and squeezed the trigger. Four bullets came out, just like he said. Three of the four men dropped. The jeep swerved. The fourth Onge in the passenger seat grabbed the wheel and got the vehicle under control. "Missed one. Pull up next to him."

Jesus Christ! James did not believe his eyes. It was only the demand of the road that kept him from trying to work out what the hell was going on.

"Come at him fast," said Edward. James brought the car around the jeep. He had no problem outpacing it.

James caught glimpse of the last jeep as he maneuvered. It was about half a kilometer ahead and had reached the curve that turned the road back into town. The jeep ignored it and ramped off-road.

How does this guy know all this? It was just as Edward had said.

When the front of the Corvette was even with the back of the Jeep, Edward launched himself with a sort of running leap from the car door. He flew through the open frame of the Jeep and jammed the Onge's head into the steering wheel with all his momentum. The jeep swerved dangerously in the Corvette's direction, but James had anticipated and already peeled off.

Edward pulled the unconscious Onge off the steering wheel and took control. He waved at James. They both stopped their vehicles and the doctor embarked.

"They're getting away," said James. Edward started driving.

Cali's captors were just a dust cloud a kilometer away. James and Edward transitioned from pavement to dirt at full speed. The jeep lurched dangerously but stayed on course. The dust cloud wasn't getting any closer.

"Put him in the back of the Jeep," said Edward, indicating the Onge. "We'll need answers from him."

drove for half an hour with his foot to the floorboard. Callista's captors must have been doing the same over the rough terrain. The dirt gave way to grassland. Still, they followed. Finally, the cloud he was chasing disappeared. He jammed his hand on the steering wheel.

"Just keep going in that direction," said James. "Look at all the tracks they're leaving. We'll be able to find them. They must have just hit some wet ground."

It wasn't long before the tracks disappeared. "We lost them," Edward said.

"Pretty good chance they're just going straight ahead," said James. "The coast is probably just about twenty kilometers away."

"Which way would we go to be closest to Sri Lanka?" asked Edward.

"Well, I don't have a map in my head, but I would guess we'd bear left a bit."

Edward dodged the Jeep around a couple trees. The jostling stirred the Onge in the back. His head was bleeding. He moaned.

"Take over," said Edward. "Bear left a bit." As soon as James touched the wheel, Edward abruptly left the driver's seat and climbed into the back with the Onge. The Onge had almost come to his senses and was gripping the front seat, weakly trying to pull himself up. Edward pointed his empty gun at the native.

65

Callista heard the crackle of the radio. The Onge kept speaking in their strange tongue. She couldn't see Edward's jeep anymore. He'd gotten so close. She had no idea what sort of training the Jesuits had put him through to be able to do what he did, but she was glad. The Onge had been beating her and he'd saved her.

Her head spun. A while back, just before Edward had come, she'd felt warmth on her temple. She was glad to feel it dry up.

The Onge chattered nervously. The two in the back seat, one on either side of her, kept their guns pointed erectly behind them from the Jeep, as though Edward might swoop out of the sky at any moment.

Her arms were bound behind her, which made it hard to stay in her seat during the bumpy ride. The ropes weren't fitted very well around her. She'd been re-tied hastily in the jeep. She worked busily at loosening them further. At present, it wouldn't do her a bit of good with a hulking Onge on either side of her, but she never knew what circumstances would present themselves.

There was a part of her that could not remain as cool as her outward appearance. That part was screaming at Edward, screaming for Edward, grieving and resentful. That part wanted her to throw herself out of the Jeep. It was the part that kept telling herself, You're going to die. They'll keep beating you. They're going to sacrifice you. They're going to rape you. You're going to die. It was the part of her mind she couldn't rest.

She contained it, though, and occupied herself with the rope. She watched the Onge. She was encouraged by their edginess. Even though she didn't know a word they were saying, she could tell they were racing toward a finish line, that they were running from her Edward.

She prayed that Edward could win.

66

Edward recognized the Onge. It was Lee'tep, Nockwe's cousin. Edward liked Lee'tep; he wished he hadn't slammed him so hard. For now, though, Lee'tep was an enemy. The Onge would kill Edward if he had the chance, if only out of fear. Edward would not give him that chance.

"Lee'tep," Edward said down the barrel of his unloaded gun. The native's head was bleeding quite a bit. Edward ripped off a piece of his own shirt with his left hand and handed it to the Onge. If Lee'tep so much as tensed a muscle, Edward would kick him off the jeep. He would take no risks. "Put this on your head. You're bleeding."

Lee'tep did so, impressed by the gun so close to his face.

"Where is the tribe?" asked Edward.

"At the village," said Lee'tep. Edward could see he was lying.

"Lee'tep," said Edward, as though scolding a child. Edward chose the traditional Onge tongue to address Lee'tep. He had to startle the man, to trick him into giving him the confirmation he needed. "As your master sees your lies, so do I. I am the devil to your god. For every fortune he might seek, I can create demise. For every blow he may strike, I may strike back. We are in a deadly dance, he and I, and I cry to see the tribe in the middle. For the tribe there should be mercy…" Edward paused, then changed the pace by slamming home a question. "How far north is the tribe off the coast?!"

"I'm not telling you!" yelled Lee'tep. *He's on the coast.*

"You shall! You are a cowardly hog!" It was quite a curse in traditional Onge. Edward saw Lee'tep restrain himself from jumping at him. "I am sure that Manassa has not the might he brags of. My only prayer is that the tribe be not armed for war. I fear an army could tip the balances in Manassa's favor."

"Well, prepare to meet your death, Devil, for Manassa has at his command one hundred and fifty men armed with the lightness and the bang-bows." Lee-tep spit at him

Edward spoke in English. "James, turn the car to the right a bit." He then resumed in Onge: "I turn to the north, to catch your Manassah by surprise from his rear."

Lee'tep examined the scenery outside the jeep and got his bearings. Edward could tell the man almost said something, but then decided better. "My Lord will give you death no matter your surprises."

Certainly, we're headed straight for them, now.

"Stop the Jeep, James," said Edward. He pitched Lee'tep out of the vehicle. The Onge watched them drive away. "Now drive. And watch out. We're about to go straight into hell and I don't have any bullets in this damn gun."

"There aren't any guns in here?" asked James as he drove.

Edward looked around more closely to humor him. He'd seen the guns drop of out the limp bodies' hands onto the road. Only a few clips remained on the floorboards, for guns they'd left in Lisbaad.

67

It was a couple hours before dawn when Edward and Seacrest finally reached the sea. Edward's trance had long since worn off and his body ached fiercely. He had many more t-pills but decided to wait for action.

At first they didn't realize they'd found the tribe. The rocky coast was unpopulated. Edward suspected they might be too far north. Half a mile to the south along the shore was a ridge which hid the rest of the coast from view. He never doubted that the tribe would be somewhere near. He was certain.

They ditched the jeep and trekked to the ridge. Just past the high point, the sea cut deeply into the island. Edward spied a dozen skiffs free floating in the harbor. He strained his eyes to catch the tribe. They would be somewhere on the coast.

At the bottom of the harbor's "U" shape, a single torch appeared. Then more. Edward could make out the shapes. They were marching to the sea. Edward and James had beaten them there.

The skiffs responded to the light, interrupting the silent night with the abrupt roar of their engines. Edward was taken by surprise at the sound. He'd expected the Onge to have oars, not motors.

"What the hell is going on?" Seacrest asked.

"They're moving. They're going mainland."

"The whole tribe?"

"The whole tribe. I don't think anyone in Sri Lanka will know, though. It'll look like the whole tribe deserted their village and disappeared."

"What do you mean? They're a bunch of primitives. Where will they go?"

Edward left Seacrest's question unanswered.

I rushed Manassa. I forced his hand. He would have waited for them all to be schooled. It would have taken another two weeks or more. It was a small victory for Edward, but he knew Manassa was adapting to his threat. Manassa would not let such a bump in the road as Edward stop him. Manassa's reaction, though, told Edward that the god took him seriously.

"What are we going to do?" asked Seacrest. His voice quavered a bit.

"Callista's with them," said Edward, as though that answered the question.

"There must be a thousand of 'em," said Seacrest.

"Yeah, at least a thousand."

Seacrest's silence arrested Edward's attention. He turned from watching the advancing villagers. "What are you gonna do?" Seacrest asked. "Shoot 'em all in the bloody head?"

Edward opened his mouth to answer, but stopped as he caught a flash of motion in his periphery. He whipped his head around.

A face hovering over a bush. Wide eyes. A tube in his mouth. A dart.

The dart was practically floating in the air towards Edward. His own body felt sluggish and unresponsive. He was trying to make it drop but it was moving so painfully slow.

The trance. He was trancing without the drug. *The danger?* He didn't know why. He didn't have time to analyze it. He was trying to make his body drop under the path of that dart.

If I just swing around… He rotated. The dart passed. His hit the ground jarringly. He lost his concentration. The world sped fast. He heard the whiz of another dart and Seacrest's body hit the ground. Edward tried to pull himself up but the next dart hit his neck and he was out.

68

Edward woke up with Tomy peering over him. The boy looked tired but victorious. Edward tried to scramble away, but he was tied.

A club came down on his head. He didn't go unconscious, but feigned it. There was no advantage in putting up a fight here. The Onge would simply club him in the head until he was dead. He made his body limp and unresponsive, despite the sickening waves of pain emanating from his crown.

He felt an Onge pick him up.

"The other?" asked Tomy.

"I have him," said another Onge voice. Edward kept his eyes closed. *Manassa out-guessed me.* He must have posted sentries around the harbor, waiting for Edward to show. Edward wanted to hit himself. He might have spotted the trap had he been trancing and not so damn tired.

The Onge lifted Edward's limp form over his shoulders. Edward waited for an opportune moment where the Onge's guard might be down. There was no such moment. They hauled him into a truck and further bound his hands and feet. He didn't dare open his eyes. He didn't want his skull bashed in.

"Bring him to the bonfire," instructed Tomy. "I will soon join you. Hurry, now."

Edward heard the tailgate slam shut. A radio chattered from the front seat. He didn't recognize the dialect. *Some kind of code.*

He almost rolled as the truck accelerated. He had to force himself to stay slack and not resist the motion. The firm hands of Onge gripped him and

303

kept him from shifting around too much. He knew they wanted their prize relatively intact when they presented him to their god.

He heard another truck's engine pull up as they sped along.

"Is that the white man?" It was one of the leaders of an Onge clan. Edward recognized his voice.

"Yes. We're bringing him to Manassa."

"I must have his blood," yelled the man. "He killed my brother last night and stole his jeep. Stop the truck!"

Edward forced himself to remain motionless. Every part of him wanted to leap up and plunge over the side of the truck bed. He knew there was not a chance the Onge would allow him to escape. The Onge had the lightness and sheer numbers, and those factors were more than enough to contain Edward.

"No, brother. His blood is for Manassa," yelled the driver.

Edward heard the click of a gun from the other truck. "Stop the truck now. It is my honor."

Edward heard another click, this time from the cab in front of him. "Back down," screamed the driver. "It is not worth the anger of Manassa. This white man will die soon enough."

Edward's mind whirred, figuring on an escape plan. His legs were tied, his hands tied, all quite efficiently. He tested them out. They had no give. There was no escape plan.

"I will remember this, Jurdan. You will get what is destined for you!" shouted the intruder. Edward heard the other truck pull off.

After about half an hour, the truck's tires started to crunch on what sounded like gravel. Edward could hear the lap of the surf against the shore. The beach.

Once they stopped, an Onge pulled him off the truck and lowered him to the ground. The pebbles felt cool and rough. He kept his body limp even as the beach dug into his face.

Edward listened. They had turned off the truck's engine, so it was an easier job. Not too far away, he heard the mutterings of a crowd, their words indistinct but definitely Onge. Another truck was noisily pulling up from behind him. Under the sounds of the ocean kissing the island and the hub-bub of the villagers was the constant breath and the sporadic crackle of the bonfire.

He heard something else: the light tap of footsteps that told him another Onge was approaching him. He almost risked opening his eyes, but resisted the urge. He felt a syringe burn into his arm, then stop quickly.

The lighter footsteps...Tomy...

He was almost certain it was. Had he given him the trance drug? No.

Poison...

Edward popped his eyes open. Tomy was looking past him, toward the villagers, watching for watchers. Edward twisted his body so he could reach the medicine bottle in his pocket. He twisted off the cap in one smooth motion and the t-pills scattered to the ground.

Tomy reacted by trying to pull him away, trying to hit him, but Edward weighed more than Tomy and was so low to the ground. His arms and legs were still tied, but he was able gyrated until his mouth could reach one of the pills. He got it along with a few pebbles; he held them all under his tongue.

Tomy got in a good blow to Edward's head. Edward rolled with it, managing to get another handful of rocks and pills. Tomy kicked him in the gut. He kept rolling, shaking his hand until only a pill remained. He tucked it into the back of his pant waist and stopped his struggle. Tomy kicked him again for good measure, but it didn't matter: Edward's trance had already begun.

He felt the poison in his body, foreign and deadly. He reacted instantly with his trance control, momentarily willing the circulation to stop in his right arm. Then he eased the circulation back, having his blood avoid the danger-ous area as best he could. He was lucky Tomy had only stabbed his arm, rather than taking the time to inject it intravenous. Maybe he wanted Edward to last a while. Managing the poison took some attention, but Edward figured he would be fine so long as he was trancing. He felt the cells dying near the injection. *Maybe the same drug used against Tien.*

Tomy gathered the t-pills off the ground and returned them to their bottle. He rustled through Edward's pockets for any more surprises.

"Bring him to Manassa," said Tomy. A couple Onge got out of the truck cab and hefted Edward up by his arms. He couldn't really walk with his legs tied but he bounced here and there to keep the weight off his shoulder blades.

Dawn still hadn't broken on the coast, but the Onge had erected their own sun on the beach. The bonfire was massive, framed of three whole tree trunks. Edward didn't understand it. If he were Manassa, he would do nothing to leave a trail. And yet here was a fire that burned bright as day. Its remains would serve as a marker for anyone attempting to track them.

No one will try to track them. No one has a clue.

The villagers were all watching him. They were turned from the fire and squinting and pointing at him. Above them all hovered Manassa, seated at an elevated throne on wooden stilts.

As Edward was carried into the crowd, he couldn't help but notice the Onge giving him a wide berth. They backed around and away as he was moved towards Manassa.

The Onge dumped him face-first before the throne. He had to twist and take the blow on his shoulder to avoid gashing his face.

He lay with his face in the dirt in an oval of Onge onlookers. There were hundreds of them, the whole tribe watching by the brilliant light of the bonfire. Warriors armed with guns formed a wall between the tribe and Edward. This was no tribal challenge. Edward was an enemy. There would be no chances taken.

Manassa ceremoniously glided down the makeshift stairs of his throne. Edward took the moment to eye the crowd. Two pale faces caught his eye.

Callista and Seacrest stood bound behind Manassa's throne. Four huge Onge held them them, one posted at each elbow.

Edward studied Callista. Her clothes were ripped. It was blood on her forehead when he caught glimpse of her at the warehouse, but that was dried now. He only glanced at her for a moment, but in the trance it may as well have been an eternity.

He smiled at her. It was worth it to get this far.

She'd be safe if it weren't for me. She would be dead soon, too - or worse. That was quite clear from the way the Manassaa loomed over him. His smile evaporated.

He looked for Nockwe. The chieftain was nowhere to be seen.

"A pill," mused Manassa. "I suppose you did something to it to make it work orally, purified it, perhaps? I know you've been trancing quite a bit in the past two days."

Edward needed to wrest control of the situation. That seemed impossible with hundreds of hostile Onge encircling, but he refused to play on Manassa's terms. Manassa intended an execution for him, and Edward had to move to change the game.

"No Jesuits? I didn't think you'd come alone," said Manassa.

"Mahanta!" yelled Edward in Onge. The crowd hushed. All that could be heard was the lap of the ocean against the shore. It was too quiet, as though the air had been sucked out of the open space and all that was left was vacuum. "End this. You know as well as I do that the nectar will only destroy your people."

Manassa laughed. He would milk this public appearance. It was clear to Edward that if he was willing to create a spectacle, Manassa would gladly take the opportunity. "You live in the past, my traitorous white servant. Mahanta is dead. I no longer inhabit such a corporal form. And the nectar - you are a snake who speaks lies with forked tongue to send my people to their death. You care for nothing but your white men, as you have proven with your treachery. Your word means nothing. You have taken the blood of my people, white man. And you have even tried to steal my powers. For that you must die."

Edward looked once more at Callista. She didn't look frightened, but rather, determined.

He drew on her strength.

"I CHALLENGE YOU, MANASSA!" Edward shouted with all his might. The ground muffled his mouth. He wasn't able to pull his head all the way up. Still, the tribe heard. There was murmuring, and then silence. "You are a liar," said Edward, adopting the cadence that he'd seen Nockwe use so many times with the Onge crowds, "and only Mahanta, a little boy afraid of a white man."

"Kill him, Manassa!" shouted someone in the crowd. The rest of the crowd joined in the yelling.

One of the inner circle stepped up and whispered in Manassa's ear. Edward could make out what was said by his lips. "There is no need to take a challenge from him. He is not a member of the tribe."

Manassa looked at Edward, then checked out the crowd. It was the same look he'd had while sparring with the panther as he waited for an audience to build. *He's building his mythos. He won't pass this up.*

"I challenge you, servant, once my champion!" proclaimed Manassa. "Your people shall come to learn the Onge rule!" And in Latin, Manassa said quietly, "Edward, you are a fool. You are dying. You may be in trance now, but that will soon wear out, and when it does, that poison will kill you. I will keep you in trance, and help you, I'll even give you the antidote, if you will just show me what you did to make the pill."

"I WILL CRUSH YOU!" answered Edward in Onge, non sequiter. The crowd was taken aback. Here was a white man with quite a bark.

Edward strained against the bindings. He felt his muscles almost pull. The ropes loosened slightly and he wiggled free. He sprang up at the ready on his own two feet.

The poison was still just in his right arm, making it feel a bit too heavy. He wouldn't be able to contain it as well while he fought.

Edward steadied himself. He felt dizzy. Tomy had given him quite a blow to his head.

Edward saw a knife flit out of Manassa's belt. He almost didn't see the gun. In one smooth motion, Manassa pulled a pistol to his hip and fired. The bullet slid out of the barrel. Edward whipped his body to the right instantaneously and the shot whizzed past and buried into the truck behind him.

He saw Manassa shoot again. Edward rolled forward and the bullet passed overhead. Manassa kept firing. Edward leaped out of his roll, flying over the third shot. His eyes were locked with Manassa's. He knew the timing of the god's shooting by the tensing of his muscles. Edward was only a few yards away, now.

Manassa aimed the gun at Edward's torso. Edward slid in reaction, but Manassa waited to shoot until after Edward committed. Edward twisted sideways but the bullet nicked his arm. He felt the poison start spreading again as his body adjusted to the shock of impact.

Edward hammered Manassa's gun hand and sent the weapon flying. He followed up with a high kick, which Manassa took in the jaw. Manassa reeled back and lost his footing, slamming into the ground. The villagers gasped.

"The white man is a god...a devil...he is a Christian devil...he might kill our god...we must stop him...we cannot stop the challenge...don't do anything." In his peripheral vision, he saw an Onge train his gun on Edward. Still, he did not fire. He would honor the challenge, for now. Once it was over, however, it would be free reign to slaughter the whites.

Edward caught Callista's gaze again. She had not wavered. He caught no sadness on her face. She looked tense but determined. She had not given up.

Manassa launched himself back to his feet with snakelike precision. He charged Edward with his knife. Edward waited for him to slash, blocking Manassa's strike by slamming his knife wrist with his fist.

Manassa didn't let go this time. He jabbed at Edward, who dodged Manassa deftly and then got hold of his wrist. He violently twisted the Onge's arm. The knife fell to the ground. Edward followed up with a body throw, sending Manassa flying. Edward jumped to land on Manassa with his knees and fist, but Manassa rolled out from under him before he hit the ground and pulled away.

The poison was moving, now. Edward couldn't stop it, not with his heart rate up, not with needing to use his right arm.

The limb felt heavy and numb. I've got to take him out quickly. Edward remembered Nockwe's duel with Dook. Nockwe had tried to eliminate Dook in the first minutes.

Manassa knows I'll try the same thing.

Edward lunged for the knife. Manassa grabbed him and tried to throw him. Edward grappled him and reversed the throw, sending Manassa back down to the ground.

Manassa pulled himself up, but Edward was right there with punch after hook. Manassa was unable to block all the blows and took a few to the face. He dropped again.

The crowd was in an uproar.

Manassa took back the initiative, throwing an upper cut from the ground. Edward tried to block, but there was so much force behind it that Manassa still managed to get the blow to Edward's jaw. Edward reeled back, blocking as Manassa followed with blow after blow. Gradually Manassa started getting in licks on Edward's right side. Punch, block, kick, block. Edward's arms and shins started aching. He shut off the pain. He knew Manassa had the same level of pain tolerance. Edward knew he'd have to practically decapitate Manassa to stop him while in trance.

Edward's right arm grew useless. More blows got through his defenses. Manassa's fists came faster and faster. Each hit was punishing. Manassa had a lot more muscle than Edward. He broke Edward's nose. Blood dripped everywhere.

Edward realized too late that Manassa had been positioning him. In an impossible move, Manassa punched twice, kicked twice, and then somersaulted backwards, picking up the dropped knife as he flew. From there he launched with his fists flying. Edward had to block the left hand with the dagger, which left the right to jolt him down to the ground.

He could not see Mahanta, only the gravel, but he saw the future. It had a knife through his back, puncturing his heart.

Only, instead, he heard a familiar voice.

"At'tan! At'tan!"

69

Where is Bri? Nockwe first looked for his wife when he reached the encampment. He feared for his family's safety first and foremost. She was in a crowd - the whole village was gathered in an oval. He watched them by the dawn light.

He was alone. The car had broken down, so he had finished his trip by foot. He had run the whole way. The others were far behind him.

He pushed through the mass of villagers and touched her elbow. "Where are the children?" he asked.

"They are with their grandmother, farther from the coast," she answered. *Near the jungle. That was wise. There is great safety in the jungle.*

"What's happening?" he asked.

"Go to the front, quickly. Manassa fights the white man."

The man who saved my life. Nockwe plunged through the crowd. His wife followed in his wake. He didn't want her to, but there would be no stopping her. They reached the front of the circle.

He couldn't help but think about his duel with Dook, and Edward's intervention. He pushed thoughts of honor aside. If he were to save his village from this tyrant, he would need to wait for his opportunity. It would not be now, with village burned and his people homeless, and all of the tribe's resources under Mahanta's thumb.

Nockwe watched the rhythms of the duel. Mahanta was winning. The Onge god landed a heavy blow to Edward's face. It looked like he broke the white man's nose. Mahanta seized the initiative, striking furiously and recovering his knife.

Bri grabbed Nockwe's arm. "Nockwe," she shouted over the din of the crowd.

He looked back at her. She sounded disturbed.

"Look at her," she said, pointing to a young white woman held hostage by two warriors. "That is the savior of our child. That is her. And this is surely her death."

70

Edward jerked his head up. He saw Mahanta, mid war cry, coming down with the knife. He saw a dark blur that yanked Mahanta's body to the side like a rag doll.

Edward tried to scramble away. The poison didn't let him. It was sapping his whole body of life. Edward only managed to drag a few feet to the side. He turned to where the blur had gone.

Nockwe! The knife which had spelled Edward's death was nowhere to be seen. Mahanta had rolled with Nockwe's tackle, and the chieftain let the god get his bearings before the challenge began in earnest.

Nockwe had intervened.

All around Edward, the crowd was in uproar. Edward forced his thoughts inward. He had to focus. He had to stop the poison.

I've got to help Nockwe. He isn't trancing. He isn't even in the lightness. Manassa will murder him.

"Nockwe!" Edward yelled weakly. He could not get any force behind his voice. The poison must have moved further than he thought.

Nockwe turned. Edward grabbed the pill from his pants and threw it at Nockwe's head.

"Under the tongue!" Edward yelled as it flew toward his face. Manassa lunged toward Nockwe, but the chieftain caught it in his mouth with his hand before Manassa could reach him.

Manassa clipped Nockwe, both rolling to the ground. They bounced to their feet, circling, their fists in the air before them.

Manassa spoke once more in traditional Onge. "Do you test the lord, your god?"

Nockwe answered in a rage, "We shall see if you're still a god without a beating heart. We shall see if they'll worship you after you're dead."

"Enough!" shouted Manassa. He attacked Nockwe in rage. Edward could tell that the trance had taken hold in Nockwe, but the chieftain was making the same mistake that Edward had at first. Nockwe was sticking to Onge fighting-style, rather than adapting his style for the moment. Manassa was much more fluid, much more agile, and was getting in blows. Nockwe was on the defensive.

Manassa did not let up, refusing to give the initiative. His fists were easy to keep up with to Edward, who was also trancing, but anyone else would have said he'd sprouted eight arms - and Nockwe, too, with his blocking.

Manassa moved in close, his fists pounding into Nockwe's chest. Nockwe fell backwards, and Manassa tried to kick him. Nockwe managed to grab his foot and twist it. Manassa went down and rolled out. They both bounced to their feet again.

One of Manassa's priests stepped into the ring slightly, as though to move in front of Manassa. Manassa waved him off, his eyes still locked on Nockwe. Nockwe charged leading with his fists, but just before he closed the distance Manassa let out a vicious jab with his foot. Edward heard a rib crack. The blow propelled Nockwe backwards. Manassa followed it up with another flying kick straight at Nockwe's head. The chieftain only managed to avoid the foot partially, the brunt of the force sending him down to the ground once more.

Had Nockwe not been trancing, that would have been the end of that duel, but instead his reaction was merely a savage yell. It reminded Edward of the medicine man's drone during the ritual. There was torture in his voice.

Nockwe got up. His neck muscles tensed, his whole body flexed. Sweat and blood shook off his dark skin. Nockwe charged again.

Manassa feinted to the right, but Nockwe read him, sending a vicious jab to the left the caught Manassa off guard. Nockwe connected ten times in the space of seconds, sending Mahanta reeling back. The bystanders had to scatter as the fight was propelled into the crowd.

Manassa buckled under the blows. Nockwe was on top of him, whaling at him.

"NOCKWE!" It was that same priest yelling. He was standing where Callista had been. Callista was gone. The two bodies of her guards lay in a pool of blood on the ground. The priest held Bri'ley'na, Nockwe's wife, with a knife to her neck. Bri's knife lay bloodied on the ground beside the fallen guards. Bri shrieked, wriggling to get away.

Nockwe turned his head to look. Manassa scrambled back to the edge of the crowd.

"Bri!"

"Your wife murdered two of the warriors!"

"Release her!" yelled Nockwe. "I am your chieftain! Do as I say!" he shouted. He had panic in his voice. The priest did not budge. "Do you dare to defy me? Do you dare to interrupt the challenge?"

"Don't move, Nockwe!" the priest shouted.

Manassa gathered his breath. "Kill them!" he shouted. "They are traitors of our people, and no longer Onge. They are white lovers. Kill them!!! Then onto the boats before they stop us!" The crowd surged inward. Manassa disappeared.

Nockwe ran toward his wife.

Edward couldn't see the chieftain anymore. The crowd engulfed him.

Edward closed his eyes. He had to stop the poison. He had to get rid of it before the trance stopped. He felt the after-pain starting to set in, and with it a gut-wrenching sort of suffocation. The nirvana effect was ending.

He did not fear the trampling feet of the tribe. The poison might kill him first.

71

Nockwe ran with his wife away from the shore. In the chaos, Nockwe eluded the Onge. A fight had broken out by the firelight. Some were taking Nockwe's side.

Nockwe held his wounded wife to him. The life was running out of her with every pulsing of her veins.

He sat down with her on his lap behind a lean-to. There were boys running back and forth, confused, but no one saw the chieftain and his wife.

"Bri…" said Nockwe. "Bri…my angel, you are so strong."

He stroked her hair for the last time. Her eyes started to empty. She managed a weak smile. Pain gripped her tense face, but there was a smile.

"I love you, my chieftain." Two tears ran down her cheeks. Life left her body. He closed her body's eyes.

"So long, my love," he said. He held her tight. He knew it was just a body, now, it was not Bri'ley'na, his beloved. He knew she was gone now no matter how much he remembered her. She had gone on to the world after. He knew she would go to the heaven of warriors and hunters, even though she was female. He would see her there.

He cried, though there was no time for it. He gripped her body one last time, then laid her down under the lean-to. She was a casualty of war, a war just begun. There was no time for a burial.

For that, he hated Mahanta and his wretched priesthood even more.

Nockwe ran back into the crowd for the white man. All were looking for the chieftain, but no one saw him. The fighting had moved even closer to the sea.

CRAIG GEHRING

72

In the confusion, Edward was left for dead. He certainly looked dead. He wasn't moving or even breathing for that matter.

James had grabbed him and heaved him up on his shoulder, running as fast as he could with Callista leading the way. Manassa had given no order about the whites, and no one seemed to be paying them any mind. The Onge's attention was riveted closer to the shore, where the skiffs had run aground to pick up their passengers and where fighting was still raging on.

James heaved Edward into the bed of the old red F-150 that had carried him in. Callista got into the back with Edward, lying low so as not to be seen. James started driving.

No one noticed them as they pulled off. James checked the rear view mirror. He heard a thud and saw a blur of dark skin.

A native had jumped onto the truck bed from out of nowhere. James slammed the brakes and leaned out of the window, frantically trying to see what was going on. Callista waved him off. It was that native that had saved Edward's life.

James punched the accelerator. He didn't want any more random natives joining them. His passengers bounced violently in the truck bed, trying to hold on as best they could.

The headlights of a couple cars flicked on. Maybe they were trying to follow them. It didn't matter – James had gotten some distance. The Ford would outpace those cars on the rough terrain.

73

Callista checked Edward's vitals.

His pulse had slowed to almost nothing. He was breathing, but just barely. He looked as though he might be hibernating. Something was terribly wrong. She checked over his gunshot wound. He'd gotten hurt, but it wasn't anything that should have sent him into shock.

Then she saw his right hand. It was blue, as though the circulation hadn't come to it in a while. His veins were discolored.

Poison?

She held his head in her hands. There was nothing she could do except pray. She was sure Edward could do a better job of it than her, but she would give it her best. There was no harm in trying.

74

Edward was aware of nothing except his cells. He could only sense the burning of his cells and the dying in his body. And of course there was the sensation of his head in Callista's hands.

The trance had stopped. It had run out. But then something had happened.

He had started it again.

It wasn't the drug trance, it was something else, something born of necessity, the same sort of necessity that let him perceive that dart so clearly.

As he'd forced himself to focus at Seacrest's house, so did he force himself into trance now. It was harder. It took all of his will, and something more. But he was doing it. Having gone to that state many times, he *willed* himself to go there again.

He willed himself to live.

The poison was everywhere in his body.

It was sending him into shock.

He felt his body trying to neutralize it, trying to kill it off. His vitals would give out before his immune system could work.

And yet he willed it. He willed his heart to pump, his lungs to breathe, his vitals to continue, barely.

It was a weak poison. It was biological. It sent the whole body into shock, but it was dying. His body could handle it, if his body had time. His kidneys were slowly neutralizing it, cleaning his blood.

He kept his body going. He kept pushing the blood through his veins. He kept pumping the air through his lungs.

He would live.

These eyes will open. I will see her.

He focused on her hands cradling his head. He heard her praying.

75

Callista sponged Edward's head with cool water. She dipped her hand in the basin and splashed some on her face, herself. She was tired. She'd been at it for days. She would not leave Edward's side.

His breathing had grown stronger and more regular. His heart was doing fine. He would wake up, soon. She wanted to be there when he woke up. She didn't want him to have the shock of wondering if she'd survived the ordeal. And she wanted to be the first to greet him back to the living.

James had rented an apartment near the docks that overlooked the harbor. Edward's room had the best view. James had taken to calling it the "sick room." Callista kept the windows open to keep the air fresh.

She stretched and walked to the window. The door clicked open behind her.

"How is he doing?" It was James. He'd come up and check on her now and then.

"Fine," she said. A couple boats dear the docks almost hit one another. She could hear the faint strains of a couple of the deckhands shouting back and forth.

"Yeah? How are you doing?"

"He should wake up any time. His vitals are strong." She turned around. "Thank you for helping. I don't know why you are, but thank you."

James rubbed his head. He looked tired, too. He leaned against the wall. "Sure," he said.

She took her seat by the bed. James had been looking at her and Edward but now was gazing out the window.

"Callista, do you mind my telling you something?" he asked after a long silence.

"No, I don't think so. No, I don't mind," she said.

He nodded. "Well, I just want to thank you, too. You see, well, I'm sure Edward will tell you all about it once he wakes up, but, well, you see, I'm not exactly good folk…"

"Nonsense, James, you're…"

He waved down her protest. "I'm not. I'm a crook, really. It's why I'm on this island. I used to doctor crooks, see. And it backfired. It's why I'm here." He sat down in the corner in one of the spare chairs. "It's why I'm here," he repeated. "And I'd gotten pretty low in my life, I mean real low. And I met you, and I wanted to be with you, and so you inspired me to try to be something that I used to be a long, long time ago. You reminded me. So now I'm here, and it's not too great a circumstance, but it's better than where I was, in spite of everything. So, thank you. That's all." He smiled.

Callista opened her mouth to respond, but she did not answer. Edward's body moved. It tensed just a bit, but it was enough to rivet her attention. His eyelids fluttered. She grabbed his hand.

She remembered James and glanced back at him. He was already taking his leave, smiling once more and waving for her to turn her eyes back to Edward. The door clicked closed.

Edward's hand tightened around hers. His eyes opened. He took in her face for a long while, then frantically eyed the room. He tried to pull himself up, but he wasn't strong enough.

He was strong enough to lie there awake for hours as she cried holding him. He was strong enough to whisper, "It's okay," "We're okay," and "I love you," and listen to her mumble and laugh and cry some more.

Eventually, she fed him soup. She helped him sit up, which he managed fine, but his hands shook too much for him to reliably get his food to his own mouth. After he got some sustenance down besides IV fluid he seemed sharper. He was the same Edward, only exhausted. He hadn't changed at all.

"I'm sorry," he said.

"For what?" she asked.

He looked at her incredulously.

"Listen," she said. "That was the worst experience I've ever had in my life. But it's not your fault. It's not your fault, okay? And we're okay, okay?"

He still looked doubtful.

"Look, if I had died, then you could have been sorry, okay?"

He chuckled.

"Eat more soup," she said, lifting another spoonful to his mouth.

76

Nockwe had left the city once he'd ascertained that Edward was safe.

Edward found him at the village, sitting against the ancient rock that marked the center of Onge civilization.

Nockwe did not react to Edward's approach. It was as though Nockwe were expecting him.

"This rock," said Nockwe. "My great-great-grandparents lived and died not a thousand paces from this rock."

Edward followed Nockwe's gaze. He was watching the ruins of his village.

"Your health?" asked Nockwe.

"Returned," said Edward. "And yours?"

"I have a sickness that can't be cured."

The grounds of the village still smelled of ash.

"I am sorry for your loss. Callista told me."

Nockwe studied Edward's face and then nodded, accepting his condolences. Nockwe didn't look sad. He looked as though he were smoldering.

"Do you know how I became chieftain over all Onge?" asked Nockwe.

"You challenged three men back to back, and you survived."

Nockwe shook his head. "Ten years ago, when Bri'ley'na was only fifteen, she had agreed to be my wife. Our chieftain, though, would not give his blessings. His son wanted her for himself. So Bri'ley'na petitioned the chieftain directly, telling him that she would not allow herself to be married to anyone but me. He finally consented. His son grew so angry, however, that two days before the ceremony he tried to rape my Bri. She escaped because I discovered them and intervened. When I charged the son with the crime, the chieftain wouldn't hear it."

"So then you challenged him?" asked Edward.

"No, then his son challenged me. And then his brother intervened. And then their father intervened. And after I killed my chieftain, I had to kill each son or else they would kill me."

Nockwe stood up and leaned against his rock. He sighed. It was the closest to grief Edward had ever seen him. Finally, Nockwe locked eyes with Edward. "The only day of my life worse than the day I became chieftain was the day I lost my Bri."

Edward felt he had to say something. He didn't know what to say, but he had to say something. "Your Bri'ley'na was brave," said Edward. "I owe her a debt."

Nockwe nodded. "So do I. I intend to pay it. Now tell me, Edward, do you come to reminisce, or is there business on your mind?"

May as well be direct. "I'm chasing Mahanta," said Edward. "I thought you might want to join me. I would be grateful if you would join me."

Nockwe considered it momentarily. It seemed he'd already considered it. He nodded. "I will join you." He sat back down against his rock.

"We'll get him, Nockwe," said Edward, looking out at the ashes of Nockwe's home.

"But we won't get my people," said Nockwe.

"We'll save who we can."

"My sons, my daughters…and they are all my sons, my daughters. Do you understand, Edward?" asked Nockwe.

"Yes, I understand."

"When my path crosses with Mahanta, I will have only one agenda. You must know this, and expect nothing else."

"I know, Nockwe. I know," said Edward.

Nockwe nodded, satisfied, and went back to his watching.

77

Darian Riley, who his general called "the fixer," did not have much to go on.

This missionary was gone. His assignment was gone, abandoned and burned to ash. It was as though the Onge had evaporated into the air, taking their missionary with them.

Riley took his time. He had all the time in the world. He only had one thing to fix at a time, and he worked at that one thing until he fixed it.

First he would search the village. He was searching for the corpse of a white man. That was what he most suspected. It wasn't long, however, before his mind turned to other possibilities.

In the ashes of one of the huts, Riley found the cross. It was badly charred, but the marking was obvious. It was an archaic Jesuit device, one that Riley was more than familiar with it.

At the southern side of the southernmost freestanding tree in the village clearing, Riley dug until he found Edward's letter.

Darian Riley found Edward's words to be quite enlightening.

Acknowledgments

Special thanks to my family and friends for all of their help and support.

About the Author

Craig Gehring writes fiction and non-fiction in a variety of genres. His passions are education and writing. Craig scored perfect scores on the ACT and SAT and then went on to found Ring Marketing, an ad agency specializing in internet marketing and design. Craig has written *SAT ACT Mastery, Norman, Nirvana Effect*, and is currently working on a new sci-fi epic. Craig lives in Baton Rouge with his wife and three children.

Contact Craig by email, on his blog, or on Facebook.

craig@nirvanaeffect.com
http://www.craiggehring.com/blog
http://www.facebook.com/nirvanaeffect